THE SORCERER'S PROTÉGÉE

ALENA JAMES

CRIMSON DOVE PRESS

Alena James

The Sorcerer's Protégée

ISBN: 978-0-6457158-0-4

 A catalogue record for this
book is available from the
National Library of Australia

CONTENT WARNING

Blood, violence, gaslighting/mind control, toxic relationships, self-harm, implied sexual assault, public humiliation and degradation, physical assault, mention of BDSM, claustrophobia, graphic scenes.

THE SORCERER'S PROTÉGÉE

THE MISTWALKER SERIES – BOOK ONE

PROLOGUE

D arren allowed himself a moment of weakness as
the orange slipped out of his hand and down the
descending path to the artificial lake. The brilliant flash of
colour rolled further away, but his fingers did not twitch.
He left the fruit vulnerable to the wolves, birds, raccoons
and tore his thoughts away. There wasn't much left for
him in the big city. Corbin had departed long ago.

Teaching his last apprentice was a short, yet marvellous
time. Darren smiled, as he always did when thinking about
Corbin—there seemed to be nothing he couldn't do. Despite the boy's arrogance and short temper, his magic potential was immense from the get-go, and iron self-discipline helped him progress quickly. Retirement seemed
Darren's only option now. He knew his legacy would carry
on strong through another.

As the sun began setting above him, the bright red and
yellow outfits of autumn trees glowed. Darren threaded
his fingers through his thinning grey hair, thinking that
he should start carrying around a beanie. The air was still

warm, but the breeze was growing chilly. Summer never lasted long enough. Maybe it was time to move to a warmer place. After all, retirement was supposed to be a good thing.

The rolling orange hit a bump and commanded Darren's attention. He wondered if it would plop into the water. There were already a few ducks with hopeful expressions in their eyes. Lazy things were too used to people throwing them bread and only looked for food themselves in the mornings, when there weren't many visitors in the park.

Darren made a few more mindless steps before he stopped. The orange pivoted away from the water and rolled to the base of a large oak, nudging the feet of a little girl. Responding to the touch, she lifted her face to look at the fruit.

The girl turned towards Darren. "Is this yours?"

Her sweet voice melted his heart. Darren stepped closer and cleared his throat. "Um, yes, but you can have it if you want."

The girl picked up the fruit and sniffled. "Thank you."

Darren looked around, but there was nobody else to be seen. The girl's face was covered in tears, her eyes puffy as if she had spent a few hours crying. She had no bag, no toys, and no other belongings one would expect to see. Just a child, seven or eight years old. Chestnut hair braided shoulder-length, with unusually bright golden highlights making it seem as if it were dyed. Her gaunt, bird-like frame was covered by a faded green sundress that complimented her olive skin and hazel eyes.

"You're welcome." Darren peeked around the tree as if the girl's family could be hiding there. It seemed like she was completely alone. In a rapidly descending twilight, the outcome didn't look good.

"It's going to be dark soon. Do you know where your parents are?"

The girl started sobbing. Taken aback, all Darren could do was search the carry bag for tissues and put the box next to her. At some point she would stop and would need something apart from her sleeve to wipe her face.

As if obeying a silent order, the girl stopped crying and dragged a tissue out of the box. She blew her nose and wiped her cheeks with the awkward grace of a child who was trying to act all proper.

"You can have more than one, I've got plenty," Darren said, pointing at the box and sitting down on the grass next to her. From some of the parenting books he had read when his wife was pregnant, he knew that it was important to speak with children on their level. As his own baby girl only survived her mother by a few days, he had never got to use his knowledge until that moment—none of his Apprentices were as young as her, nor ever felt like children to him. Maybe he could help this poor soul get back to her family. Her parents were probably worried sick.

"My name is Ayla," the girl blurted. "Someone should have picked me up at noon, but nobody came. They said it would be a couple, a lady with ginger hair and a blond man. They were supposed to take me to my new home so I could have a family. But they didn't come. This was a cruel joke, and now I can't find a way back!"

"Hey, it's okay, Ayla," Darren soothed, sensing that she was about to start crying again. "I can take you back to your old place if you want. Do you know the address?"

She shook her head. There was nothing she remembered about her old life. She couldn't tell him the names of people she used to live with, or those who were supposed to have picked her up. She didn't remember anything apart from her own name and that she was ten years old. And the fear she felt before she was brought to the park, by people she couldn't remember either.

"I have an idea. Would you like to come with me? I don't want to leave you here on your own, and there aren't any other options left. I'll give you some food and a warm bed. Tomorrow morning, we'll go to the police station and see if anyone's filed a missing person report for you. We'll find your family, I promise."

It must have been the hopeless expression Darren saw in Ayla's eyes that forced him to make a promise he didn't know he could keep. This girl needed to be safe. Darren guessed she must have suffered some kind of trauma, which blocked her memories. He was confident that they would come back with time.

That wouldn't be his business, though. Children belonged in loving homes, surrounded by the affection of people who cared about them. Not with strangers who found them in a park.

The child dug into the simple roast as if she hadn't eaten for days. Darren only shook his head, wondering about her background. She must have come from an orphanage, judging by her behaviour and inexplicable fear. The existence of potential foster parents who should have picked her up would explain a lot. Why in a park, though? Why without any authorities in sight? And why was this child left there completely alone?

The visit to the police station was fruitless. Nobody was looking for this girl; nobody had heard about her. Together with Ayla, Darren composed posters that they spread around the park. Every day, they kept expanding the search area, but there was no luck. Nobody recognised her, as if she never existed.

Darren spent countless nights awake, pondering his future actions as the poor child cried herself to sleep. He could find no explanation for the situation. Children didn't just appear out of nowhere. Someone would be looking for this girl, and he had to figure out a way to help. After all, he promised her.

A promise he was never able to keep.

PART ONE

CHAPTER I. AYLA

The beautiful, cloudless day had already passed the peak of its glory. As the sun began its inevitable journey down, painting the roofs of the neighbourhood a soft shade of gold, Ayla freed herself from the weight of the amorphous bogeyman that once swung from her shoulders. Her future was no longer disfigured by the unknown. The quiet street was almost deserted at this hour; the only sounds were cheerful birdsong in lush green bushes and an occasional soft rustle of autumn leaves floating on the wind of Indian summer.

Ayla pedalled on her bike and looked around, enjoying the smell of fresh pies that always lingered in the air from the town's only bakery. She wanted to bask in all the friendly, familiar faces of this place she'd called home. Darren had gifted her a peaceful life this past decade, one that she never wanted to leave unless he was by her side. The furthest she'd strayed was the prestigious university in the neighbouring city, just about an hour's bus ride away.

She always rode her bike home from the station, the trip a reminder of her happiest years.

Each person Ayla encountered was delighted by her news—that day she found out her latest test results placed her among the top students of her graduate year. Her relentless pursuit of linguistics and translation granted her the choice between a post-graduate scholarship and an entry-level position interpreting for the ambassador. She was too happy to be bothered that the dean spelt her name *Isla* in her letter of recommendation, as people often did based on pronunciation. That imperfection could bother her later, once she came down from her high. Her delirium could've turned cancerous polyps benign, rid swollen pustules of infection, reversed the rot of decaying fruit.

She needed to discuss her options with Darren. Oh, he was going to be so happy!

Ayla's pedals began to slow, a strange feeling nipping at her heel. Too quiet. No birdsong in the air. No chattering from the neighbouring houses. No sounds from other streets that would normally be a never-ending background hum. Ayla frowned, a shadow of uncertainty touching her mind. Just another thing she would have to discuss with Darren. Once she had shared her achievements with him, they would make sense of today's unusual atmosphere. Together.

When she arrived at their house, she slid off her bike. The front door was slightly ajar. Ayla pushed it in, wondering why Darren wouldn't have closed it. Perhaps, he was too busy with his studies and didn't realise he forgot to lock it properly after she'd left. The wind must have pushed it open, but the well-oiled hinges didn't make a sound to alert him. She smiled, thinking about his absent-mindedness. He was a fantastic example of a true scholar. Once in his zone, there was hardly anything to distract him from the task at hand.

Smiling from ear to ear, she flew into the living room forgetting to take her shoes off. That was always the rule in the house—you come in, you take the street shoes off, you put on the house shoes. A transition for both Darren and her from the busy life outside to the serenity and peace of home.

As she ran into the room, the abnormality struck a blow to her stomach. Why wasn't Darren at his desk but lying on the floor instead? Why was there red paint all over the white carpet—that would take ages to clean up! Ayla blinked, suddenly snapping out of the bliss. That stain reeked of blood, not paint. And there was a lot of it. She nursed an invisible wound on her belly. Darren wasn't moving. His body lay limp, dismembered from memory and laughter and language and all intellectual thought.

Ayla stopped in her tracks, breaths quiet and hollow, as if any perceptible noise or movement would make things worse. Her bag dropped on the floor, the sudden thud making her flinch. Pale and shaky, she leaned against the wooden door frame and stood there, unable to avert her eyes from the gruesome scene in front of her.

Darren's hand twitched, and she lunged towards him. Hope gave her strength as she lowered herself to her knees and took his cold hand in hers.

"What happened, Darren?" she cried. A world without his mood, his mind, wasn't something she was ever prepared for, and now she didn't know what to do. Call for help and leave him all alone in this room? Bring bandages for a wound that drew out that much blood? He needed to guide her through her next moves, step by step. Which limbs to move, which thoughts to have.

But he didn't respond, his breath ragged as he focused his eyes on her.

"Tell me how I can help," she pleaded, looking for the sparkle of life in his pale blue eyes. There had to be something, anything that she could do. Darren had always been so strong and reliable. His form was definable, inviting security and confidence and familiarity—a solid pillar of safety in the fog. It was impossible to imagine life without him... *No*, she told herself. *He's not going to die. I'll fix it. He just needs to tell me how.*

His eyes darted to one of the drawers of his desk. Ayla reached inside and pulled out a small notebook bound in black calfskin leather. "What's this?"

Darren beckoned her to come closer and she instantly obliged. "Take it... They'll... come... back... You must... run."

Wide-eyed, Ayla struggled to process the sight. Her head spun with numbness that was spreading all over her like a forest fire. She clung to Darren's hand as if it were a lifeline. He was telling her to run, she had to do it. But that would mean leaving him alone. Leaving him to bleed out on the white carpet, while she got to live.

"Go... now!"

The words seemed to have taken all his strength as Darren pushed her hand away. Ayla got up, blindly obeying his order. Heart beating in a violent drumbeat, she took her time to turn around. Her mind was frozen, all thoughts blocked out. All she could do was do as he said, trusting his knowledge. His wisdom gave form to her body which was dissolving at the seams—yes, Darren was going to make it better. She had to listen to him. But maybe if she dissolved, no one would find her.

Darren's rasping voice broke the silence again. Ayla startled, realising she never moved from her spot.

"Go, Ayla! Run!"

She turned on her heel and rushed outside. Light shadows of the afternoon seemed to engulf familiar houses in a strange haze. With blurry eyesight and a pounding heart, Ayla ran until she was out of breath and had to stop. She found herself in a small neighbourhood park that boasted all shades of bright yellow, orange and red—bright red, like the blood on her white carpet. The flowers appeared as if carnivorous and cannibalistic, eating themselves and staining each other. Red took over her vision and coloured everything around her.

Ayla collapsed onto a neat wooden bench. Someone had carved the words "A + B = Love" on the seat, and she traced the letters with her fingers, too numb to think. The wood had absorbed the sunshine throughout the day and was still warm to the touch.

Ayla lowered her head and let unshed tears annihilate her body. She had no strength to contain them. Darren was now surely dead. Nobody could survive the loss of so much blood. She knew he had sent her away to spare her. What was it he said about mysterious "them" coming back?

She shuddered at the thought of someone wishing Darren dead. He was a quiet, private person who was happiest surrounded by his books and the studies she didn't understand. In the years of her life with him, she hardly saw anyone visit, or him leaving to visit someone. Being a hermit seemed fitting for him, and after a while, she accepted it as his way of life. Unbeknownst to herself at the time, she adjusted her own life to match his, though he always encouraged her to go out and make friends outside of the house. She didn't have many, being determined to be the best student in her class. To make him proud. He deserved nothing less.

Bitter tears flowed down her cheeks as Ayla wept over a future that dissipated to nothing. Her adoptive father's figure that had always shone light over her flickered and ceased. A gentle breeze grew stronger and colder. Indian summer was nearing its end, and the chilly night wouldn't show mercy to her lightweight cotton dress. Ayla trembled again, reality hitting her like an untrained incision into the solar plexus. What was she going to do?

The soft leather of the notebook in her hands felt warm, bringing a bittersweet smile to her face. The last piece of her old life, something that Darren passed along to show that he cared even after he was gone. Holding back another wave of tears, Ayla opened it.

To her surprise, she found nothing extraordinary. The pages were full of Darren's handwritten notes as he was pinning down his ideas about Ayla's origin. He described in great detail the memory exercises they did to stir remembrance of the past, and the leads he followed that all went nowhere.

The last page didn't fit in with the rest—not quite a diary entry, more so a letter. Addressed to her. As if she would ever go browsing through his things. Unless...

Ayla let out a shaky breath and gently pressed the creases before reading.

"My dear Ayla,

If you're reading this, something terrible has happened. I need you to know that you are in great peril once I'm no longer around to keep you safe. The world is cruel and unforgiving to any weakness. I made a terrible mistake by sheltering you from all the dangers instead of teaching you how to protect yourself. A mistake that I'll never atone for.

The mystery of your origin kept me awake for many nights as I was trying to pinpoint the reason why you appeared the way you did. You didn't just lose your memory. It was erased on purpose. Perhaps, it was too dangerous for you to know who you were or where you came from. I have a few leads, but don't think I'll be able to pursue any of them now. My time is running out.

Before we met, I was part of the society called Sorcerers. We are people with various magic talents. My gift, for instance, was passing along knowledge and seeing magic potential in others. I believe you have some yourself, even though it never manifested. One of the most powerful Sorcerers in our society was my Apprentice once. I wrote to him about you not too long ago, hoping he can find you if things go sour. He never replied, so my letter must have been lost.

Some Sorcerers capture people with hidden or underdeveloped magic abilities to use their power for themselves. That's what I fear most for you. I'm begging you, please run as far away as you can. It's very important that..."

The letter ended abruptly as if Darren was interrupted. The handwriting, rushed. Maybe he knew someone was coming. They had never spoken about anything like magic or Sorcerers before. Ayla's head spun with questions. Why did he never tell her that she might have magic powers? Was that the reason they moved to this little town? Most importantly, who was that former Apprentice of his that was supposed to find her?

Ayla rubbed her forearms and stood up. The night had already fallen and the streetlights cast a warm yellow that didn't radiate any real heat. She sighed, weighing her options for the near future. She had no money on her as she usually used the multi-pass for her bus rides to the city, and she'd spent her allowance for the day on coffee and a hot cheesy bun at the university's cafe. Her friends were in the city that she couldn't get to. She didn't have a coin to call someone, and Darren didn't have a phone in the study. The shops were closed. She had no spare clothes and her bike was still at the house. So was her bag with the multi-pass.

Ayla's thoughts spun in her head. *If Darren is dead, there's nothing for these people to look for. Especially if he sent them off somewhere else. And I need to get my stuff, otherwise, I'll freeze—besides, I'll be quick. In and out, just in case. I'll grab my bag and some clothes and run away.*

Checking every corner and staying in the shadows, she made her way back to the house. The little street was quiet as usual. Families were gathering around dinner tables, laying out cutlery, bringing out fresh roast and drinks.

Just like she used to do when things were normal. Darren taught her how to make sure the meat was always mouth-wateringly tender and the vegetables were cooked to perfection, not mushy or raw but the golden middle. She used to lay the table and he served the food, and then they both laughed and talked about the day's affairs and plans for the weekend...

The windows of her house were uncharacteristically dark. Nobody was waiting for her with a hot meal and a kind word anymore. The door was still ajar as she left it, the hall with her pictures on the walls open for everyone to see. Ayla stifled a sob, tiptoeing inside. Now wasn't the time to grieve. She had to collect her things and get out.

Not a sound disturbed the still air of the hallway. Alert to the slightest drift, Ayla crept to her bedroom, averting her eyes from the living room. She couldn't break down, not now. Even though Darren was still there, on that fluffy white carpet. Eyes glassed over. A pool of dark liquid under his chest no longer warm.

Ayla took in a shaky breath, trying to pull herself together. *In and out*, she reminded herself. *Only the necessities. Figure out the rest once I'm safe.*

The silence grew thicker as if foreboding of something terrible to come. It crept towards her, blended with the deep shadows, its tentacles brushing over her skin. Putting a blanket of deaf nothingness over the unsuspecting victim. It already reigned in the empty hallway, eating at her recent joy that now seemed surreal. It must have spread all over Darren's body in the living room. His study. Creeping towards her bedroom, deceitfully sluggish yet unstoppable. A silence to stifle any scream. Any plea for help.

Ayla shuddered, her skin covered in goosebumps. Her time was running out. Whatever this thing was, it was bad news. Something else was coming, something terrible. And she was the target.

She grabbed her overnight bag and started shoving in warm clothes, anything she could grab in the dark. A ticking of an invisible clock broke through the strange spell that covered the place. This eerie sound echoed in her ears, sending chills down her spine. Ayla paused for a moment, putting her hand on her chest to tame her racing heart. It was no use panicking now. Of course, it was the clock in the spare bedroom. It wasn't anything scary, not at all.

Yet somehow, this was the only sound she could hear.

Ayla whimpered, feeling the bag for her multi-pass. There was no sign of it—no wonder, she did leave it in her backpack when she came home. It would still be there, at the threshold of the living room where she dropped it. That was the only thing left. Once she had it, she could leave town and lose herself in the city. If only she had another second.

The silence abated, disrupted by somebody's voice. Someone was talking out in the street, bringing the conversation closer and closer to her house. The unintelligible mumble turned into sentences. Soon, Ayla was able to make out more of the conversation.

"...to be any good at what you do," a man's voice said, finishing the sentence. "One of the most important things for a Tracker is figuring out the thought process of your prey. A hunter yourself, you can only guess what the prey will do or how she will act during confrontation. Where will she run and how long will she hide before believing it's safe to come out? Getting into her head can be tricky, especially when you're just starting out."

The front door swung open. Millions of feet—but most likely, half a dozen—stomped around the hallway as if they owned the place. Ayla felt it impossible to shuffle even one centimetre.

"Is that why we brought Alicia, Master?" asked a younger voice. "To use her abilities so we can find our prey?"

"Exactly so." The first man sounded pleased. "Now, sweet Alicia is going to help us if she wants to see the light of day again, won't she?"

Alicia whimpered, the hopeless sound making Ayla's head spin.

The visitors' steps echoed along the hallway and disappeared into the soft carpet of the living room. Ayla's thoughts were racing. If they left the hallway to go through the living room into the study, she had a chance to dart out unnoticed. She'd just have to make do with the things she already packed. The multi-pass would have to stay behind.

"I'm alone and scared," a high-pitched voice sounded from the living room, approaching the hallway again. "I have no food, no money. It's cold outside. The hunters left, so I can get something from the house."

Ayla curled into a ball, trying to contain her fear. How did that girl know all this?

"I'm going to my room so I can get my things and some money," the voice went on. The steps stopped at her door, and Ayla quietly snuck into the large wardrobe. Hopefully, they weren't going to check this room first.

"Which bedroom is hers?" the younger man asked.

The one called Master scoffed. "That's easy to find out. If she's not here yet, we can wait until she comes. You better be right, Alicia. I hope you don't disappoint me."

"Yes, Master," Alicia blubbered, her voice shaky.

Ayla tried to hold her breath. If they wanted to wait, let them. She could stay here until they thought she wasn't coming and went looking elsewhere.

The wardrobe door opened. "Got you," the old man celebrated. His firm hand grabbed her forearm and dragged her out of hiding. Ayla blinked at the bright light of a torch shining in her face, helpless in its blinding glare. She closed her eyes, but the foreboding figures never left, floating around her vision as a nauseating phosphene.

CHAPTER 2. AYLA

An elegant black car with heavily tinted windows made its way through an upscale neighbourhood. The ride was so smooth Ayla could hardly believe they were moving. Neat, perfectly trimmed evergreens adorned the road, with a wild flash of red maple every now and then. Wrought iron fences protected beautifully landscaped gardens, paved and stone walkways, manicured lawns, marble statues, and flowers that were still in bloom. Daytime rapidly slipped away, replaced by the silver twilight that heralded the arrival of darkness.

Ayla had never liked the night. She spent most days studying—evenings were for dinners and chats and the occasional board game. Unknown places drew unease and going out at night felt like a waste of time. If she stayed up late, she would be too tired to study the next day. Being wild was something others did. Something she might have done once she finished school and graduated from university. An activity to enjoy with a very special person she was dreaming she would find one day. Not that the day was going to come anyway. Not the way things were now.

The desperate attempt to run away from her captors at the house ended with her being knocked out. When she first came to, she was lying on the plush back seat of this fancy car. The safety belt wasn't holding her in place, so even with her hands bound in front of her, she still had some freedom of movement.

The back area was separated from the driver by an obscure panel, which Ayla found out soon enough was soundproof. There wasn't much she could do in her position, no one to ask the burning questions, so she just sulked, staring at the scenery framed by the window. This was just unfair, how easily she got caught! Looking back now, she saw how careless she'd been. With her mind clouded by the stress and grief she was hardly able to make a better decision anyway.

The car slowed down gently, turning into the driveway. Ayla watched automatic gates close behind them, with a flashing red dot of the security camera on top. As they pulled over to the front door of the opulent mansion, she shivered at the sight of armed guards in bulletproof vests. One of them walked to the car and Ayla curled up in the far corner of the seat, hoping he wouldn't notice her. As much as she hated being restrained here, the thought of going into that mansion terrified her more.

The car door opened with a soft click and Ayla gasped quietly, tightening the grip of her arms around her knees.

"Out you go," a steely voice ordered, and she froze on the spot. "Come out or I'll drag you out!"

Ayla took a deep breath and slowly climbed out of the car, taking in her surroundings.

The house looked warm and welcoming, with all its lights illuminating the ample yard. The guard with an unsmiling face that looked as if it were carved from stone placed an unyielding grip on Ayla's arm and firmly led her to the sophisticated iron door. Just before it opened, she was able to catch a glimpse of a cluster of cameras above her head, and a wave of panic overcame her. What was with all the security?

A middle-aged butler in a tuxedo welcomed them in. Without a word, the guard nodded and made his way up the side stairs, with Ayla struggling to keep up but too scared to show any weakness.

A quick glance to the side revealed a massive door opening into a breathtakingly large ballroom decorated with flowers, candles and statues, and a cocktail buffet set up next to the opposite wall. The middle of the room was taken by rows of chairs with crimson sashes over them. All chairs were facing the wall Ayla couldn't see, but before she could even wonder about it, she was forced up the stairs and the ballroom disappeared from her sight.

A long corridor brought them to an unremarkable door. After a short double knock, the guard opened it and pushed her inside the brightly lit room.

"Hi there," a pleasant feminine voice purred, startling Ayla. A tall woman with a fashionable short haircut smiled at her warmly. "My name is Melody, I'm here to help you get ready for the auction."

Ayla looked around the room, noting the rich heavy curtains blocking the windows, the sophisticated leather-bound sofa, the intricate stonework of the small fireplace. This was undoubtedly a house of a wealthy person who most likely owned many, many more.

"What auction?" she inquired, the hair on her arms rising with the pitch of her voice. She ached to be out of there as soon as possible. Her foot angled for the door.

Melody ruffled her auburn hair and checked herself out in the tall mirror. "Oh, that's really exciting! You've never been to one before?" she asked. Ayla shook her head, and Melody continued. "Well, this is one of the best events of the year, excluding the Solstice galas, of course. A lot of influential Masters come here to get rare enchanted items. Sometimes it's something as simple as a branch of lovehaze captured in amber. Not the most unique item but quite powerful still, if you know how to use it. Other times it can be a cursed tiara or potion of truth. And the greatest thrill of all is when we're introduced to someone new and get to see the Masters compete for a fresh Apprentice!"

"Compete?" Ayla suppressed a cold shiver.

Melody leisurely walked to the small oak table and reached for a crystal decanter. The drink flowed into the sophisticated glass like a crimson river. The tall girl handed it to Ayla, giving her a kind smile. "Here, have some of this. It will help you relax a little," she advised.

Ayla politely took a sip and put the glass back. She wasn't sure if the drink would help tame her increasing anxiety. It tasted nice, but she wasn't going to let herself get drugged in the case it was laced. She had to stay alert.

Melody opened the door to the bathroom with a welcoming gesture. Ayla reluctantly stepped inside.

"Have a nice hot shower and then I'll tell you the rest."

The door clicked shut and Ayla caught her breath. A quick assessment of her surroundings brought her bitter disappointment. The window was a tiny rectangle under the roof, secured with fancy iron lace. The only door was the one she walked through, with Melody on the other side and potentially guards watching the door of the bedroom.

The air was infused with relaxing notes of lavender, aiming to create an easy-going, safe feeling. This room was much larger than the bathroom back home. A dedicated rest area with a small vanity table and a red velvet poof looked inviting and cosy. Ayla exhaled sharply, then took off her clothes and stepped onto the warm textured tiles in the shower, hoping the hot water would help her think of a solution to her situation.

Standing under the hot stream, Ayla couldn't stop worrying. What did it mean that the Masters "compete" for an Apprentice? Who were these Masters in the first place? What did she have to do with it all? Even considering Darren's words about her hidden magic, she didn't think she was worth all the fuss. There were so many questions, yet so few answers.

Ayla recalled the fancy ballroom set up for exquisite entertainment, the security cameras and armed guards throughout the whole house. She shuddered at the thought that those people were clearly incredibly rich and very likely insanely powerful. Would there even be any limits for them?

The shampoo smoothed out her hair and the fragrant shower gel glided over her body with delightful ease. All the luxuries were so relaxing, so welcoming—no doubt intending for Ayla to drop her guard and succumb to a veneer of safety before she was thrown to the wolves.

Ayla lowered herself on the poof and stared at her reflection in the mirror. At the dark circles under her eyes. Pale cheeks. Haunted expression. The troubles were only beginning. How was she going to find a way out?

A sharp knock on the door startled her.

"Are you ready? I'm sorry to disturb you but we don't have much time." Melody's voice cut through the door like a dagger.

With a sigh, Ayla opened the door. Melody gave her a sharp nod of approval and gestured to the plush sofa, where someone put out a beautiful outfit.

Before her lay a forest green corset dress that she came to realise fit her snug on top, with a long silk skirt that flowed like a waterfall with her every move. A hardly noticeable beading outlined the waistline, creating a shimmer effect. The alluring neckline descended to the crease between her breasts that was deepened by a lacy bra. An outfit like this served only one purpose—seduction.

Melody looked her up and down approvingly as Ayla shifted her weight from one foot to another.

"You're gorgeous! Let's do your hair and makeup now, and then you'll be good to go."

Ayla lowered herself onto the swivelling chair, her concerns inching their way back into her mind. Was there a way for her to escape this golden cage before something worse happened? Melody ignored her nervousness as she got along with her work, chirping away.

"Let me tell you more about tonight. As you may know, Masters are ascended Sorcerers. Having an Apprentice increases their authority in society, especially if it's a gifted one. An Apprentice can bring glory and power to their Master, but this is a thin line. Once powerful enough, an Apprentice ascends with their Master's approval. If a Master doesn't allow this, an Apprentice might challenge their Master. In case of victory, the old Master will lose all their power which will go to the new one. Does that make sense?"

Even though it didn't, Ayla still nodded, her mind racing. This was all so new and bizarre she decided to find out as much as possible to know what to brace herself for.

"What does it have to do with tonight? Why am I even here?" she inquired quietly, wary of upsetting the only person who chose to give her some of the much-needed information.

Melody giggled. "Hang on, I'm getting there. So, there are Apprentices and there are slaves, two completely separate things, even though it can become hard to distinguish between the two. Slaves come from various sources, the most common one being the BDSM scene. They enter the relationship for their own kink, without realising that the game is not actually a game. Another way is if they get into debt they can't repay. In any case, there's no way out for them. They are owned property that can be used by the Master as they please. Slaves can even be sold off to another Master without their consent, sometimes at an auction like tonight, to the highest bidder. Easy-peasy."

Ayla shook her head in disbelief. "Is this some kind of joke? Slavery was abolished centuries ago! Besides, I don't have any debts or magic powers."

Raising a perfect eyebrow, Melody gently glided her fingers through Ayla's hair, sculpting it into soft waves just below her exposed shoulders. "Nobody told you? How did your old Master explain his relationship with you?"

Ayla shrugged and her eyes widened as she met Melody's gaze in the mirror. "You mean Darren? I was never a slave and he was never a '*master*'. He picked me up from a park years ago when I was just a lost child. We couldn't find my parents, so he adopted me and raised me like his own daughter."

Adding the final touches to the hairdo, Melody chuckled. "Okay, I'll tell you then. Darren was one of the Sorcerers. We are a group of people who possess the gift of magic and are able to cast spells using an artefact charged with power. Every one of us either has a special talent or a set of mediocre abilities that help us fit into our society. Darren was one of the weaker Sorcerers, and all he could do was give a strong foundation to new Apprentices. His teaching was great, but he wasn't good for much else. He preferred to stick to his own ways, never joining the proper education system at the Academy. Living in the regular world among regular people seemed to suit him, and nobody really cared." She paused to admire her reflection over Ayla's head. "I myself love playing with style and fashion, and I even have some spells I created on my own! So far I'm still an Apprentice, but my Master says I'm going to ascend very soon and get an artefact of my own.

Anyway, now that Darren is dead, you have no Master. This means that you'll be assigned to a new one who will figure out what to do with you. Before becoming part of the auction, you will be assessed. If you have no potential powers, you will be sold as a regular slave to compensate for the expenses of the Hunters. But if you do have a hidden talent, you will be positioned as an Apprentice, which is quite rare. Masters don't die very often, you know. I bet you'll get lots of bids then!"

Ayla shuddered as the chills crept down her spine. "What if I don't want to be sold?" she demanded. "I'm a human being, and I haven't done anything wrong to any of these people. I don't have any debts to them, and I don't want to be an Apprentice to do magic or partake in whatever it is those Masters do. I just want to be left alone to have a chance to grieve the loss of my father and then figure out what to do with my life."

The tall girl's fingers dove into a large makeup kit and picked up a jar of foundation. Her movements were so swift and seamless that Ayla couldn't separate the moments when she changed from sponge to brush, or when her eyelashes were curled and the eye makeup went on.

"Oh honey, you'd better fix your attitude before you go on that stage. Your life is no longer yours, and the sooner you understand this, the better. A new Master may not like the sassy demeanour, and then you'll be in trouble. Trust me, the things they can do for punishment are something you only want to experience once. You'd do well to obey whatever they say and keep your snarkiness to yourself."

Sassy? Snarky? Ayla couldn't believe her ears. Was she expected to remain silent and let things happen as if she had no will of her own?

Melody's hands fluttered in front of Ayla's face and within an instant, the look was complete. Ayla quietly gasped as she took in her reflection. Despite her past beliefs, the long dress didn't make her look shorter than she already was. It hugged her figure without suffocating her, while the fine beading threw tiny sparkles all around. The purposefully loose waves of her hair seemed to be glowing, bringing out the golden highlights the way she'd never been able to before. Her eyes looked almost green as opposed to her usual light hazelnut, enhanced by the colours of her eye shadow. She turned her head from left to right, stunned by the view. A pair of gold hoops appeared in Melody's hands and she quickly clipped them into Ayla's ears.

"No necklace?" Ayla said flatly as her peer covered her shoulders with an airy light green scarf.

Melody scoffed, stepping back for a final glance over her handy work. "Not just yet. Don't you worry though, your new Master will give you one."

The door suddenly opened, letting a swift gust of air into the room as a man in his mid-forties walked in. He stopped a couple of steps away from Ayla and gave a short nod to Melody who bowed gracefully in response. Without acknowledging it, the man's steely grey eyes focused on Ayla, looking her over—she'd seen that look before, on the face of a man as he compared salami at the butcher. Ayla lifted her head defiantly, but before she had a chance to speak, the man used the opportunity to put his index finger under her chin, forcing her to look into his eyes.

"Lesson one. Don't ever do this in the presence of a Master. Be humble and look down unless told otherwise," he said in a low voice. Ayla stepped back and jerked her head to the side to get away from him. Who did he think he was?

The man scoffed. "Not the smartest one, are you? Well, being cheeky might just raise your price. Some Masters would love to tame a wild thing like you."

Ayla's mouth transformed into a frown as the man approached her again and grabbed her shoulder to keep her in place. Out of the corner of her eye, she noticed a massive gold ring with a bright green stone on his finger, seemingly glowing a little more as his grip tightened.

"Now, let's see if you have any other value. *Abre!*" he declared as she shied away from his penetrating stare. A foreign presence invaded her mind like a wave of unstoppable force. The man's will quickly overwhelmed her belated resistance. It ripped through her thoughts like steel wool. Pushing away her good memories. Stomping over her silent pleas for mercy. Careless of her pain to achieve what he wanted. Ayla shuddered when he stopped somewhere deep inside her subconscious, probing at something she didn't realise was there. Time froze as she was trapped in this iron cage, unable to move, to get out of his steel claws.

The torture was over as abruptly as it began. Ayla blinked, restoring her eyesight and bringing herself back to reality. The man turned away to leave without heeding her any further attention, as if she was nothing but a piece of furniture.

Melody rushed to open the door in front of him, unable to contain her curiosity. "Did you find anything, Master Sawyer?" she bounced on the spot.

The man smiled at her eagerness as he stopped for a moment to reply. "Indeed. The little brat definitely has potential—and quite a decent one, mind you. I believe the bids are going to skyrocket. It's going to be a great show. Enjoy!"

Ayla sat down on the chair, wrapping her arms around her as she shivered after the unpleasant experience. The temperature in the room left her freezing.

"What did he do to me?" she whimpered quietly. The aftertaste of the man's presence in her mind, bitter and disturbing. All of a sudden, her desire to run away disappeared. The only thing she wanted now was to hide under a fuzzy blanket and get this awful discomfort out of her system. To stay there until this nightmare was over and things were back to normal.

Melody glanced at her with a shadow of sympathy deep in her eyes. "Hey, it's okay. He just made an assessment to see if you had any magic potential. I know, it's not a great feeling but at least now you know that one day you'll be free to do whatever you want! If you get a good Master, you might actually enjoy being an Apprentice. Like me!"

Ayla covered her face with her hands. She had no more energy to fight, to try to escape, to stand up for herself. Fatigue fouled every fibre inside, casting indifference. She didn't care what the future held for her. If only she could get just a little sleep.

The door opened again, heavy steps announcing another presence. "Time to go," declared an authoritative voice, and a security guard grabbed her by the arm.

Melody followed them along the narrow corridor into the little room behind the stage and gently wiped Ayla's tears away with a soft cotton ball. "Good luck!" she whispered to Ayla. "Remember, do as your Master says and everything will be alright."

In an instant, she was gone. Ayla stood there alone, staring at the dark heavy curtain separating her from the noisy ballroom on the other side. Residual pain settled in her head. Nobody was there to help her. The thing that man, Sawyer, did to her should have been illegal.

Ayla rubbed her forearms, wishing she had something warmer to wear. It was so cold she half expected her breath to come out as steam. *Probably not actually cold*, she told herself. *Must be the effects of that nasty spell or whatever it was. I hope someone does it to him some day.*

The auctioneer made an announcement. As the curtain raised, so did rapturous applause. The little, flat circle Ayla stood on raised itself to a pedestal. She wavered, nearly losing her balance as she ascended higher and higher. Once her position settled, she straightened her back and braced herself to face the crowd.

CHAPTER 3. AYLA

B right stage lights overwhelmed her as the applause slowly abated. Eyes wide, Ayla looked around the ballroom, trying to mask her fear. A massive vintage chandelier reigned over the open space, with hundreds of bright candles nestled among pristine crystals. The modern stage Ayla was standing on brought about a stark contrast with the rest of the room. Polished black glass and immaculate steel skirting with built-in LED lights gave the impression of a state-of-the-art theatre. Studying her surroundings, Ayla wondered if this stage ever hosted a formal orchestra playing a *minuet* while elegant couples exchanged bows and curtseys before indulging in classical dance. A dreamy smile crossed Ayla's lips. The captivating symphony of perfectly tuned instruments flowing over the crowds like a gentle river... She loved the timeless classics, even though a good performance was hard to come by in the little town she had lived in before. She didn't belong on this stage.

With a nervous gulp, she rubbed her shoulders again. A mocking giggle lashed at her like a whip and she flinched, struggling to keep her balance. Annoyed by this moment of weakness, Ayla looked around to pinpoint the source of that laughter, but everyone was quiet now, studying her with the curiosity of a child gawking at animals at the zoo.

The crowd looked like a giant dark mass with white spots, largely consisting of men in tuxedos and black dinner suits. Only every so often there were flashes of sparkling gemstones on stunning necklaces gracing the necks of stern-looking women. Some of the guests were standing on the opposite side of the room by the cocktail buffet. With glasses of sparkling wine in their hands, they seemed indifferent to the auction, more preoccupied with the selection of finger foods on display.

Ayla looked over the sea of faces in a desperate hope to see sympathy, when one of them caught her eye. Unlike the other spectators, this man stared at her so intensely she could swear she saw tiny beads of sweat forming on his forehead, despite the cool air of the room. His dark eyes seemed to emanate danger, and Ayla felt the chills starting their inevitable journey down her spine. She gulped nervously, resisting the urge to curl into a ball and cry.

"I'm not afraid," she whispered to herself. "He can't hurt me, I'll find a way to escape. But I need a cool head for that. I'm not afraid. I'm not afraid."

The man leaned forward, his eyes never leaving her. Ayla shivered and rubbed her arm, barely stopping herself from digging her nails into the skin. Pain used to help her in scary situations, but here this would undoubtedly be seen as a vulnerability. Something told her these people wouldn't take kindly to any signs of weakness.

The auctioneer slammed his hammer to announce Ayla, nearly making her jump.

"And now, the exciting last lot today is our latest arrival, ladies and gentlemen. This shy little lamb has a sassy attitude that she showed our Maestro during the assessment. No prior knowledge or experience with magic, yet a fair potential to develop into a moderately powerful Sorceress. This rare find came to us as heritage from Master Darren, who is now, sadly, deceased. All profits are going to Master Asher who captured her with his fantastic team of two Apprentices. As you can see, this innocent sweetheart is a pretty little thing too, so she could become a worthy addition to your parties or bedtime routines. Provide a bit of motivation for her to learn quickly."

A few people laughed at the comment, and even before the starting bid was announced, several hands shot up in the air. The auctioneer chuckled, calling the crowd to order. Ayla studied the faces in the audience, squinting from the blinding stage lights. Eyes sparkling with excitement. Smiles plastered on faces. Hands in the air to raise the bid. What were these people? How could they even do this to a human being?

"Three hundred."

"Three hundred quills on the left, going once! Anybody give four hundred?"

"I give five!"

"Five hundred in the third row! Anybody give six hundred?"

Ayla gulped, realising he didn't mean mere hundreds. They were dealing with hundreds of thousands of quills. Darren's whole house would have cost less than the first bid. And these people were just throwing the money around as if it were nothing. To get her as their... Apprentice? What was the purpose of an Apprentice? What would happen to one that failed? After all, she never thought things like magic were real. And she doubted that she truly had any, as her aptitude had not made itself known.

They're all wrong. If I'm so special, why didn't this Master Asher keep me for himself? He knows I'm a fake, that's why. They just want the money, and when the new Master learns I'm worth nothing, he'll kill me.

The dark, bearded man was among the first ones who raised the bets, beating his competitors by far every time his hand went up. The room grew quieter as there were fewer and fewer bidders able to match his price.

Isn't he going to run out of money? There has to be a limit for everyone. Or does it not exist for this guy?

Ayla shuddered as she caught his triumphant gaze. The man was clearly ready to celebrate his victory. Eyes sparkling, a grin on his face, he leaned forward as if he were to grab her there and then. Almost unknowingly, she made a small step back. Her whole body was screaming for her to run away, but how was that possible? With all these people watching her, all the armed guards across this giant property, all the security cameras. There was no chance of escaping. She had to wait and see if she'd have a chance during transit to her new location.

"Sold to Tamil Asfour. Please, proceed to the Velvet Room on your left, sir." The auctioneer slammed the hammer to finalise the sale, the echo of the impact tearing through Ayla's body.

The podium whirred and slowly went down. Trembling head to toe, Ayla saw the dark man stand up and make his way towards one of the doors. He didn't pay her any more attention as if she didn't exist anymore. The crowd relaxed and switched to leisurely conversations and the beautiful cocktail buffet on the other side of the room. Ayla's eyes scanned her surroundings. The guards were chatting about, with guns carelessly hanging off their hoists. Nobody looked at her.

With a gulp, she stepped off the podium before it lowered into the tiny room under the stage. No doubt, someone would be waiting for her there. But now, she had a second or two. Her whole body covered in goosebumps, Ayla turned towards the side exit on her left, lit up by a cheerful green arrow. The guards must have left and it promised a quick escape. What next? She would figure it out later.

Ayla drew in a sharp breath, grabbed the long hem of her dress and sprinted towards freedom. She never was that quick in her old life and she'd always hated running. This time, her speed surprised her. Crazy how danger could enhance her physical abilities.

"Hey! Where are you going?" Someone's raspy voice slashed her hearing like a knife, but she didn't look back. *Keep running. The door is so close...*

She rushed down the steps of the stage, careful not to trip. Falling down would be the worst. All the run-aways were captured if they fell. Not something she could afford right now. A strange sensation pricked her skin. Danger. Something bad was about to happen.

"Don't shoot, you'll ruin the goods," another voice commanded, and the sensation disappeared. Ayla crossed the threshold of the door and stopped for a split second. The corridor behind it stretched in two ways. Where did she have to go? Heart racing in panic, she tried to clear her mind and remember the way she was brought in. Which would logically lead her outside? *Think fast! Which way?*

A strong hand gripped her arm, making her yelp. "Stupid girl. Where do you think you're going?" The guard turned her around and shook her by the shoulders. "Masters will beat you to a pulp if you try this again and get caught. Or do something way worse. Is that what you want?"

"I just want to go home. Please, I didn't do anything," she pleaded, searching the guard's dark eyes for mercy. He had a harsh look to him, but maybe, just maybe he would hear her desperation. Maybe he had a daughter her age, or a niece. There had to be something that could help her. A soft spot for someone in her position. Kidnapped and sold like a piece of meat. Forced to do who knows what against her will.

The guard shook his head, a shadow of sadness on his face. "Not with the fortune he paid for you. It's all about money here, little girl. And politics. You have no idea what you've gotten yourself into. This is serious. One thing you should know is that you can't run away now. You must obey him and hope for the best."

"Come on, time to go and meet your new Master," a new voice boomed behind her. Another firm grasp locked on her other arm.

"No," she whimpered as the guards dragged her back through the auction room and into another corridor. "I'm not a slave, this is a mistake!"

The guards remained silent as they lugged her further along. With a sharp push between her shoulder blades, they forced her inside the familiar room, nearly making her fall. "Wait here," the second guard ordered and slammed the door shut. A soft click of the lock brought about another wave of exasperation. The beautiful lounge with a cosy fireplace was warm, yet Ayla was freezing. Fear of the unknown squeezed her heart in its iron grip. Surely, she would suffocate. She slowly lowered herself onto the soft couch, wrapping her arms around her. Her head was spinning so much she was afraid she might faint.

It's going to be okay. I'll think of something. There's always a way, I just need to collect my thoughts. Once I've calmed down, I'll figure it out. I'll be okay.

There was a little technique that Darren taught her when she stressed herself out before exams. "Breathe in on 4... hold for 3... breathe out on 4... and again..."

The technique never seemed to work at first, but eventually, Ayla's heartbeat slowed down and the dizziness faded away. She opened her eyes and looked around, taking her time to study every object in the room for usefulness. The armchairs and the sofa wouldn't be much help, but what about the wardrobe and the chest of drawers?

The lock clicked again and Melody flew through the door, her cheeks rosy and her auburn hair slightly dishevelled. Ayla dropped her hands to her sides, pretending that she was only checking herself out in the mirror. Luckily, Melody was so excited she didn't seem to notice.

"Congratulations! You've set a new record by far! Nobody has ever seen a bid like the one you got!" she exclaimed, taking her makeup kit out of the drawer again. Ayla pushed Melody's hand away from her face in annoyance. In a moment like this, she didn't feel the need for a touch-up. This girl was either stupid or completely lacking empathy.

"What's so great about being sold like a slave?" she snapped and stopped to take a breath. After all, Melody was the only one who seemed agreeable... Maybe she would be able to help? "I'm sorry, it's just all new to me," Ayla apologised, hoping that her words sounded convincing. "I'm very scared, surely you can understand."

Melody gently brushed her hair, restoring the waves and freshened up her makeup, ignoring Ayla's alarmed tone. She stepped back to admire the result and cocked her head to the side, a dreamy smile on her face. "You just have to trust him. It's going to be okay," she replied in a soothing voice. Before Ayla could object, the heavy door opened again and the unpleasant Master Sawyer walked in, followed by the dark man who had purchased her, Tamil. Looking her up and down, he grunted approvingly and walked closer to her.

"Last formality, and she's all yours," Sawyer grinned. Tamil rolled his shoulders and tapped his foot impatiently.

"Let's get it over with. I don't have much time," he barked in a hoarse voice. Ayla yelped as Sawyer's strong hands ripped the silk scarf off her shoulders and wrapped a thick leather collar around her throat. The soft click of the lock sounded unnaturally loud in the ensuing silence. The cold metal ring stung her chest, and she instinctively stepped back, pulling at the collar with her fingers to loosen it as panic rapidly took over her mind.

"Take it off! I can't breathe!" She fought against Sawyer's grasp, writhing and panting. Her body betrayed her, letting a survival instinct loose. It didn't matter what consequences she would face in the future, even if it was the near future. All that mattered now was the collar. It had to be taken off immediately!

Sawyer turned her around in one swift move and clicked his fingers in front of her face. The gold ring on his finger flashed green as he quietly pronounced, "*Cálmate, pequeña.*"

Ayla breathed out and went quiet as her consciousness grew fuzzy. Peace descended upon her, and nothing mattered anymore. Why fight if it was futile anyway? She had nowhere to go. It was much easier to comply, wasn't it?

As she dropped her hands, Sawyer quickly bound her wrists together with a piece of silken rope. Melody gingerly picked up a silver chain and fed one end through the ring on Ayla's chest, handing the other to Tamil. He forced her to step closer to him.

"That's better. Now, a crash course on how to behave, since you seem to have zero idea about etiquette. When your Master asks a question, you must answer straight away. 'Yes, Master' or 'No, Master' are acceptable answers. Forget the formal address, and you'll be punished. Don't obey your Master's commands, and you'll be punished.

Misbehave or let your Master down, and you'll be punished. Even the toughest ones break, and you certainly won't last long. Do you understand?"

Ayla nodded, and added hurriedly, "Yes, Master."

The man gave her a half smile. "Good girl. You'll be on the leash until you are trained to obey your Master completely," he stated plainly. "Trust me, it's for your own safety. Don't get it in your head that you can run away. You have nowhere to go. But your Master will treat you well if you're good. He won't hurt you unless you misbehave."

A strange thought made its way through the haze in Ayla's head. She carefully raised her eyes to his face, almost flinching as she half expected him to hit her.

"Aren't you my Master?" she asked faintly. A weak ray of hope suddenly lit up her thoughts. Maybe things weren't as bad as she imagined.

Tamil scoffed and motioned her to the door. "Hell no, I wouldn't so much as touch a weakling like you. Now hurry up. We've lost too much time on this nonsense."

Downstairs, a chauffeur in a black dress suit bowed his respect and opened the back door of a luxury car with lightly tinted windows. The chain was removed, but before Ayla realised her sudden freedom, a sharp push on the back landed her on the soft seat. With her hands bound, she barely managed to keep her face from hitting the perfectly cured leather. An engine whirred and the car softly pulled away past the mansion's lights and guards, through geometric-shaped dwarf trees and into the night streets.

Beautiful mansions blurred and fell out of sight as the car merged flawlessly onto the highway. Bright city lights became more and more scarce until nothing but darkness reigned over the deserted world.

CHAPTER 4. AYLA

A yla could not give clear definition between what she witnessed or hallucinated during her car trip, but nevertheless she saw a figure of a large white tiger racing alongside their vehicle, following whatever strange whim or compulsion a wild animal does. The car slowed down, turning into a brightly lit service station, but the tiger turned east, where if it ran for long enough it would meet the inevitable rising sun. They pulled into one of the parking spots away from the entrance to the little shop, and Ayla scoffed. Of course, they wanted to avoid cameras. How predictable!

The driver and the passenger got out, voices muffled by the thick glass separating them from her. She pressed her face to the window, trying to catch what they were saying.

"I'm sure I've told you to get a full tank before the auction," Tamil raised his voice.

A grimace crossed the driver's face but he remained reserved, or perhaps Ayla was simply trying to give definition to his indiscernible features. "Yes sir, and I did. That was before Camilla wanted to go out and then ordered me to drive around the clubs".

Tamil sighed, scratching the back of his head. A bitter smile touched his lips. "There's always something with her. Well, this delay, and in a public spot of all places, is going to cost precious time that we don't have. Hurry up!"

The driver nodded his agreement and retrieved a fuel card from his pocket. Tamil walked towards the small corner shop as the car doors made an unmistakable locking sound. Ayla moved to the opposite window and checked the other side of the small service station. Two other cars were fuelling up, their drivers too busy chatting. Neither of them looked in her direction, lost in an animated discussion with occasional bursts of laughter.

Hope came where she least expected. A slender teenager in a dark hoodie was standing just a couple of metres away, staring at the expensive car she was in. The plastic bottle of orange juice in his hands froze half-way to his mouth as he gaped at the image of pure luxury in front of him, something he would probably only see on TV.

Ayla waved her tied hands in the window, hoping he could see her through the lightly tinted glass. She banged on the glass a few times, then pressed her palms to it. Soon enough, the teenager noticed. His eyebrows went up in surprise as he realised what was happening. Ayla mouthed "*help me*" a few times until she was sure he got the message.

As the driver finished topping up the fuel and got back into the car, the teenager turned his back and walked towards the payphone at the corner of the shop. The passenger door opened and slammed shut as Tamil returned with a small bag of food and a tray with two steaming coffees. Ayla's eyes didn't leave the slender figure dialling a three-digit number until the car pulled away again and the bright lights of the service station disappeared in the dark.

The smooth highway once again swallowed the captors and their prey. Ayla curled up into a ball on the backseat, hopelessly clawing and biting into the unyielding rope around her wrists. She had been doing it on and off ever since they left the mansion, but the only result she got was angry sores that were becoming itchier as the minutes crawled by.

A sudden wail of the police siren made her jump. She twisted herself around to see the blinding flashes of red and blue rapidly approaching them. An uncertain smile appeared on her face as thoughts of hope rushed into her mind.

The siren was now straight behind them, and the car started slowing down to pull over at the curb. Ayla bounced impatiently as the police officer with a flashlight approached the driver's side.

An unwelcome thought bisected Ayla's happy thoughts—what if they were going to shoot the officer and keep moving? She had seen too many movies where things ended just like that. Shaking with fear for the unknown man in uniform, she pushed herself into the seat as if it was going to help him somehow.

The driver calmly slipped his licence through the window and sat patiently while the officer studied it.

"Do you mind if I check the back?" Ayla heard him say and her heart skipped a beat. She was sure now it was the teenager's call that made this happen, and she said a silent prayer for him. The bright glow of the flashlight went through the back window and Ayla banged against it with all the strength she had left.

"Help me, please! Help!" she screamed, showing him her tied hands, tears running down her cheeks as a wild hope conquered previous thoughts. Help was right there in front of her. The officer had to do something, to get her out of there. She would tell the police everything that had happened and maybe they would raid that cursed place and stop the slavery and kidnappings and whatever else those people were doing. After all, it was their job.

The policeman turned back to the driver, but before he could say anything, Tamil leaned toward the window.

"This is a gift for Corbin Blackbyrne, officer. Is there a problem?"

A small object in his hands bloomed bright green. The officer's face blanked. Eyes wide, Ayla watched the policeman shake his head. "No problem at all. Have a good night, sir," he replied with a salute and turned away.

The engine roared back to life, and Ayla was once again alone on the leather seats. She leaned back and stayed quiet. Though shapeless, the figure of this Corbin weighed heavy. He elicited anger and anxiety in those who spoke or heard his name. Maybe, if she said it three times in the car window, he'd appear over her reflection and pull out her teeth.

It wasn't long before the car slowed down for the exit off the highway. Ayla sullenly looked out at the faceless buildings that seemed to be abandoned warehouses, and the gaping darkness between them. Soon the road disappeared into the thick forest and Ayla lost track of time. It could have been minutes or an hour before they decreased speed once again, turning into a hidden driveway.

As the car crept along, tall trees gave way to the spacious yard dimly lit by a few solar lights scattered along the paved driveway. The tyres softly rustled over the fallen leaves and the vehicle came to a halt. Ayla cautiously looked out the window, trying to estimate her chances in this new environment. The building she was brought to looked like yet another mansion, but of an older build than the ones back in the city. Black stones and dark windows, all guise and no warmth—a tomb built for an ancient king, the kind who ordered for all his household to be buried with him when he died. This house was no home.

The car door opened. A silver chain locked on her collar before Ayla had a chance to protest. Tamil roughly yanked on it, forcing her out. She pulled at the collar, rallying her anger to smother her terror. How could she be so naive to believe she could run away after the auction? She should have made a run when they were still making bets. The guests would have been overwhelmed and this would have caused just enough confusion to let her out of there before they figured it out.

Tamil's iron grip dragged Ayla towards a impenetrable wooden door with an iron framework. The sound of the bell resonated deep within the mansion's walls, bringing back an echo that sent shivers down her spine. Maybe nobody was home. As sweet as that thought was, Ayla knew better than to believe it.

The door creaked open, revealing a woman in a maid's outfit, whose friendliness belied the command of her stocky build and confident posture. The woman's greying hair was pulled into a neat bun on the back of her head, similar to the way the skin on her face and arms pulled against her bones, dark and hardened, as if she had spent most of her life in the sunny fields or the open sea.

"Welcome. Master Corbin is expecting you," her voice relayed, mellow and relaxed. A gracious smile rested on her lips, and not a muscle on her face showed any surprise. People in collars and chains mustn't have been out of the ordinary.

The maid bowed and closed the door behind them. As she led the way, Ayla caught a whiff of freshly baked pastries, and feelings of loss rose with bile in her throat. Immersed in her thoughts—using her tongue as a levee to contain her emotion—she didn't pay much attention to her surroundings, and only when they entered a luxurious study did she realise something important was about to happen.

The maid silently bowed and stepped back. "Your guests are here, Master."

A tall, slender man rose from a leather chair and walked around the large wooden desk he'd been sitting at. Beetles spread, pinned in frames by his head. Ayla diverted her gaze to the floor. She remembered the instructions. The man stopped in front of the desk, and his polished black shoes crossed Ayla's line of sight. Feeling his eyes on her, she remained perfectly still, not even blinking. If he liked her, she might be granted some freedom. For now, she would play by their rules until she figured out a way to deceive them.

"This is the girl, Corbin," Tamil said, his voice a drastic change from what she'd heard before. The arrogant, annoying brute that brought her here was reduced to a puppy before its superior. Ayla frowned at the peculiar transformation. Corbin didn't reply straight away, studying her.

Compelled by the eerie silence, Ayla raised her eyes to his face and accidentally met the gaze of his deep black eyes. But holding it for even an instant was far too long. Oh, in just one second he'd pinned her to the wall with an invisible toothpick or needle or probe. Thankfully, he chose to look away and focus on her companion, so she was able to take a shaky breath.

"Are you sure she's the right one?" he asked in a low, velvety voice.

Tamil responded straight away as if finishing a trick in hopes of a treat or belly rub. "Yes, absolutely! Everything aligns. Asher caught her in Darren's old house, and she was brought straight to the auction. I spent half of my fortune buying her. I guarantee it's the right one. Is this enough?"

He produced a piece of paper from his pocket and hurriedly placed it on the table. Corbin glanced at it and paused for another lengthy second.

"Greedy bastards. Asher should have brought her straight to me, I would have doubled anything they got at the auction." He shook his head. "And you, Tamil. You know better than to try and deceive me. If she is indeed the one, I will honour our arrangement."

"Thank you, Corbin." The man carefully handed him Ayla's chain as she stood still, eyes fixed on the new Master's polished shoes. "She's a bit unruly, I must say. No manners whatsoever and I wouldn't be surprised if she tried to run away. Sawyer had to sedate her so she would shut up about the collar and how it was suffocating her. Some sort of claustrophobia, I guess."

Ayla's cheeks reddened with anger and embarrassment. It wouldn't do any good to show her feelings now, even though being talked about as if she were an object was not something she was used to. Emotions were flying high, and she bit her lip hard, until a hot salty liquid seeped into her mouth. Everything in her body was shouting the need to run away, and she struggled to maintain a calm appearance. Luckily, neither of the men seemed to notice.

"I appreciate the intel. You're free to go," Corbin replied, and the dark man left the room.

Ayla was alone with her new Master. When Corbin's hand reached for her, she flinched. He retracted, only to reach for her again and gently touch her collar.

"Don't be afraid," he soothed as the lock clicked open and her neck felt the sweet cool air for the first time in hours.

Ayla took a shallow breath, wary of something terrible that might come after. It was strange not to look at the face of the person talking to her. Reminding herself of the darkness she saw in his eyes, she thought that might have been a good thing.

"You don't need this when you're with me." The chain rattled as he put the collar on his study table. "Or this." He touched the rope on her wrists and the stubborn knot fell apart as if it was barely tied.

"Thank you... Master," Ayla croaked, throat dry.

Corbin shook his head with a sad smile and ever so softly ran his fingers along her jawline. She was startled by the unexpected touch but reminded herself to keep still. His hand was warm like any regular human being. Nothing deadly at all. "No need to call me Master when we're alone, just Corbin is fine. What's your name?"

A subtle strain in his voice made Ayla tense harder. Something told her it was an important question, one that she should give the right answer to. She dared to look into the impenetrable darkness of his eyes but there was nothing to tell her what he expected. "Ayla. It's spelt A-Y-L-A," she replied and closed her eyes, as if this would protect her from whatever was coming if the answer was wrong.

Nothing happened, though; the air was just as still and quiet, with only her accelerated heartbeat breaking the silence.

"Darren's daughter, right? He told me about you, and I've been looking everywhere to make sure I was the one to take you in. Poor thing, you must be terrified. I'm sorry you had to go through so much, but things will get better now. You're safe here."

Ayla blinked, chasing away the unwelcome tears. The strain of the past hours settled in her bones. She thought about the last time she felt safe, when she got off the city bus and rushed to tell Darren her big news. How she'd hoped to see his bright white smile that always seemed to erase years off his tanned face. Oh, if only she'd come home earlier that day!

The thought of being back home overpowered all others. This was all just a nightmare. Darren was going to come into her room and gently shake her awake, and then they'd say a quick mantra to push the bad dreams away.

Dark is the night, but bright is the day,
It's going to chase all the terrors away.
So all you can say and believe that it's true,
They'll never come back, because I've got you!

That mantra never failed her. Ayla smiled, silently repeating the little rhyme, entranced by its power that she believed in with all her heart. With a quiet thud, she slumped to the floor as her consciousness left her strained body. A lone tear slowly ate its way through the makeup on her cheek, glistening in the cosy light of the study. The last image that impressed upon her was of one of the larger, heavier insects on the wall. Corbin had used far too many pins to pose the beetle in its natural stance. The image blinked away. Everything went quiet.

CHAPTER 5. AYLA

Golden rays of morning sun gently touched the silk pillows, slowly making their way to Ayla's face. Half awake, she stretched and smiled to herself. The bed was comfortable and warm, just like back home. In a moment, her alarm would go off to announce the beginning of another productive day at university. Darren would pour her a cup of black coffee with a slice of lemon and they would chat about their plans.

"You're safe here," an unfamiliar voice said inside her head, and she jolted awake.

Rolling over to another side, Ayla spotted an array of happy chrysanthemums in pots by the window. Darren used to buy small bouquets of seasonal flowers to bring home on Fridays, to signify the end of the hard work of the week and the beginning of a time to rest and rebalance. They had a little vase made from green frosted glass that Darren had inherited from his mother, which complemented every flower that rested inside. He used to say that the vase would be Ayla's once he was gone and hearing him say that used to upset her to no end. She wiped away an unwelcome tear. Now was not the time to properly grieve.

The door opened with a soft click, and Ayla turned to see her visitor. A young maid walked in and offered a polite smile. In the bright light of the morning, her sun-kissed skin was in stark contrast to the brilliant white collar of the traditional maid's outfit. Her jet-black hair sat in a smooth bun without the slightest imperfection. Her smile was that of an impeccably schooled professional, though there was no trace of warmth in her eyes.

"Good morning Ayla, my name is Dolores. I run the household here." Her voice level, she set a neat pile of skilfully folded clothes on the bed. "These are for you. Please choose what you'd like to wear to breakfast and come downstairs when you're ready. The meal will be served in the small dining room."

Before Ayla could ask any questions, the maid turned on her heel and briskly walked out of the room, closing the door behind her. Ayla sighed and rolled out of bed. A closer examination of the clothes revealed a few lounge outfits and a couple of long dresses, all in the same natural colour palette. Not willing to make herself late, she quickly put on a pair of wide-legged pants and a beige cotton jumper. A trip to the bathroom revealed a modest hygiene pack consisting of a small hotel-style tube of toothpaste, a brand new toothbrush, a bar of lavender-scented soap and a comb. With the morning routine out of the way, Ayla rushed downstairs.

The delightful smell of freshly baked pastries guided her through the long corridor and into the small dining room. Ayla realised she hadn't eaten for nearly two days now, and steadied her step not to appear too eager. The beauty of the place went unnoticed as she saw the feast set up on the table. Piles of pancakes, seasonal and exotic fruit, cheeses and waffles—her eyes could hardly process it all. She swallowed nervously, glancing around to make sure there was no potential trouble. The room only held her and the friendly old maid from the night before; there was no sign of Corbin or anyone else. Was she allowed to start in his absence?

"Master normally comes down to breakfast later." The maid's eyes were kind and understanding. "Help yourself to anything you like, no need to be shy."

Ayla gingerly picked up a small dessert plate and started with a couple of pancakes with some fresh whipped cream on top. On a separate dish, she placed a few slices of seasonal apples and pears. It seemed like she'd only sat down when her plates were already empty. Thankfully, the maid was observant.

"Would you care for some omelette? It's one of Master's favourite recipes, brought from one of his travels to the East."

Ayla nodded her agreement, grateful for the maid's keen eye. Her eyes sparkled as a generous serving of steaming hot perfection was placed in front of her. Deliciously fluffy, the omelette had a creamy texture that almost melted in her mouth, with a touch of cheese, speckled with sun-ripened tomato, juicy ham, sweet pepper and a rich bouquet of spices she couldn't distinguish. Coming together, the omelette was an impeccable symphony of tastes. Ayla signed happily and leaned back on her chair once she cleared that plate too. She might have eaten too much, but this wasn't important now.

Sated and relaxed, she inhaled the refreshing aroma of skilfully brewed coffee that was placed in front of her in lieu of the dirty plates. A snow-white macaroon waited on the porcelain saucer with a delicate blue ribbon around the edge, and the creamy froth on the drink was twisted into a little heart. Ayla smiled her gratitude to the chef who created all of this for a stranger in the house. Her face dropped at the thought. That was all she was. A stranger at best—but most likely, a slave without rights—who was brought here in chains, on a leash like an animal. This breakfast masterpiece wasn't created for her. It was for the Master of the house who was now holding her fate in his hands.

Ayla startled at the sound of approaching footsteps from the corridor. Frozen on her spot, she watched Corbin appear at the threshold. Today, he was wearing a fitted shirt in pastel blue, and a pair of classic-cut jeans. Some strands of his short dark hair were accentuated by gel, giving him a perfect casual look. The polished black shoes from last night were swapped for a pair of stylish sneakers.

The whole room seemed to have transformed with his arrival. The maid straightened up and threw back her shoulders to try and match the impeccable posture of the Master. The air filled with silent yearning to serve and please. Ayla carefully studied the plate in front of her. Was she even allowed to sit at the same table? She held her breath when he lowered himself onto a leather-bound chair at the head of the table, just one seat away from her.

"Good morning Ayla," he greeted her warmly, as he took the skilfully folded linen napkin and spread it on his knees. She kept looking at the little spot in front of her where she had accidentally dropped a tiny piece of ham from the omelette. Her cheeks grew hot with shame. There was no time to remove that piece.

"Good morning Master... um, Corbin," she whispered. The movement in the corner of her eye told her that he shifted his weight and leaned on the table.

"Please look at me when we're talking, this is unsettling. You can follow the etiquette when we're out, but this is your new home. It's a safe space, Ayla, and I intend to keep it this way. You are not a slave here."

Ayla filled her lungs with air and slowly breathed out. She looked at Corbin's face, for the first time having a chance to properly study it. It was cleanly shaven, with high cheekbones hinting at a potential Nordic bloodline. A friendly smile on his lips found a reflection in his deep-set midnight eyes. A hint of fine lines on his forehead and in the corner of his eyes betrayed his age as mid-thirties. There was no sign of the dark aura she sensed the night before, and Ayla wondered if she had imagined it. After all the trauma of the past couple of days, she wasn't sure she could trust her judgement.

"If I'm not a slave, does it mean I can leave?" she blurted, surprising herself. Immediately, she covered her mouth with her hand. "I'm so sorry," she rambled. "I didn't mean to..."

Corbin raised his hand and she went quiet, seeing it as a sign to stop. "This is a valid question. After all, why wouldn't you, after everything that's happened? The answer is, yes you can leave. Where will you go? I don't know, and it won't be my problem once you walk through that door. You've been assessed as a Sorceress with good potential, but it needs to be trained. With nobody around to help when your gift manifests itself, who knows what can happen? Best case scenario, you panic and make a few serious mistakes that are likely to cause serious damage to yourself or others. Worst case, you implode trying to contain the force you don't understand. There are also some people out there who hunt amateur Sorcerers to drain their power, but if you're careful, you might just survive."

Shocked by his blunt answer, Ayla couldn't find the words to reply. She watched him nod to the maid who filled his cup with steaming hot coffee from the French press and carefully placed a white porcelain jug by his side, with just enough milk for his drink. Ayla's eyes followed the reserved movements of the head of the house as he took a couple of sugar cubes out of the glass jar and dipped them in the coffee. As he stirred it and poured the milk into the cup.

Taking a sip, he cast his gaze upon her again.

"So, I have an offer. You have until the end of the day to figure out if you want to stay or not, and this choice will be irrevocable. If you decide to leave, make sure you allow some time to get to the highway before nightfall. You can keep the clothes you're wearing, just remember it gets chilly at night. However, if you stay, you will accept the rules of the house. I will provide my protection and guidance to help you nurture your talent safely until you're ready to follow your own path. In return, I expect full compliance."

Ayla needed to stay calm until she was alone. There was no need to make her decision right now. The maid returned, serving Corbin his own fluffy omelette. Without paying her much more attention, he started his meal with the reserved grace of someone who had been raised in an aristocratic family. She wondered if he did belong to high society when he was a child or if he made his place in it. Her thoughts wandered into a strange limbo as she avoided the pressing matter of her fate.

If what he said was true, she couldn't afford to lose control of her dormant magic. Even though she had never seen it manifest, another Sorcerer was sure it was there. And Darren, too. Considering she had never suspected that her father could be one of them and that she never learned about magic being real until that fateful afternoon, it was easy to assume she wouldn't be able to find someone to help her if needed. As much as she wanted to leave, it seemed like her safest option was to stay.

Ayla startled when Corbin pushed his chair from the table and stood up, placing his napkin next to his empty plate. She was so lost in her thoughts she didn't notice him finish his meal. Maybe if she stayed, Corbin could help. Magic was supposed to be a cure for everything, wasn't it?

"I have some business to attend to, but I should be back by nightfall. Have a think about everything, take a tour around the house—there's a lot to see and consider. If you're still here by the time I'm back, I'll take it as an acceptance of my offer. The paperwork is ready."

"Paperwork?"

Corbin raised two fingers in the air and the younger maid rushed towards him with a stack of papers. "Thank you, Dolores." He nodded his permission to leave, and the maid quietly disappeared, hastily grabbing the dishes to clear the table. Turning back to Ayla, he continued. "This one is a certificate of your purchase. I signed it to prove my consent to let you go and free you of any slave claims. If someone recognises you from the auction, they will have no grounds to recapture you. This piece of paper will set you free from any future harassment."

He pushed the single sheet of paper across the table to her and switched to the neat pile that was held together by a series of staples. "This one is an Apprentice agreement for you to sign in case you decide to stay. All your rights and obligations are listed there, including potential breaches. It also explains what level of magic mastery you need to achieve before you are free to follow your own path. Any questions?"

Ayla opened her mouth but no words came out. Her mind blanked, as if someone had wiped all thoughts out of her head. She dared to look into his midnight eyes, barely catching a glimpse of emotion she couldn't decipher. Something dark touched his gaze for a fraction of a second and his aura thickened with danger, just like the night before.

"Good. Everything you need is here." He pushed the stack of papers towards her to settle next to the lone page of the certificate. "I have to go now. If you choose to leave, I won't be seeing you again, so this is goodbye."

Before she had a chance to say anything, he stood up and walked out of the room, leaving a faint trace of minty aftershave in his wake.

Shocked by the sudden revelation, she sat there immobile for a few minutes or maybe an hour, she couldn't tell. The choice was obvious. She had to take the certificate and run as far away as she could, to hide and live her life among normal people in a normal world. To forget all about the horrible auction and cruel Masters, to properly grieve the death of her father, and to slowly move on like a regular person. She would find a way in the world, even without a penny to herself. Things were going to work out somehow.

Ayla looked at Corbin's confident, sophisticated signature on the certificate. She could leave right away. All she needed to do was take this paper and walk out the door.

Almost against her will, her gaze switched to the agreement. Knowing that she had magic was strange and scary. What if Corbin was right and it would manifest in the strangest way? There would be nobody to guide her, to explain how to control it. Things could go terribly wrong. Would it be worth staying here for who knows how long?

With a deep sigh, Ayla opened the first page of the agreement and dove into the fine print. She had always read the terms and conditions and scrutinised every dash and comma, of every contract she had ever signed.

Hours passed by as she studied the lengthy document. An Apprentice didn't seem too different from a slave, with all the obligations and next to no rights. Their Master could let them go on a whim at any time, but it would take years of studying and hard exams to prove herself as a Sorceress before she could leave on her own journey. Every wrong move carried potential punishments at the discretion of the Master. Lashings, starvation, public humiliation, mutilation—and potentially, death.

No way was she going to accept these ridiculous terms. Without a right to appeal anywhere, and no governing body having authority to step into a Master-Apprentice relationship, how could she ever agree?

She stood up to stretch her legs and paced back and forth in front of the table. Both of her options were terrible, and there was no third. Stay or leave. Potentially live or potentially die.

But Ayla always played by the rules. In all her life, she never got in trouble. Perfect student, perfect daughter. Corbin would have no cause to punish her. And if so, taking the offer to stay wouldn't be so bad after all.

Ayla glanced back at the pile of papers. Even considering that agreement was the worst idea ever.

She was going to sign it.

CHAPTER 6. AYLA

The cold, stone hallways of Corbin's house never seemed to end. Silence reigned as if there was no human presence, yet there was still life under the surface. Breathing that could only be heard when you pressed an ear against a lip. Somewhere in the kitchen, the maids and the cook were clanking dishes and exchanging the latest gossip. Ayla lingered outside the door but chose not to enter.

When Corbin had returned the night she signed the agreement, he hardly spoke to her. He checked her signature and got Dolores to take the papers away. The maid mentioned a binding spell to secure it, but Corbin refused it. The mystery of their conversation niggled at Ayla's mind. Perhaps it was her Master who had been making wrong decisions.

Because curious women opened doors.

When Ayla woke up the next morning, there was no trace of him. From the friendly old maid, Maria, she found out that it was normal for Corbin to go on lengthy trips that sometimes took weeks. There was no way of knowing how long he would be gone. All she could do was try to make sense of this cold house with its odd rules. And that was how she found herself lingering at the kitchen door.

She made her way to the front of the house. Large French windows let in bountiful golden rays of sun over a green lawn, glistening after the morning shower. Out in the garden, a gloomy man was trimming the lush bushes while keeping an eye out for any imperfections on the lawn. Birds sang cheerful tunes outside, their high pitch voices barely audible behind thick walls. Ayla stepped closer to the door and reached for the handle.

An authoritative voice stopped her. "Where do you think you're going?"

Ayla surprised herself with her own bite. "Dolores, right? Why am I not allowed to have a look at the garden? I've signed the contract. I agreed to be an Apprentice and now I live in this house, too. Corbin made a point that I'm not a slave and encouraged me to look around the place. I can go inside and outside as I please, can I not?"

Dolores scoffed, rolling her eyes. She didn't look like someone who would hold her tongue in front of Ayla. "*Master* Corbin is too kind, but you shouldn't test his patience. Until you've proven your magical talent, you're nothing but a slave, just like any slave in any other household. It would do you good to learn how to obey the rules. Master gave you his grace, but he can just as easily take it away. And then what are you going to do?" With a firm gesture, Dolores pushed Ayla's hand off the door handle and blocked the entrance.

Ayla stepped back. This maid clearly forgot her place. "So you're the one setting the rules in the house, are you?"

The maid glared at her. "I told you this when we first met. Pay attention. Until Master comes back, I'm taking care of his property. This includes you, *slave*."

"I'm going to tell Corbin about this." Ayla hissed back, fighting the urge to slap her opponent's perfectly made-up face. She felt the red flame of anger burning in her chest, lit up by the arrogant maid. The chilly fear of failure was counteracting it. Yes, she could tell Corbin about the maid's behaviour. However, she didn't know anything about their relationship. Dolores had been there for a longer time, and he might take her word over Ayla's. Which of the punishments would he choose then? Besides, what if she couldn't prove her worth to him? Would he really turn her into a regular slave, as the contract said?

Dolores didn't bother with an answer as if she didn't hear anything. She locked the door and hid the key in the pocket of her tidy white apron. Without a word, she turned her back to Ayla, and her brisk steps echoed in the empty hall.

Ayla exhaled and started counting to ten again. Once she reached the top number, she held her breath and then slowly exhaled, counting backwards. Switching her attention to the mundane numbers was little help but there was not much else she could do. She waited a little longer to regain her composure and then straightened her back to return to the dark belly of the mansion. She might be banned from going outside for now, but there was a lot more of the house she hadn't seen. With the intent to make the most of the day, Ayla went on her journey of discovery.

The sun started climbing down and the house filled up with shadows that were becoming longer by the minute. Ayla's stomach reminded her she hadn't had lunch, but nobody offered anything, and the maids were nowhere to be seen. Her pride didn't let her go to the kitchen, and she could only hope Corbin wouldn't take too long. They'd serve him dinner for sure!

Room after room, she made her way around, trying to memorise the maze of the mansion. Very soon, she discovered that they all looked similar to one another—spacious, with sophisticated yet simple furniture, heavy curtains that blocked out sunlight, cosy rugs on the floor. One of the rooms was much bigger than the others, with a huge plush sofa boasting an array of soft cushions, and a few leather-bound armchairs. The fireplace was quiet and dark at this time of the day, and a fluffy hide of a rare white tiger in front of it made her sad. Ayla never liked to see hunting trophies, and witnessing yet another one of them brought back the feeling that she didn't belong here. Not in this mansion and not in this strange world where people were sold and bought, and fear reigned supreme.

She left the room, absent-mindedly walking further down the long corridor. Another door seemed to be darker than others, and she pushed it open. What she saw stopped her in her tracks.

It was much larger than other bedrooms. Heavy atmosphere hung thicker here, the air saturated with a cacophony of smells. Leather, mostly. Some cardamom and spice. Something sharp and ferrous. Not daring to step in, Ayla realised it must've been Corbin's bedroom. The place was dominated by black, creating additional darkness in the barely lit environment. Black armchair next to the silent fireplace, black curtains letting in only enough sunlight to show silhouettes of things, black sheets on the bed. Everything in Ayla's body was screaming for her to leave, that it wasn't safe to stay any longer. Approaching steps behind her signalled that she'd been caught red-handed, even though she hadn't done anything wrong.

"This is Master's bedroom." The old maid's voice came from behind, and Ayla sighed with relief. At least it wasn't the hostile Dolores!

"I'm sorry," Ayla muttered, unsure of why she was apologising in the first place. After all, she'd been told to explore the house, yet she never received any guidance on what she was and wasn't allowed to see.

The maid stepped towards the door and carefully closed it. "It's okay, sweetheart, you didn't know. It would probably be best for you to stay away from it in the future."

"Why is everything black?" Ayla dared to ask, fearing the answer.

The maid's face twitched for an instant before she gathered her composure. "It's a practical colour. Covers up a lot of things." She stopped, her expression hesitant.

Ayla's imagination conjured all the terrible things that could have happened in that room. All the possible reasons why even the air there felt black and full of suffering. Of course, it was all too good to be true. Getting out of there had to be her priority, so she needed to learn everything there was to learn as an Apprentice and leave. Next time she'd have to be more careful with the outside door. Maybe she'd wait until everyone was gone before she tried to go out again. Just to see the garden, nothing else. Not until she was secure enough to try to run away.

The old maid cleared her throat, breaking the dead silence. "Actually, I was just looking for you. Master Corbin has returned and wishes to see you."

Ayla's heart leapt in her throat. This was the moment of truth. Now he was going to find out her true worth and decide her fate. Slightly shaking, Ayla turned her back to the black room and obediently followed in the maid's tracks. Maybe if she gave her full compliance, he would show mercy. This would buy some time to plan her further actions and hopefully make sense of the system. There had to be a loophole that would give her more rights. At least that was what she told herself.

As they walked down the hallway, Ayla couldn't help but notice that the house had a different feel to it now that Corbin was back. The walls were lit up by vintage lamps, and passing by the large dining room, she saw the massive chandelier throwing rays of light through the plethora of crystal teardrops hanging off the edges.

The maid led her towards the living room and crossed the threshold, stopping at a mere pace from it. "Master." She bowed in respect, her hands perfectly still along her sides. "Ayla is here, as you requested."

"Come." His low voice froze Ayla's blood. On rigid legs, she walked into the room, her whole being screaming for her to run away. Not a single muscle obeyed her command as if he put her under a spell. Had he?

Following his order, she approached the fireplace and lowered herself to the floor, just opposite Corbin who was taking one of the large armchairs. Something told her that was her place and she wasn't supposed to be at the same height as him. He smiled and nodded approvingly.

"Good manners. That's nothing like what Tamil told me. I knew you would try your best." He beckoned her to come closer and she obeyed once again, changing her position to the spot next to his feet. She stared at the reflection of the cheerful fire in one of his armchair's polished legs, not daring to look at him. Corbin spoke again, with amusement in his voice. "I think I mentioned before that I would like you to look at my face when I'm talking to you. At least, when we're alone."

Understanding his silent threat, she quickly lifted her face to his, looking anywhere but his eyes. Something told her that would be the most dangerous thing of all.

A small smile touched his lips. "That's better. I hope you remember it for next time."

Ayla quickly followed his words with a series of nods, hoping he didn't get angry. She thought about Melody's words that if she did everything right, there would be no punishment. And Sawyer's hiss that this would be something she'd only want to experience once. The contract was more than clear that their words were true. She had to obey no matter what she truly thought.

His face lit up with a more genuine smile, making him look almost like a regular person. Just a normal man having a chat, and definitely not someone who could kill her with a snap of his fingers. Ayla wondered if that was how it happened in this world. Did they say some sort of a spell? Or was there some kind of magic wand?

"Good girl. I brought you some gifts." A wide gesture of his hand included part of the room in front of the fireplace. At her confusion, Corbin sighed. "*Mostra*," he ordered, and a few objects around her slowly gained a faint blue glow—a golden goblet with fancy writing circling it;

a necklace with a blue stone encased in a metal claw; a piece of burgundy red fabric; a thin, elegant silver ring so small it would only fit a child's finger; an ivory comb; a tiny, transparent vial with clear liquid. All those things were placed on the white tiger hide, yet somehow she missed them when she looked around for the first time. "Some of these artefacts contain magic in one way or another, while the others are just what they appear to be. Magic is all around us, you see. It's stronger in some places than others, and there are locations in the world where it's so potent it's almost palpable. There are, however, others where magic can hardly exist. For our daily spells, we use objects charged with magic that's the easiest form to control. Now, I want you to have a good look at each of these things and tell me what you feel. Take your time, don't rush."

"Do I have to say any special words?"

"No, Ayla. You can use any words from a language that's not your mother tongue to facilitate the spell, but this is not necessary. Once you reach a certain level of mastery, these things come to you naturally. For now, just try to pick up the energy of these items. Some of them vibe differently from others."

Ayla took a deep breath and chose the ivory comb first. She stared at it so intently her eyes hurt, but felt nothing that would point to her this was any different from the comb she had used back home. Next, she examined the goblet. It felt completely ordinary, too.

"You can pick them up if that's easier." Corbin's voice betrayed some impatience, and fear rose in her chest again. This was definitely a test of her abilities. She could not fail.

Tracing her finger along the writings on the sides of the goblet, the only thing she felt was the intricate carving of unknown words. It must have had some kind of significance and Ayla wondered if she could fake it. Would he be able to tell she was lying?

No, it wasn't worth it. She had to be honest and show that she was trying her best. Someone like him would scent deceit. Like Dolores said, trying his patience was a bad idea. Not something Ayla wanted to do during her very first test—or was it a lesson?

She took the piece of fabric that felt soft and ordinary. The necklace was just a necklace, the ring only a ring. Lastly, the glass vial felt like a cheap toy from the souvenir shop. Nothing told her any of them held power.

"Anything?" Corbin asked, making her body tense up even more.

Tears clouding her vision, Ayla shook her head. "I'm sorry, I didn't feel like any of them were special in any way. I can learn how to do it though, I *will* learn. I'm really good at learning, I was one of the best students in my grade."

Corbin shook his head. "I haven't seen an Apprentice who wouldn't be able to feel magic in these artefacts. A couple of them are among the most potent ones in the world." He picked up the necklace, and the blue stone flashed an eerie green in his hands. "For instance, this one can break through any enchantment, and there's almost no way to stop its power."

Ayla shattered. If she wasn't able to pass the easiest test of all, it meant she was indeed incapable of magic. Sawyer was wrong. "Is there any other way I can try?" She searched for mercy in the darkness of Corbin's impenetrable eyes. There was no indication of what would happen next, and that was the most terrifying thing of all.

"I don't have the time or patience to delve deeper into this matter." He stated plainly, every word sounding like a death sentence.

Ayla pushed a painful lump down her throat and bit her lip in a desperate hope that the pain would help her keep herself together. "Are you going to... get rid of me?"

Corbin's face changed expression to mild amusement. "Of course not, why would you even think that? I'm going to send you to the Sorcerers' Academy. There are plenty of teachers there who will be able to detect your particular talent and assist you in developing it. I just don't have the time to teach you."

A delicate knock on the door interrupted her line of thought as she was about to thank him for sparing her life. After all she'd seen today, she was sure he'd kill her if she was of no use to him.

"Apologies for interrupting." Dolores's slender figure hovered at the threshold, waiting for Corbin to allow her in.

"We're finished here. What is it?" he asked calmly as she bowed before approaching and carefully handed him an envelope of rich brown paper with a single word on it. *Corbin*.

Ayla glanced at the fancy handwriting on the envelope, unsure if she was expected to go or wait until he dismissed her. Corbin unfolded the letter and quickly scanned it before looking at Dolores again.

"Is the messenger still waiting?" As Dolores nodded in confirmation, he continued. "Good. Let them know we'll be there."

With a flash of a snow-white apron, Dolores left the room and silence regained its dominance. Ayla chewed the inside of her cheek and suppressed a sniffle, second-guessing her choice. She imagined herself pedalling on her bike and enjoying the smell of fresh pies. Letting her hair catch in the wind, trailing behind her like a cape. Between her and freedom stood the mighty ink of a pen.

"Here's your chance to shine, Ayla." Corbin shot up and urged her to follow him. "We've been invited to the annual Royal Gala."

CHAPTER 7. AYLA

You don't belong here. There is no power in you. No secret ability. You're a fraud and everyone will find out at the gala. You're nothing but a slave, just a toy for your Master's entertainment. And when he tires of you, you'll be dead.

Ayla woke up shuddering from the harsh words echoing in her mind. Pulling the sheets to her chest, she whispered Darren's mantra to soothe herself in vain. When that didn't work, she got up and splashed some water on her face, hoping that something cool would ward off the terrors.

The nightmares started their haunt after her failed attempt to show Corbin any magical ability. After that day, he left on another one of his trips and Ayla hadn't seen him, to her relief—*mostly*. Meals were only served when he was home, so she had to go to the kitchen and ask for food. The days she had to ask the young maid, Dolores, were the worst. Her air of superiority was humiliating, infuriating. She wanted nothing more than to yell at the snobbish girl.

Ayla always caught her temper, reminding herself that she had to be very careful not to upset the balance in the house. Her position was shaky. Strategically, it would be best not to attract any attention.

Other servants kept their distance. The cook never said a word to her, setting a tiny meal on the kitchen table and walking away, as if Ayla was contagious. The gardener who came occasionally only stayed outside and probably didn't even know about her existence. The old maid, Maria, was not around much, always running errands under the heel of Dolores. It looked like Apprentices were supposed to keep to themselves and maintain minimal interactions with the servants. Their main focus must have been studies, refining their magic and serving their Masters. How lonely.

There were no explicit orders to let Ayla go outside, so she could only enjoy the sunshine from one of the house's large windows. Her stares were endless, watching as the sun coloured the tops of the trees a bright gold at dawn. Reds and oranges at sunset. The gardens were always trimmed to the standards of a perfect estate, but Ayla noticed land beyond the house's public facade. Wild—the trees and bushes of that land weren't clipped as much, attracting plenty of birds. Ayla could observe them from the small dining room. The sight always gave her peace.

She got pretty good at finding her way around the house and knew the behaviours and routines of those in it. When the doorbell rang and hurried steps ensued, Ayla listened carefully. From Dolores's intonation, she knew the visitor was someone who didn't visit often.

"This way please," Dolores's sweet voice purred, the tone she always kept for the guests and Corbin, but never for Ayla. They approached the room and the door opened with a tiny squeak. Ha, Corbin should learn about this! A squeaky door in the perfect house? Someone would get in trouble.

The visitor flew in, her outfit a brilliant green with flashes of organza and sparkles. The hem of her dress dragged behind her on the floor, forcing Ayla's gaze along her long, flirty silhouette. Slitted sleeves bared her arms, and her neckline showed just enough skin to highlight a beautiful, shiny choker seemingly made from moonlight.

"I'm so glad to see you!" Melody exclaimed, wrapping her arms around Ayla for a short hug. Once she stepped back to restore the distance, she automatically fixed her shimmering perfection of a dress. Ayla couldn't help but admire her once again.

"Me too, Melody. You have no idea how much I missed real people," Ayla confessed, hoping it wasn't oversharing.

Melody laughed as if a dozen tiny bells went off at once. "Oh sweetheart, you'll be meeting a whole lot of people tonight at the gala! Everyone of significance will be attending, even the Crown Prince is rumoured to be coming down! And I've made huge progress lately. Tonight is my official graduation from the Academy. Now all I'll have to do is pass my Master's last test and then I'll ascend! How wonderful is that?"

Ayla tried to hide her disappointment at the thought of her losing the only friendly person she knew. Ever since Corbin confirmed he wouldn't be teaching her, she'd been having nightmares about going to that dreaded magic school and being just as useless as she was at the mansion, without any support. But the happy Melody didn't deserve to have her night ruined, so Ayla squeezed out a fake smile. "Congratulations! Going to the Academy must have been hard."

Melody's lips stretched with a cheeky grin as she began to unpack the small cosmetics bag she had brought in. "Not at all. I really enjoyed my time there—all the lessons were too easy! I'm sure you'll love it there too." Taking no notice of Ayla's discomfort, she continued chirping about her joyful times at the Academy. About the boys and the lessons. None of the information she provided was of any practical use, though. Melody walked away from obstacles and adversity without a single scratch and believed anyone could do the same.

Anecdotes Ayla didn't need to hear, too distressed about her own potential failure. She stifled her frustration as Melody brushed her hair perfectly straight. Not a single hair stood out as it fell down Ayla's shoulders in a shiny sheet, her golden highlights a stark contrast to the rich chestnut. Melody's delicate hands moved to Ayla's face, creating dramatic smokey eyes against her paleness. Despite all her reservations about the party, Ayla couldn't help but admire Melody's skills once again. The girl had an obvious gift.

Melody stepped back and smiled in content. "All done. Now, for your dress." She pointed at the plush sofa that held a backless halter-top dress. In a blink of an eye, Ayla was sheathed, her skin feeling the tight fit. Was this dress tailor-made for her body, she wondered, or was it enchanted to always be a perfect fit?

A clanking noise startled her.

"Last step." Cold metal bit into the sensitive skin on her neck, replacing the warmth of Melody's soft hands.

Ayla's heart stopped. She raised her hand to feel the familiar, degrading collar that snatched her freedom at the auction. Tears welled up in her eyes. "I wish I didn't have to wear this," she whispered in a desperate attempt to provoke pity in the tall girl.

Melody shook her head sadly. "Sorry Ayla, you know that these are the rules. Until you've shown your magic abilities, your status is no higher than a slave. Master Corbin might keep you on the leash or not, this will be entirely up to him. Remember the etiquette though, and try not to get in trouble. There are lots of influential people at the gala tonight. Keep your eyes down and stay low. You'll be okay."

A series of steps in the hallway announced another person's arrival. With a sigh, Ayla ran her hand along her smooth hair and stood up. She was right to assume it was her Master.

Corbin was almost unrecognisable. His jet-black hair was slicked behind his ears. Perfect posture brought out the dark suit he was wearing, the only splash of colour a crimson handkerchief skilfully folded in the front pocket. Dark buttoned shirt, dark leather shoes, calm expression devoid of any emotion. Ayla shivered, thinking about the blackness of his bedroom. She'd always believed one's bedroom was a reflection of their soul.

Corbin stopped a few paces away from the threshold and threw a small glance at her before turning his attention to Melody.

Her face bloomed with a ready smile in return. "She's all ready, Master Corbin."

He nodded approvingly. "Thank you, Melody. I appreciate you coming over on such short notice. Your work is impeccable, as always."

He turned his back to leave. Melody gently pushed Ayla between her shoulder blades. As Corbin walked out of the room, Ayla hurried behind, annoyance growing at the things she didn't understand. How was she supposed to know she had to follow him when he made no motion to tell her? They descended the stairs in silence, walking past countless doors and windows until they found themselves outside. Ayla's indignation transitioned to disappointment when she saw a pair of heavily armed guards flanking their ride. Corbin got into the low sports car and closed the door without waiting for her. Ayla froze, too stunned to react. Was she supposed to have jumped in there with him? As the car sped out of the driveway, one of the guards grabbed Ayla's arm and manhandled her to another car, a much simpler one. She wilted as she thought about the last time she'd been in a car. That seemed like it was months ago, though she couldn't tell the time. In a house where every day was the same as the previous one, only the slow change of the seasons could tell her she'd only been there a couple of weeks. They were currently in the first week of October.

Guards got into the back seat with her, squeezing her from both sides. She wriggled for some more room, but they wouldn't budge. Once settled, their bodies went stiff as if made out of stone. Eyes were fixed on the road ahead. Not a single muscle moving. The driver she didn't see was separated from them by a dark sheet of heavily tinted glass. An eerie silence settled, only interrupted by the sound of tires slowly making their way down the driveway, winding among fields with abandoned warehouses, and finding themselves on the familiar highway. The steady hum of an engine started to lull Ayla to sleep again. She closed her eyes for a second.

A sudden jerk of the car would have sent her flying if she weren't restrained by the safety belt. Ayla looked around drowsily, realising she'd indeed fallen asleep and they had already arrived at their destination.

The castle before her was overwhelming in its grandeur. Built in the Renaissance style, perhaps, though it boasted a share of Baroque features—a mixture of geometrically precise arches and mouldings, alongside bold, lush adornments, taking the best of both styles. The symphony of its beauty... Ayla stepped back to take it all in. She had never seen a castle before, nor did she know of any castles anywhere in the country. How was it possible to keep such a place secret from the public? Surely, someone would have said something.

Rude guards pushed her along. Annoyed, she moved forward but stopped short. Corbin was already there, waiting for her.

"Keep your eyes down, remember? Looking around will only get you in trouble. Now, I'm not going to put you on a leash tonight, but you'll have to be careful. Follow me everywhere I go unless I tell you otherwise. You have to always keep a small distance, about a step behind in free areas and half a step where it's crowded. You're not allowed to talk to slaves, only to Masters—and only if they ask you a question. It probably won't happen as you're with me and I can take care of any inquiries for you. In short, keep a low profile and behave. Do you understand?" Corbin was not satisfied with Ayla's simple nod in response. He shook his head, voice like the crack of a whip. "Use your words, please."

"Yes... Master," she hurried, feeling ashamed and sorry for herself. She thought about the irony of her situation, standing in front of the castle of her dreams, every bit as beautiful. It probably had a king too, or a prince—didn't Melody mention a Crown Prince? People getting out of cars were dressed to impress, with expensive fabric and exotic leather everywhere she looked. As her gaze met another, she hastily looked away. Corbin warned her not to stare. She had to remember that.

Ayla blinked, dragging herself out of her thoughts. Corbin's back disappeared through the large front doorway, under a decorative keystone that illustrated many ripe fruits. Panic saturated her senses as she rushed towards the entrance. Thankfully, there were no guards there to stop her and the ones that came with her had stayed in the car. Ayla nearly ran, silently cursing the high heels she was wearing. A crowd of similar black suits filled the large ballroom, and a lot of men had black hair styled like Corbin's. She looked to her left, to her right. Her heart beat violently against her chest. Hyperventilating, she leaned against the wall. The car was gone and she couldn't go back and ask the driver. Corbin was nowhere to be seen, and she didn't know anybody else. She feared his presence but needed him like a little child.

Conscious she was catching curious glances, Ayla decided to move to a quieter spot to gather her thoughts and calm down a little. Sooner or later, Corbin would notice her absence and then he'd find her. She had no doubt of that. The only thing she needed to do was stay out of sight of other Masters until then.

As she backed away from the crowd, she felt herself falling. Not used to the high heels, Ayla couldn't keep her balance and crashed on her back. Shattered glass and angry curses landed at her feet. Her eyes fixed on the bright chandelier lit up with a thousand candles, straight above. Her head was buzzing, and she carefully slipped her hand around the back to see if there was any blood. A small amount of hot liquid met her skin. Hurting herself in the first five minutes at the gala was not keeping a low profile.

She looked up, terrified to meet the gaze of whoever she was at the mercy of. The cruel eyes of an older man, dressed in the same dark suit as Corbin, bore into her.

Sawyer.

He reached down for her, and for a second Ayla believed he was going to offer her an assisting hand. But a harsh reality hit when he grabbed her by the collar and yanked her to her feet. A whimper escaped her lips despite all effort to stay quiet.

His unforgiving glare made her remember she wasn't supposed to even be looking at his face. With a shaky breath, she turned her attention away, but everywhere she looked, she saw faces upon faces of curious observers who huddled around to watch what happened next. Ayla wanted to curl up into a ball and pretend like nothing happened, like it was all another nightmare, but the iron grip on her collar kept her in harsh reality. Sawyer slowly lifted his arm, keeping hold of her until her toes were barely touching the ground. A crooked smile crossed his face as he kept moving her upwards until she could no longer feel steadiness under her feet. Ayla gasped for air as she writhed and clawed at the unyielding hand on her collar. How cruel, how simple of an end this would be.

When Ayla almost lost all hope, Sawyer lowered his arm, placing her on the ground. She greedily breathed in the air of the crowded ballroom. What a luxury it was to be able to breathe. His hand kept her steady when she wavered, losing her balance.

Sawyer shook his head from side to side as he clicked his tongue. "Tsk, tsk. I knew you were rude from the get-go, but this? What a disaster. Trailing so far behind your Master when you should always be nearby. Not watching where you're going. Stepping on another Master's foot and making him spill his drink. That's a serious offence, little girl."

Terror seized control of Ayla's body. *What is he going to do? With so many witnesses around, knowing that Corbin is in the same room somewhere? Would he risk conflict with him? Or is this part of some sick game?*

Her expression must have betrayed her when she noticed a sudden change in Sawyer's face. He let go of her collar and sighed.

"Such a pity," he stated quietly. The crowd went silent, and Ayla glanced around nervously to find out the reason. All eyes were fixed on his hand that raised ever so slightly, then struck at the speed of lightning. Ayla yelped at the force of the hit, hot blood rushing out of her nose and ruptured lip. She stumbled back in shock, wiping it with the back of her hand. Sawyer made another step towards her, and his hand shot up as he prepared to hit her again.

"What's going on here?" A young man's voice cut through the crowd. People parted for him, listening intently to catch every exchange from the emerging conflict.

Ayla dared a glance at her saviour. He had an impeccable posture like Corbin, but his hair was a much lighter shade, dark brown rather than black. The suit he was wearing was a stark contrast to the other Masters. The material held a lush green colour, decorated with golden embroidery throughout and an emblem of a falcon on the left side. Royalty. Ayla's eyes widened. The man's eyes flashed green as he gave her a small smile, before turning his attention to her attacker.

Sawyer dropped his hand and gave the prince a quick bow. "The slave here wreaked havoc in your ballroom, Your Grace," he stated in a clear voice. "She stepped on my foot and elbowed a glass of champagne out of my hand.

Instead of apologising, the little brat dared look me in the face as if she were to challenge me. I demand satisfaction."

A murmur passed over the crowd like a wave.

The prince wrinkled his nose as if he smelled something foul. "You know the rules, Sawyer. Only her Master can deliver punishment, otherwise, there would be chaos everywhere." The audience gushed at his authority. A series of steps pierced the quiet. People made way for another newcomer as Corbin emerged from the sea of faces. He stopped a couple of paces away from Sawyer and Ayla, his face impenetrable as always. The prince turned to him and said, voice devoid of any emotion, "Your slave offended Master Sawyer, and he demands satisfaction."

Ayla watched as Corbin paused in his usual manner, thinking of the optimal response. She sniffled and wiped blood off her face. Wasn't this enough for Sawyer's *satisfaction*?

Corbin's eyes landed on Ayla's wounds, carefully studying her open lip and the bloodied nose. He looked her over as if she were a pet who got into an unfortunate accident, deciding whether or not to take it to a vet. "Punishment will be delivered as requested. I'll take care of it at home." He turned around intending to leave the scene, and Ayla stumbled after him, worried about losing him in the crowd again.

She winced as Sawyer stepped into her path, shaking his head in disagreement. His crooked finger pointed at her accusingly. "I think I'll speak for all of us when I say the punishment has to take place here, not at your house. Everyone has witnessed the offence, now everyone needs to see the consequences."

Corbin let out a heavy sigh as the crowd started murmuring their agreement. The prince raised his hand and silence was restored. "I agree. There is a post at the end of the ballroom, and my servants will bring the tools. Come." He gestured for them to follow him. Ayla marvelled at his grace as he turned on his heel leading the way, his pace brisk yet elegant, his steps almost silent in calfskin shoes with intricate engraving. Only when pushed between her shoulder blades did she realise what he actually meant.

Corbin took her by the arm, forcing her to match his pace as he started after the prince. Not a word was said, but the heavy aura about him grew thicker. Dozens of thoughts were racing through Ayla's mind. She was dreading what was coming, her imagination readily feeding heart-stopping terror. Would they cut off her hands? Burn a mark on her body labelling her as a disobedient slave for the rest of her life, preventing any possibility for her to be recognized as an Apprentice? Force a rat into her mouth? Confine her to a tiny cage so she couldn't move?

The last thought instilled the most fear. Claustrophobia anchored her to the ground. Surely, the greatest satisfaction could only be met by witnessing the greatest of suffering. She started dragging her feet as they neared the end of the ballroom, and tried to stop when she saw the small pedestal with a tall post on it. Corbin's steady hand led her forward, nearly making her fall as she resisted.

The post had metal loops built into the solid wood, two at each side at shoulder height and one in the front a little higher. Corbin's grasp forced Ayla onto the pedestal. Someone clipped a thick metal bracelet on each wrist, both of which had small hooks on them that matched the loops on the post. Ayla's head went spinning as she soaked in the situation. The polished hardwood had stains all over, barely noticeable against its natural colour, but unmistakable—dried blood. The same thing she was afraid to see in Corbin's bedroom.

Her Master let go of her arm and motioned for her to step against the post. A servant brought forth a small foldable table and placed it by his right hand. Glancing at the setup, Ayla caught sight of a plush black bag unfolding on it, revealing hooks, chains, silk ropes and ribbons, whips and lashes, and some metal tools she preferred not to identify. Corbin's hand grazed over them all until he singled out a small hook. Ayla stepped back as he shortened the distance between them and clipped the hook onto her collar.

"Listen carefully." He pulled her close so that only she could hear what he said. "Don't fight me now. This will be over soon, I promise."

Ayla shuddered as he clipped the other side of the hook to the front loop of the post and her wrists to the sides. Now she was restrained to one spot and wouldn't be able to move around if she so desired. Through the corners of her vision, she checked on his movement. She gasped upon seeing a thick leather belt in his fist.

"Twenty lashes, Corbin." Sawyer's raspy voice rose from the crowd.

Nobody protested against the barbarity, their shouts of anticipation showing that Ayla's suffering was the highlight of their evening. She let out an indignant breath. She was getting out of here as soon as she found a way, agreement or not. Then she would run and run, out of the city and away from all these mansions and castles and expensive cars, to settle somewhere in a small town like the one she used to live in with Darren. Maybe deep in wild land where the trees and bushes weren't clipped as much, among flocks of indifferent birds going about their days. Peace. A new life, different name. And no magic, not that she had any.

"She's never been punished before." Corbin's every weighted word was met with full attention. "I can offer five lashes as this is her first offence."

The hum below told Ayla that people were unhappy. The crowd reached a peak and then abated again as the young prince's voice demanded silence. "Five lashes might teach a child to obey, but not an adult. I agree that twenty is too much for the first offence, though. Ten lashes, Corbin."

Ayla squeezed her eyes shut, bracing herself for impact. Corbin's cool hand slid under her chin and turned her face towards him. The smell of leather filled her nostrils, and she opened her eyes in surprise. What was he doing?

"Bite on this," he said, offering the folded belt to her.

"Please, Corbin, don't do this. I'll be good, I swear. It was an accident!" she rushed, knowing that she wouldn't get too much time to talk.

He shook his head, a sad expression in his eyes. "It's too late. Do not beg, this will only make it worse. You have to be strong now, Ayla. Keep biting and try to be still. No matter how much it hurts, you can't pass out. Do you understand? If you faint, the punishment will have to start over. Be brave." He gently ran his fingers down her cheek.

She obediently took the belt with her teeth.

With her head down and fingers intertwined behind the post, Ayla tried to shift her focus to something else. Anything at all. Happy memories, no aches. A safe space.

A swift movement in the back and a gust of air announced the arrival of the first lash.

"It's not too bad," Ayla thought, leisurely tapping her teeth on the leather. Then the true pain hit her, overwhelming all senses. The force sent her into the post. It made sense now why there were hooks in place. Without them holding the disobedient slaves still, there would have been a lot more blood stains on the pedestal.

She squirmed, trying to adjust her body in a way that would make it hurt less. There was no feeling of blood on her back, but with the hit so strong there were undoubtedly some welts forming. She resisted the urge to spit out the belt and lick her lips. If the first strike was so powerful, the others might render her near unconscious, and she remembered Corbin's words about staying in her mind until the punishment was over.

"One," his steady voice pronounced behind her. Another gust of air ensued. Without giving her any chance to process the first blow, he struck her again, making her shiver head to toe. "Two."

Again and again the sharp sting of the whip bit into her flesh. This backless dress that made her feel gorgeous an hour ago felt like a curse now. After three, she lost count and her only thought was to stay conscious. Her blank stare was fixed on the clean white wall a few metres away, behind the excited crowd. The shimmering light of the chandelier was creating shallow shadows gently swaying from side to side. She absently looked at the minuscule changes of light and shade, growing numb from the pain. A sweet feeling of emptiness crept closer and closer, until a sudden thought blocked it—*I have to stay conscious until this is over.*

She shook her head, noting that it felt light and ethereal. Was she in her body still, or did she get detached and this was nothing but a dream? "Nine," someone said, and she giggled. Why was someone counting out loud?

"Ten."

Someone pried her teeth off the leather that she nearly bit through. A metallic sound made her hands suddenly drop, and another one sent her to her knees. Strong hands kept her from falling on the floor, and her head rolled to the side. Ayla squinted her eyes at the change of lighting, now facing the whole glory of the crystal chandelier, not its pale shadow.

"So pretty," she whispered, giggling again. There was no more pain. She was walking on soft, fluffy clouds, still conscious but no longer suffering. It was over. She survived.

"How are you feeling?" Corbin's eyes searched her face, and she was surprised to see a hint of concern in his dark eyes.

Ah, he wants to know if I'm conscious, she realised, and a dreamy smile crossed her lips. "I'm happy," she replied, singsong.

Corbin's look grew more concerned as he gently stroked her hair. Ayla realised they were still on the pedestal. He was sitting cross-legged and holding her head on her knees as she faced the ceiling. The audience was gone. Cheerful voices came from all directions now. People continued with their night as if nothing happened. There was food to be eaten, drinks to be had, announcements to be made. Everything was back to normal.

Ayla looked at her Master's face and admired his chiselled cheekbones and strong jawline. The touch of his hand on her hair felt like heaven, even as a small voice in the back of her head reminded her of who he was and what he'd done. "It feels so nice," she breathed out, closing her eyes. Something moved her body, but she no longer cared. A soft grey fog rose around her, enveloping her in its soothing embrace.

CHAPTER 8. AYLA

Ayla spread healing ointment across the welts on her back as far as she could reach, slow as if stalling would help her forget her shame. She felt the phantom touch of Corbin's fingers guiding her own across her raw skin, sorry for what they had done. Her wounds numbed, but she had to remind herself that the ointment was not a gesture of kindness or nurture. There was no such thing here.

She tried her best to temper her optimism, but she smiled when she realised that Corbin cared for her in his own way. Surely some of his gestures measured beyond duty. She found herself waiting in the small dining room. Even though he wasn't in the house, she was invited to breakfast, and did not have to humiliate herself by begging. Patient, she scanned the empty room. In the light of day, it was unrecognisable. All the darkness tucked in the corners, the table set up welcoming and pleasant.

Her smile faded when Dolores came out of nowhere and dropped a bowlful of porridge in front of her. The first spoonful made Ayla gag. Dolores might have been told to serve her breakfast, but she made sure Ayla didn't enjoy it. The food was bland and tasted like ash, with clumps of undercooked pieces that stuck together. She forced the porridge down her throat and looked around the table for water, coffee, or any liquid to wash it down. As expected, there was none to be found.

Pushing the bowl away, Ayla indulged in self-pity.

The gala could've given her a good night, considering what Melody had said. The introduction to the prince could've gone smoother, maybe she would have learned a thing or two. That castle was enormous; surely, there would have been plenty of room for her to avoid collision with Sawyer.

Unless he sought her on purpose.

Ayla seethed, beginning a pace to the living room. He must have been following her close, otherwise, how would she have stepped on his foot? He wanted to see her punished. And it was no coincidence that he demanded twenty lashes. He knew very well that she wouldn't have been able to take that much, and the punishment would have had to happen again.

Ayla had just found a plush lounge to sit upon when light steps announced a new visitor's arrival. She dug her nails into the palms of her hands. Nothing good could come out of this, no matter who it was.

Melody flew into the room with a toothy grin on her face and opened her arms for a warm hug. Her short auburn hair was styled in a single wave, leaving her left ear and its three silver rings exposed. Ayla blushed, remembering that she was at the castle last night, too. A myriad of thoughts ran through her mind, all trying to come up with an excuse to mend her reputation.

"Hi there, Ayla, how are you feeling?" the tall girl asked in her cheerful voice, eyes sparkling with mischief. She landed on the armchair next to Ayla. Today, she was dressed in an ankle-length plaid skirt and a black top with a silver brooch pinned to the soft fabric. The brooch resembled a bird, like a smaller, simpler version of the emblem she'd seen on the prince's jacket last night.

"Today is a very special day!" Melody announced without waiting for a response to her question.

Ayla smiled politely, avoiding any negative thoughts about this new development. It wasn't Melody's fault that every time they met so far, something bad was to follow. She only did what she was supposed to do, undoubtedly by her own Master's orders, who must have had some kind of arrangement with Corbin. Unlike Dolores though, Melody actually made an effort.

"Why's that?" Ayla asked cautiously.

Melody clapped her hands in excitement. "You're going to the Academy!" When Ayla's face dropped, Melody giggled. "Last night, the prince had a word with Master

Corbin, and they decided that it would be best for you to enrol now, even though the term has already started." She paused. "Especially after your... accident."

No doubt that every student at the Academy would know about her *accident*. Ayla cleared her throat but couldn't speak.

Melody slid her hand across the wave of her hair, making sure it stayed perfectly in place. "Okay, let me tell you it's not that big of a deal. Lots of people have been at that post, and it's not unusual to see someone getting a lashing at every gala. Sawyer was just nasty, to be honest. Twenty lashes are a standard punishment, but not for a first-time offender. The prince did the right thing when he ordered only ten—although let me tell you, Corbin did a great job haggling! If he offered ten right away, you could have ended up with fifteen, seeing how determined Sawyer was to make you suffer."

"Why would he do that?" Ayla wondered, grateful for Melody's unfiltered speech.

Melody jerked her shoulder and her face darkened for an instant. "Some people are like that, Ayla. They enjoy seeing the suffering of others, or even better—inflicting pain themselves. There were quite a few of those in the audience last night, thirsty for fresh blood. To avoid the crowd's unrest, the prince ordered a public punishment instead of letting Corbin take you home. You would have probably gotten away with a slap on the wrist then. In any case, Corbin still managed to put Sawyer in his place by picking the lightest of the whips. The way he hit you was the most sparing technique. If it was Sawyer, you would have been left bleeding all over, and undoubtedly passed out after the third strike."

At Ayla's silence, Melody continued. "Corbin stayed with you after the punishment was over. He was worried and actually carried you in his arms all the way to the car, driving you back himself. We were all shocked. After all, you haven't proven yourself yet, and he could be putting his reputation at risk if you were to have no magic. No Master would take such care of a slave. He must have strong faith in your abilities."

Ayla moved closer to the arm of her sofa, hoping to steady herself on something solid. Corbin put his reputation at risk for her. Why would he do that?

Melody chewed on her lip as if seeking another topic, then looked up with a brighter face. "Oh, you missed my graduation ceremony! My Master arranged for it to be a surprise. I received my graduation ring. Then he announced that I was no longer an Apprentice and had granted my ascension! The prince congratulated me himself! I wish you saw that, Ayla, it was so special! And then, there were fireworks, and lobsters—and let's not forget pink champagne that was brought all the way from the prince's hometown in Laseilles. Some young Apprentices from the Academy were there, too. I was really hoping you'd make a few friends before you were enrolled."

That must have been why Corbin took her to the gala in the first place, to meet her future peers. She should have been paying attention to him and not getting distracted. Now she only had herself to blame for falling for Sawyer's little trick.

Melody slapped her hands on her thighs and rose from her seat. "Let's get you ready. You don't want to be late on your first day!"

"I don't think I have any clothes suitable to wear out. My closet is full of pyjamas and loungewear," Ayla confessed, making her friend laugh. Melody swept her hand towards the door. Eyes wide, Ayla spotted a small black suitcase that she could have sworn hadn't been there before.

"That's why I made sure to bring you the uniform. You'll look really nice in it!" Melody clicked the locks of the suitcase open, revealing its belly stuffed full of dark-hued fabrics. She dug in, unspooling like intestines a pair of knee-length stockings, a modest V-neck top, and a short plaid skirt, all in various shades of black and dark grey.

Ayla lifted her eyebrows at the length of the skirt which barely touched her mid-thigh. "Is this a proper school uniform or another test?"

Melody shook her head, fetching the last piece of the uniform—mid-heel boots. "This is how you start. Beginners all wear short skirts or shorts. The higher you progress, the longer they become. And once you receive the skirt that almost reaches the floor, you'll get an invitation to take the final exam. And then you graduate. See, it's not too hard."

"Are you going to have your own Apprentices now?" Ayla suddenly realised the full meaning of Melody being a graduate. She was like Corbin now, as crazy as it seemed. Maybe there would be a chance for her to figure something out sooner than she expected.

Melody burst out laughing. "That would be awesome, right? But no, I'll have to hone my powers for another ten years before I can choose if I want to become one of the Masters or not. Not everybody takes Apprentices. That's a huge responsibility!"

Ayla wanted to ask so many more questions, but Melody nodded at the dark outfit she spread out on the armchair. "I'll tell you more, but we really need to hurry. I'll be taking you to the Academy, and we don't want you to be late on your very first day."

With a sigh, Ayla got up and changed into the strange new clothes. The fabric felt odd, and after a little while she understood why—it wasn't strictly warm, but it wasn't light either. It seemed to be changing its properties depending on the temperature. With the strange October weather, she welcomed this oddity. Ayla shook her head in astonishment. If her guess was right, this meant she never had to bother with summer and winter clothes, or with wearing a coat when it was cold.

"Pretty cool, huh? The uniform will maintain magic properties as long as you are a student. I can only wish to invent something as amazing as this someday!" Melody helped fasten the straps on Ayla's boots.

Ayla straightened and glanced in the mirror across the room, ready to go. The finished image of a new student alarmed her. What did they do to failing students in magic schools?

The two of them made their way to Melody's scarlet convertible, its roof down on a sunny day. The engine purred like a cat as Melody strapped herself in with the safety belt and signalled for Ayla to do the same. Trees were flying past as they sped through the forest and out to the highway.

Ayla leaned back in her seat and closed her eyes, willing the sunshine to soak into her skin. She tried her best to calm her anxious mind. "Why isn't Corbin here?"

"Oh, Ayla... Master Corbin is an extremely busy man. You'll hardly see him around, he's away most of the time." Melody sighed. "He didn't even want to have another Apprentice after his previous one... didn't work out. Darren was his old teacher though, and I guess he wanted to pay his last respects by taking you in. He made sure you were in good health after last night, and that was pretty much all he had to do for you."

They drove in silence for the rest of their journey. Fresh mountain breezes stroked Ayla's face, never too harsh or gentle. The drive would've been a joy if she wasn't impossibly tense. When the convertible's engine relaxed and the murmuring of students met her ears, she finally opened her eyes.

The building before Ayla—a castle, but not quite—spread its glory across her vision, stoic and sunbathed among the surrounding trees of a large park. The Academy. It was crafted from a stone similar to the prince's castle. Students in dark uniforms, contrasted with the golden aura of dawn, were getting out of cars and stopping to say hello to their friends. Everything seemed strangely normal.

But then Ayla lifted herself out of the car and stood frozen to the spot. Everyone's uniforms were longer than hers. Of course, the term had already started, but it looked like they had all progressed much too fast. Aware of the increasing interest, she made a couple of steps towards the entrance.

Melody raced up behind her. "Come, I'll introduce you to your teacher," she urged, holding Ayla by her hand. She led her through a hallway, too fast to allow Ayla to take in her surroundings.

Clutching onto her chest with her free hand, Ayla tried to soothe her growing anxiety. How was she going to make it, starting the year at such a disadvantage, especially considering that she might need more time to learn than everyone here? They reached an open door.

"I'll take it from here." The words rattled like a clap of thunder. As if emerging from fog, a man appeared in front of her.

Ayla dared meet the gaze of her new teacher, praying that she was mistaken. It was no use. Her intuition was right. Nothing good was waiting for her in this school. Dread overcame her senses.

"Sawyer."

He flashed a toothy grin. "*Master* Sawyer for you, my dear. Welcome to the Academy."

Quick-thinking Melody flashed a dazzling smile. "Master Sawyer, you're the new teacher? Oh, congratulations!"

Sawyer didn't return her warmth. He ignored her, looking at Ayla as if she were a curious bug, and scoffed. "You. Get in class, and make sure you're never late again. Here's your schedule," he snapped, pushing a piece of paper into her hand.

Ayla's cheeks burned a scorching red. She rushed through the door and stopped, unsure of what to do. Her head darted around, aware of the hushes and curious glances. There was nowhere for her to sit.

Sawyer's iron fingers latched onto her shoulder. She winced. Why did he try to hurt her every time they met?

"If there's no room, you make room. Next time, kindly arrive early and secure your desk."

Ayla ended up sitting on the floor, earning a constant stream of glances and whispering behind her back. Thankfully, she wasn't asked any questions. Sawyer kept the lesson to the point, only asking the students who were willing to answer. After that, every student received a thick book with runes that were to be studied until the end of the class. Once the bell rang, the books found their way back to Sawyer and students left the room, chattering in pairs and groups. A few of them spoke about extracurriculars like chess and dance and metallurgy. Ayla felt a pang of jealousy and anger against her chest—their skirts were long, so they were successful, but they still had the time and confidence to pursue something other than magic. Would their Masters not be angry? Would they not feel guilty allowing time for anything but study? Ayla would have to work hard for a single lick of their prestige. She rushed for the exit but found herself stuck behind all the others. Her neck grew cold when she realised that she was left alone with her spiteful teacher.

"Go on, little girl, scurry along. I can't wait to see your *talent* shining through," Sawyer hissed through clenched teeth.

Ayla didn't have to be told twice. She twisted on the spot and ran for the door, out the corridor, and to the nearest empty room she could find. The girls' bathroom. Her back met the wall of a cubicle and she sobbed until her bottom met the floor.

A knock on the door of her cubicle startled her.

"I'll be right out." Ayla tried to sound nonchalant. The person outside was quiet, waiting for her patiently, even though the door wasn't locked and she could have opened it herself. Ayla wiped away her tears and straightened her short skirt. No matter what, she had to catch up to the others. She couldn't show weakness here.

A pair of large, unblinking blue eyes greeted her when she opened the door. The beautiful girl they belonged to was about her age, with a rich brown complexion and bright orange ribbons keeping together her neat braids. Her skirt, Ayla noticed, was not much longer than her own.

Ayla squeezed past the girl towards the wash basin. When the girl followed her, she looked at her reflection caught in a fancy frame on the wall. "Sorry to keep you waiting."

"You're Master Corbin's Apprentice, right?" the girl said bluntly, her eyes never leaving Ayla's gaze in the mirror. Tiny beads of sweat formed on her forehead.

Ayla stepped back towards the door, trying not to seem like she was about to run for the hills. People seemed too strange here and she was itching for the moment this torture of a day was over and she could go home. Even the mansion's cold walls were better than this. "Um, yes. I suppose."

The girl's eyes sparkled as if she just found out a most desired secret. "I'm Camilla, we're in the same class," she shared with a wistful smile. "It's so nice to meet you!" Camilla's warm hand folded around Ayla's, dragging her out of the bathroom to a dining hall. "Let me show you around." She moved her hand in a sweeping motion over the hall.

The room boasted a rib-vaulted ceiling pierced with tracery, so tall its peak disappeared into shadow. Large French windows overlooked the green lawn in the back of the building, scattered with colourful wildflowers. Some students were taking their lunch there, sitting on the grass or snacking as they walked. Inside, students sat in groups around polished wooden tables. There were many more boys than girls—no, they were far from being children. Young men and women, lots of them her own age. They resembled crows in their black uniforms, gathered for a feast. Ayla gulped nervously, wondering what happened to failing students here. Did any of them fail in anything? She looked up at the ceiling. Just how great of a height could one fall?

"Oh, of course," Camilla said, and Ayla realised she asked her question out loud. "Everyone has a weakness. Students try their best though, as failure means punishment—which can be very..." Her voice trailed off, eyes filling with tears.

Ayla furrowed her eyebrows, trying to read Camilla's face. Sensing that no good would come from prying, she asked, "Where do I order food?" There wasn't anything that resembled a service area.

Camilla pointed at the tables. "When you sit down, you have to put your hand on the wood, like this." She dragged Ayla to the nearest table and took a seat, placing the palm of her hand on the smooth surface. "These tables are enchanted to answer your call, no matter how weak your powers are. Think about what you'd like to have and order by saying, *Serva*. Very easy, look!"

She tapped her hand on the table and pronounced, "*Serva!*" A plate of ripe cherries and blueberries, a bowl of yoghurt, and a glass of water appeared in front of her. Popping a blueberry in her mouth, she winked. "Your turn."

Ayla hesitated. She thought about Sawyer stating that she had hidden powers, and then the disappointed look on Corbin's face when she failed his simple test. How Sawyer sarcastically said that he couldn't wait for her talent to shine, almost as if he didn't expect it to. How he humiliated her in front of everyone the night before.

They say he's never wrong. I must have magic in me, Darren thought it was possible, too. I can do this.

"*Serva*," Ayla exhaled, picturing a plate of pancakes. The space in front of her stayed as clear as before. She closed her eyes and took a deep breath. "*Serva*," she repeated, determined to make it work this time. Aware of catching glances from other students, she stared at the empty table.

Camilla shifted her weight. "Um, maybe your power is somehow concealed," she said in an unsure voice, making Ayla conclude that this was probably the first time someone hadn't been able to order food. "That's okay, you can have my fruit. I'm not very hungry anyway."

Ayla thanked her new friend, took a couple of cherries, and went quiet. None of this made sense. The fact that she couldn't make use of artefacts at home would explain why she couldn't interact with the enchanted table here. But Camilla said it was made in a way even the weakest students could use it.

Sawyer with his sarcasm and animosity, and Camilla who suddenly decided to be friends once she brought up Corbin's name—Ayla could not see the full picture, but she knew that they were both pieces. She needed to start planning her escape from this odd society with its barbaric customs. To return to the normal world and live a normal, successful life. Her powers might never manifest, so was it worth signing that dreadful agreement? If Darren was one of the Sorcerers, it explained a great deal why he wanted to keep her away from all this. And if Corbin didn't want an Apprentice in the first place, it was understandable that he wanted to keep living his life the way he had before she moved in. A cherry burst inside Ayla's mouth. There was no place for her in his heart. She was just taken in as a favour to his old friend. It was up to her to prove her worth—or perhaps, to make sure she was never caught if she did decide to run away.

Another bell caught her unawares. Ayla had been too immersed in her thoughts to notice that Camilla was about to leave. Her new friend pointed to the exit of the hall that was now filled with hurrying students. The crowd got denser as they moved through the narrow doors, and they got separated. One moment and Camilla's back was gone, undistinguishable among all the black uniforms. Ayla stepped aside, cursing herself. Twice now she had lost track of someone in the crowd. She hoped this time she'd be able to find them.

Ayla's knees smacked into the ground. Just as she was steadying herself, a firm hand on the nape of her neck pushed her back down. Whoever this was, they were much less subtle than Sawyer.

She raised herself to a young man blocking her way. He seemed vaguely familiar with light brown hair spiked up, much too styled for a casual, ruffled look. His mischievous blue eyes held a touch of wickedness. Ayla tensed. She had no way to defend herself, but she took a deep breath and matched his challenging gaze. Even if he called her bluff, the least she could do was try. "Can I help you?"

He grinned. "You sure can. I thoroughly enjoyed your little performance last night. The way you tripped on Sawyer's foot was remarkable. Spilling his drink everywhere. Making him furious. I haven't had so much fun for a long time! And then, your pathetic punishment. You looked like such a delight."

Ayla bit her lip, determined to fend him off. She straightened tall and proud to spite the fear inside. "What do you want?"

The young man laughed. "Just a little fun. Play with me, little bunny. See if you can get away before I catch you." He pulled a fox figurine from a hidden pocket inside his jacket. "Come on now, run!" he gestured to the hallway behind her.

Ayla did not budge.

With an exaggerated sigh, the young man uttered a few words she didn't understand, and the figurine on the palm of his hand flashed an iridescent green. Something strange started happening to the air—it seemed to have fled her lungs, making her gasp. Ayla scratched at her throat to relieve the invisible pressure. Her hands met nothing but her own flesh.

"You shouldn't be taking artefacts outside of the classroom, Julian," a steady voice bounced off the empty walls of the hallway, and the pressure suddenly released.

Ayla fell on her knees once more, breaths shallow and fast, trying to make up for the lost seconds that seemed like hours. She turned her head to her saviour.

"Calm down, Eric, we were just having a little fun." Julian grinned at the newcomer, putting the figurine back into his pocket.

The one called Eric walked closer to Ayla and stood by her side. "Doesn't look like she was having fun. Maybe you should educate yourself on a little thing called consent next time."

Ayla's torturer gave him a mocking bow, a wicked grimace on his face. "You're boring. This is the best place to do whatever you want, without having your Master around. Why not enjoy it?" He winked at the stunned Ayla. "Don't worry, little bunny. I'm sure we'll get a proper chance to play soon."

His footsteps echoed, never losing sound despite his growing distance.

Ayla rubbed her shoulders and shivered. While she was glad about her unexpected rescue, she wondered whether she may have gotten into bigger trouble. What if Eric was capable of greater harm?

"Hey, it's okay." Eric's gentle tone relaxed her worry. He was almost a head taller than her, though most people were. His strawberry blond hair reflected the golden sunrays that seeped from the dining hall, and his face was friendly and open. Deep hazel eyes matched hers, but his high cheekbones and broad forehead were much different. A hint of a smile in his gaze mirrored the one on his full lips.

Ayla paused, taking in the image of this handsome stranger. She wanted to smile but could only muster up a frown as she scanned for danger. After one moment passed, then two, she sighed dreamily, allowing herself to feel safe. Nobody existed, except him, and he would never hurt her.

The touch of his hand on her shoulder made her lean forward to shorten the distance between them. Sweet, foreign anticipation filled all her being, longing for more.

He jerked his hand away and stepped back awkwardly. "I'm sorry. I shouldn't be looking at you like that," he said. His voice sent a wave of warmth down her belly.

She blinked hazily when he looked away, and reality slowly swam back into focus. Ayla made a step back too, blushing. What was she thinking? "Oh no, *I'm* sorry! I feel so bad, I don't know what happened—but I promise I'm not like that." She rushed into an explanation, gradually getting redder as she found herself talking too fast and making little sense.

Eric raised his hand in a calming motion. "That's completely my fault. See, my father was an incubus and I inherited some of his natural powers. They do come into motion every now and then."

Ayla blinked so fast she could've taken flight. "An incubus. Right."

Eric motioned her towards the doors in the hallway, all shut now for the lessons. "I think you're late for your class anyway. Let's go to the library and I'll tell you more."

As he was leading the way, she stole a glance at his masculine figure, noting that his uniform was almost down to his shoes. One of the higher-level Apprentices. She wondered what his interference might mean. Maybe he'd help her find a way to survive without constant attacks. A chance she couldn't afford to miss.

The library was a massive labyrinth of rows upon rows of books. Pointed arches along the walls supported the incredible height of the vaulted ceiling, seemingly even higher than the one in the dining hall—or perhaps that was the illusion of perpetual shadow, as there were no windows in their vicinity, the only light coming from downward-facing chandeliers hanging over the bookshelves. The air was musty yet not stuffy, so this place somehow had good airflow throughout.

Ayla smiled, tracing textured spines with her fingertips. She loved books, and places like this made her feel at home. Volumes of all sizes were taking up the entirety of her vision. There was a system to the library's layout that she was curious about, which Eric quickly explained. Closest to the entrance were textbooks for lower levels like hers. Further away, more advanced books. Hiding in the barely lit corners were almanacks on rare subjects, undoubtedly meant for scholar use only.

Eric walked her through the narrow rows towards an area tucked away. The world brightened around them. Large windows were facing the courtyard on this wall, flooding the small study area with light. There were a few desks with hard wooden chairs, as well as sizable cushions scattered on the floor for an informal setting. Eric pointed to one of them and, once Ayla settled, sat down himself.

"You're a new student, right?" Eric's voice was a pleasure to her ears after her uncomfortable encounters. She nodded, trusting him to lead the conversation until she felt confident enough to take over with her own questions. "How come I haven't seen you before?"

Ayla shrugged, her cheeks growing warm. "It's my first day."

A puzzled expression crossed Eric's face. "You've started at a huge disadvantage. There are only a few weeks left before the exams. It would take you an awful lot of studying to catch up on theory, not to mention spell-casting and Halloween prep. There must be a good reason why your Master would enrol you so late. An extraordinary talent, perhaps?"

Ayla let out a heavy sigh. She couldn't feel further away from the delight of a gifted student she possessed back at her old university. The place where the teachers praised her, and peers showed respect seemed to be in another life. "Not that I know of. He tried to teach me at home but didn't have enough patience. Apparently, I wasn't able to pass the simplest test, so he thought I might have better luck learning from the teachers here. Even though Sawyer said I had potential power, I don't feel like there's anything to prove it."

"How odd. Who is your Master?"

Ayla startled. "Corbin Blackbyrne," she replied cautiously, watching for his reaction. This wasn't a test she could fail. She was sure of it.

A shadow of sympathy appeared in Eric's eyes, and for a moment she thought he was going to take her hands in his. "I'm sorry. That must be very hard for you."

Ayla paused, waiting for an explanation. The last thing she expected was someone feeling sorry for her. After all, Corbin showed more kindness and mercy than most.

Seeing her reservation, Eric continued, "Corbin announced he wasn't planning to take in another Apprentice after the previous one died. I'm surprised, is all."

Her ears cocked like a rifle. She leaned in, ready for more, but it was Eric's turn to hold a pause. He studied her face as if weighing possible consequences before deciding to continue. "There's something you may not be aware of yet. Corbin was the youngest Sorcerer in history to get his graduation ring from the Academy. He mastered the program in less than two years and easily passed all exams by the age of seventeen. The required ten years of honing his skills afterwards were spent overseas. Nobody knew where he went until he came back and quickly gained a secure position in our society. Following the example of other people in power, he decided to become a Master and took in an Apprentice—"

"—and then?" Ayla couldn't lean any more forward.

Eric sighed and once again she had a feeling that he was going to touch her hand. Instead, he gave her a sad smile. "Having an extraordinary talent makes things different. Corbin is used to effortless learning and doesn't have much compassion for those who take their time. His Apprentice was gifted, but he kept pushing for better results. And then, one day he pushed her so hard she broke. The spell she was casting needed total control and once that was lost, it turned on her." He sat silent for a moment, letting Ayla digest his words. "Corbin was devastated. Right after that, he declared that he wouldn't be taking on anyone else. I wonder what happened to make him change his mind."

The sharp sound of the school bell sent Ayla out of her seat. She scrambled to her feet, alarmed and disheartened. If he had so little understanding and patience, it explained why he sent her to the Academy—to make her someone else's problem. Proving her worth now was more urgent than ever. "Thank you for sharing with me," she said. "I feel like I'm always trapped in the dark as he never tells me anything."

Eric stood up too and nodded. "Happy to help any time. Let me know if Julian gives you grief, okay?"

The library slowly filled with other students, bringing about the hum of rapidly approaching voices. The shuffling of dozens of feet on the wooden floor filled Ayla's ears as she thanked her new friend for help and grabbed her school bag to leave.

"Wait! What's your name?"

Ayla turned around to face him one last time. "Ayla Summerfield. Nice to meet you!"

"Likewise! I'm sure we'll meet again soon."

With his words resonating in her ears, Ayla rushed towards the exit. She ambled around in a daze until she was swept up by a tight-lipped Camilla who was obviously displeased by her disappearing act. Their next lesson was history of magic, and she was determined to get Ayla to one class on time. They made their way to the end of the corridor and ascended the narrow staircase leading to the second floor. The heavy wooden door on top was decorated with intricate standalone symbols that seemed to consist of straight lines and sharp angles. Ayla tilted her head, studying them. There was no doubt that this was some kind of magic, yet she couldn't feel a thing.

Seeing her interest, Camilla chuckled. "Impressive, isn't it? These runes of protection are as strong as the ones we have on the front door. You're feeling it too, right?"

Bewildered, Ayla thought of nothing better than to nod. Maybe she was better off pretending until she figured out how to find the magic on her own. She paused at the threshold, taking in a familiar atmosphere. How many hours had she spent in similar auditoriums during her five years at university? All those lectures were highlights in her memory. Lessons in places like this were a time of rest for those who were running behind on other subjects. A few of her fellow students would camp out in the back rows and secretly do homework for practical lessons, and those who worked night jobs used the opportunity to catch a small nap. She preferred to take seats closer to the front, yet not the first desks—third or fourth rows were her favourite.

Camilla coaxed her to the back.

Settling behind a white wooden desk with her textbook, Ayla couldn't help but finally feel at ease. Camilla noted her glow, looking at her sideways as the steps of other students resonated throughout the room. The unspoken question hung in the air until Ayla could no longer contain her desire to share her excitement. "I met someone. A student from another class, Eric. He saved me when I was nearly attacked by this guy Julian, and we had a good chat. He's been very kind."

Camilla's eyes widened and she shook her head. "Unbelievable. There he goes again. Tell me, did he use his power on you?"

Ayla's smile faded, her moment of feeling special over.

"He's got a bit of history with that. I mean, we all understand that he can't control it, but it feels like every term he's got a new girl. Things always happen so fast with him, it's terrible. Everything is peaches until he finds someone else, and then the ex-girlfriend has to take academic leave to recover because that's how deep the wounds are. You must be careful. Please, don't fall for him."

Camilla's warning pressed heavy on Ayla's gut. She glanced down at an elevated pedestal with a stand-up desk, steadying her focus on the hunched slender figure of the new teacher, a purple cashmere shawl wrapped around her shoulders. The teacher fixed the old-fashioned glasses on her nose as her pale blue eyes scanned the room, taking note of every student. "Her name is Mestre Arrhea," Camilla explained. "You may not know, but not all Sorcerers are Masters. A Master is a Sorcerer of a high rank who takes in Apprentices, which is a huge deal. Other Sorcerers have no capacity for mentoring or simply don't want to deal with the extra responsibilities. Teachers without a Master rank are called *Mestres*, which was a word for 'teacher' in some old language."

For someone her size, Mestre Arrhea had an incredibly powerful voice. Ayla tried her best to hang on to every word, but images of Corbin and Sawyer and Julian and Eric flashed like cards through her mind. Her fingers trembled around her pencil. How could men be so different, yet so equally capable of harm?

She didn't want to know.

CHAPTER 9. AYLA

Long, sharp claws framed the bald soles of the rat's feet as it kicked.

Ayla screamed and dropped her bag, scattering papers across the floor. The rat emerged from an upturned textbook and locked onto her with large eyes. Its hairy body closed the gap between them with ease. Lacking any semblance of grace, Ayla jumped on a dining hall chair.

Eager for entertainment, a gathering crowd giggled, watching her struggles as the rat clawed the legs of her chair. As the days became colder, most students preferred to have their meals indoors. The enticing smells of casserole dishes and hearty soups pointed out the favourite flavours of the season, and every meal was followed up with a spiced drink. The allure of food granted extra eyes on Ayla.

Desperate, Ayla looked around. Camilla had stayed back after the class and Eric was nowhere to be seen. The sea of faces surrounding her showed no sympathy, no mercy.

"*Repele*," a familiar voice cut through the hum of excited conversations and the crowd slowly parted. Eric elbowed his way towards her as the rat scampered down the hallway, following his command. He helped Ayla get down and put both his hands on her shoulders, looking into her eyes. "Are you okay? Did it hurt you?"

Ayla shook her head, shedding her fear state. She couldn't believe someone was able to sneak a rat into her bag that she had put together this morning with her own hands. The bag never stayed behind all day.

She breathed out as a tiny red flag emerged in her consciousness. When she was walking to her table, she passed by Julian. He must have snuck the rat in somehow as she kept her eyes low, avoiding getting his attention. Maybe he cast some kind of spell to get the creature into her bag after he stole another artefact. She wouldn't put that behaviour past him.

"I'm scared of rats," Ayla confessed, returning Eric's gaze. She spotted Julian in the corner of her eye, circling the rim of his glass of mulled wine with a spoon. "Certain rats more than others."

Julian gave Ayla an arrogant salute. She shivered, thinking about the list of the Academy's punishments for misbehaviour that Camilla showed her the other day. Julian's pranks would be considered a mild inconvenience and he would get away with a slap on the wrist. Disruptive actions during a lesson would vary, depending on the severity and the teacher. Someone with a Master rank like Sawyer could beat the student black and blue without any consequence, as the rules of the outside world didn't apply to the Academy. The teachers' power was only limited by the principal, and no one had seen him for months.

As far as Ayla knew, full-scale fights would result in a much more serious punishment. The student could get detained and forced to clean out the back room of the alchemy lab. The place contained old potions and artefacts that had been there for so long that nobody knew what they would do if touched. Only two weeks ago, students carried out a stretcher from the room that had a horribly mutilated corpse resting on top. Ayla nearly fainted upon sight of the skin blackened, as if it had been torched, and chunks of meat missing off the bones. Camilla told her that a student had been sent to that awful room for fighting.

"I'm glad it's over now. Promise I'm okay," she reassured Eric, determined to keep him out of trouble. She put her hand on top of his and smiled.

Eric threw a suspicious glance at Julian who was now busy talking to his friends. It was clear that her words didn't convince him, but he understood her intention. Letting go of her shoulders, he gestured towards the exit.

"Let's get out of here. If you don't have a lesson now, we can study at the library." He gathered Ayla's scattered books back into her bag and slung it over his shoulders. "After you."

Following his gallant gesture, Ayla walked out of the canteen. She didn't bother looking at Julian again. For now at least, she was safe with Eric who was becoming a reliable friend and rescuer as the weeks went by. It felt natural to stand close to him, to sometimes exchange a slight touch on the hand or the shoulder. There were moments when she doubted herself, catching Camilla's disapproving look whenever lunchtime was over and Eric took her to the library to study. She was torn between contradictory thoughts. Was she just blinded by his kindness to see the dangers Camilla spoke about? Or was her other friend just jealous of her happiness? After all, things never got physical with Eric. He was playful, yet respectful, and never made a move on her. There was nothing there to think of any ulterior motive he might have had.

"Hey, I was wondering... if it's okay to ask, of course..."

Eric gave her an encouraging smile as he cleared the table for them. "Of course it's okay. What would you like to know?"

"Can you tell me about your special abilities?" She braved the question that had been haunting her ever since they met. "You told me that your father was an incubus and you've inherited some of his powers."

His gaze wandered to the crystal clear glass of the French window they were sitting by. The greenery outside was wilting, and large fluffy snowflakes were falling from the sky, melting before they touched the ground. Eric sighed, sorting the books in tidy piles in front of them before replying.

"It's complicated. I can't change what I am, only how I act. People look at me and see an incubus, a sex-driven demon. If their feelings are unreciprocated, they blame it on me. It's awful to be judged for what you are as opposed to who you are."

"Yeah, tell me about it! I could be the sweetest person in the world but without magic, I'm nothing but mud under their boots."

"Exactly. No matter how nice I am, they will always see me for my bloodline," Eric leaned towards her. "But you are different. When I look into your eyes, all I can see is kindness, not lust. This has never happened to me before."

For a moment, Ayla thought he was going to kiss her. It took a serious conscious effort for her to break away from the power of his mesmerising eyes.

He's an incubus and can't control it. It doesn't mean he actually likes me that way.

Eric smiled as if he could see her internal struggle. Maybe he did, being so used to people always assuming the worst of him. He pointed at the book he had opened in front of her and cleared his throat. "Anyway. I've got the runes here if you want to have another go."

Relieved, Ayla readily moved closer. Runes were one of the major problems. Her magic stubbornly remained hidden and she couldn't stomach the simplest spell. Corbin had been away for a couple of weeks now and the house was cold and depressing. She spent hours upon hours trying to learn but everything was in vain. No matter how hard she tried, she never remembered a thing once the book was closed.

"When I was a child, my tutor taught me a cool trick to learn runes," Eric was as patient as ever, supporting her through her rough journey. "You start with the basic runes, right? Now, we need to trace it with a finger and quietly pronounce the rune's name. Keep doing it and say it three times, then close your eyes and picture it, and say its name again. If you do that for a couple of minutes, you should be able to memorise it."

Ayla took a deep breath and tried again, for the hundredth time. Like before, the sharp loops and angles of the runes made her think of sticks and triangles. She traced one with her finger and silently said its name. The two connected triangles lying on their sides with a single interlapping point in the middle, looking like a graphic bow, or infinity sign.

"Dagaz," she read the description underneath. "It means *dawn*."

"Good." Eric nodded. "It's the symbol of hope, awakening, certainly, completion, and it is commonly used to start the spells that are based on creation of something new. For instance, the *spell of new life* is used to help a woman conceive. Another example is for gardening, if you want the seeds to grow faster."

Ayla kept tracing the rune over and over, repeating Eric's words in her mind until they became a monotonous mantra. She closed her eyes, but the moment she lost visual contact, her mind went blank.

Deep concern lay in Eric's eyes when she lifted her face to him. Her cheeks were wet from tears, her lower lip trembling. He pulled a tissue out of the richly decorated tissue box on the table and gently wiped her face.

"I don't understand," he admitted, shaking his head. "Do you still have the mind blank?"

"Yes! I've always been so great at learning, always at the top of my class at school and then at university. Why can't I memorise the simplest things now? As soon as the book is closed, everything disappears from my memory and I start again as if I've never seen anything like it before."

"It's okay," he reassured her in a rushed tone. "Tell me what you *do* remember."

Grateful for his patience, Ayla dug in her memory for anything that stood out after all her lessons at the Academy. At that point, she'd been to all the required classes for her grade. Her schedule included History, Introduction to Alchemy, Practical Spells, Botanics, and Runes which were the basis of all spell-casting. There was a short course on Etiquette which ended in a pass-or-fail test. Ayla had no problem with it, for a change. She already had great manners from her old life. Learning about the ways of this society had been difficult to understand, but once she figured out a logic, it wasn't that hard to do the rest.

At least, that's one thing Corbin won't be angry about.

"Are you alright?" Eric's gentle voice brought her out of the sadness she always felt whenever she thought about the mansion. Ayla straightened her back and put her hands on the white pages.

"Sorry, I got distracted. Yes, I do remember that the spells in Alchemy are generally formed by a logical sequence of runes. The beginning that opens it, the description, the crown, the catalyst and the ending."

He nodded in appreciation, his eyes lighting up. "Excellent! What runes are commonly used for the beginning?"

It was terrible to see the spark of excitement disappear from his eyes when she finally responded. "I don't remember. We were talking about one of them just now, right?"

This time Eric took her hand and gave her a reassuring smile. Despite the disappointment in herself, Ayla couldn't help but smile back. There was something secure about him that made her feel comfortable sharing her constant failures. It was as if they had known each other for years and he was her dearest friend, her most supportive ally.

"Maybe we need to change the environment. I have a feeling that your potential is somehow locked away and it only needs a little push to come out." He held a pause, as if gathering his thoughts. "There's a little coffee shop in town. Would you like to have a nice cappuccino after classes? We can try to study there if you want."

Ayla's heart somersaulted in her chest. This was the most excited she had felt in a long time, and she would be lying if she said she hadn't dreamed of him asking her out. Even if it was only to a local coffee shop to study. Did it count as a date?

"I would love to! But Corbin's driver has strict instructions to get me straight after school. I'll be in a lot of trouble if I'm not there at pick-up time. Once I'm back, the maid doesn't let me out of the house," she confessed bitterly, cursing the ill fortune that forced her into her Master's care. Her stomach rumbled at the thought of a nice meal at the coffee shop. It would be good to have something to eat apart from whatever she could get at the Academy.

A dark cloud crossed Eric's face and he frowned. "We missed lunch today, you must be starving." He studied Ayla closely. "You've lost a lot of weight since we met. Do they not serve you food at home?"

Tears of shame filled her eyes as she tried to stay composed. All those hours spent entombed and alone at the mansion, the driver who only used one-word sentences with her, the indignant Dolores who made sure her stay was as miserable as possible. She held back too much, and Eric's simple question broke her defence. Her composure crumbled.

"Hey, it's okay." He gently wrapped his arm around her shoulders as she started crying. "I'm sorry, Ayla, I didn't realise how hard it was for you. We'll think of something, I promise. I can't let you starve. That's just messed up."

It felt like only a few moments passed, but the school bell announced the beginning of the next break. Ayla startled and pulled away, realising she had been sobbing with her head buried in his chest, holding on tight. Ashamed of showing her weakness, she smiled awkwardly, trying to hide her embarrassment. Eric's steady hand wiped tears off her cheeks, and once again she felt safe and comfortable. There was nothing wrong with being vulnerable with him. She knew she could trust him. It would just take a little getting used to.

CHAPTER 10. AYLA

A quiet knock on the glass brought an excited smile to Ayla's face. She rushed towards the window and gently pushed the frame up. The masculine figure in a black leather jacket and matching pants lowered his feet on the floor, the sound of his arrival muffled by thick carpet.

"Good evening," Eric purred as he dragged his bag across the threshold. He closed the window and pulled the blinds to keep any unwanted observers unaware of his presence. As always, he was there 15 minutes after the household went to bed and all the lights went out.

"Hey." Ayla matched the tone of his voice. He had been visiting for a few nights now, and she was getting used to having him around. She was a little annoyed that he strictly kept to their arrangement and was only there to bring her food and help prepare assignments for her lessons. When he climbed through her bedroom window for the first time, she was sure their relationship was going to progress past study buddies. So far, every touch they shared was when she was upset and in need of comfort, or if he was showing her the right position of hands for an incantation.

Eric opened his bag before her. He revealed a small lunchbox with a selection of cheeses and charcuterie, accompanied by assorted vegetables and artisan bread. Ayla nearly clapped her hands in excitement. She knew how difficult it was to come up with ideas for cold meals that would have no strong odours. Eric was incredibly crafty and thoughtful when it came down to taking care of her, making sure there were no traces of his presence while he was there and when he was gone. He would only bring enough food for one meal and cleaned every crumb afterwards to keep all compromising details out of the maid's watchful eye. He didn't wear cologne during his visits and he always had dark clothes on, covering as much of his pale skin as possible. The heavy blinds were always carefully pulled to block out the light that he would test from a distance before he came inside. Everything was carefully planned to keep Ayla out of trouble.

She whispered thanks before they busied themselves with the late dinner. Once the food was gone, Eric put the box away and routinely checked every nook and cranny for crumbs. Ayla couldn't hold back a smile. He wouldn't be doing all of that if he didn't have any feelings for her or if she was only a friend. She could only wonder why he chose not to act on his feelings, and that was bothering her to no end.

Putting the books on the bed, Eric threw an inquiring glance at her. "Is everything okay?" he asked in a low voice, as always keeping the noise to a minimum.

Ayla let out a sigh as she braced herself. If she needed to know the answer, she had to ask him. Otherwise, she would be speculating forever, never getting any closer to the truth. "There's something I wanted to ask you," she croaked, her throat suddenly dry. Eric gallantly handed her a glass of water and waited for her to take a sip and continue. She nodded her thanks and cleared her throat. "Camilla mentioned that you... um, see a different girl every term and that... things happen."

The hurt in his eyes made her stop mid-speech. *This was a terrible idea*, she scorned herself, reshuffling the books on the bed to make an appearance of looking at something other than the wounded expression on his face. Eric gently touched her hand and she turned towards him again.

"I'm part incubus, remember? My powers activate without my consent, but at least it doesn't happen all the time. Only when I am with someone I like. This means, however, that I can never tell if someone actually likes me back or if they fell prey to my demon side. I didn't figure it out until the end of last term when the girl I was dating ended up locked away by her Master. I was the one to blame for her suffering, of course. She was acting the same as the others, unable to accept the fact that the term was over and she had to spend the holidays away from me, wherever it was that her Master wanted to go."

"Like an addict," Ayla commented, covering her mouth as she spoke.

Eric nodded, a shadow of sadness settled deep in his eyes. "Yes. My presence in their lives, their relationships with me, were nothing but an addiction to my power. Maybe they never really liked me but my curse forced false feelings into their minds. I don't want to cause this pain to anyone."

He went silent, studying her face. Ayla's thoughts were in dismay. This certainly explained the reputation he had at the Academy and the snarky comments from Camilla. Maybe she did mean well after all. But had anyone actually listened to his side of the story?

"So this is why you stay away from... the people you like," she managed, trying not to sound bitter. It was naive of her to think he had romantic feelings for her. After all, she was a misfit at the Academy, possibly the worst student in its history. She was sure to fail every single exam, and being a decent human, he took pity on her and shared his free time by trying to help. This was only a gesture of goodwill, nothing more.

"That was the plan," he admitted, gently squeezing her hand. "Until I met you. Remember, at our first session at the library, I told you that without prior knowledge you looked at me like I was a normal person? I've kept eye contact to a minimum to spare you from my curse. I've tried to stay away but Julian's constant attacks would have driven you crazy, and you couldn't protect yourself." He lifted her hand to kiss it, and Ayla's heart nearly jumped out of her chest. Eric slowly returned her hand to its position on the bed and looked into her eyes.

"I like you a lot, Ayla. I wanted to be your friend, to make your studies bearable and to protect you from bullies. I couldn't tolerate the thought that you were abused and ignored at your own home, too. There is so much suffering in your life, I don't know how you manage it all. From what I've heard, you had a hard time transitioning from your old Master. Life has been so unfair, and you deserve so much more than this. The only thing I can offer is to help you as much as I can, while I'm still at the Academy. I simply have no right to cause you even more pain."

She blinked, putting together the pieces of the puzzle. So that was why he was putting distance between them. He was being a hero, saving a damsel in distress, and a true gentleman by not using the opportunity to get what he wanted. But she had feelings for him, too. It wasn't only up to him to decide.

"I like you, too," she responded, keeping eye contact. "I don't think it was your powers that did it, though. You've been so kind and caring, never implying at the slightest that you were interested that way. I felt that something was there, but wasn't quite sure if it was just my imagination."

Ayla stayed still as his hand glided through her hair, past her neck and shoulder, all the way down her arm. The gentle touch of his soft skin against hers fired a hidden desire she had been pushing away for as long as she had known him. Her lips parted as she leaned closer to him, her whole body responding to his touch and craving more. Eric's deep eyes grew more hypnotic than she had ever seen.

"You are an incredible woman," he whispered, pushing a loose strand of hair behind her ear. Ayla inched closer, enjoying the warmth of his breath on her lips. Her pulse quickened, sending waves of adrenaline through her veins. This was finally it. The moment she had been waiting for.

Eric suddenly placed his hand on her shoulder, gently restricting her from moving closer. He restored the distance between them, looking into her eyes with concern. "We can't, Ayla. I'm sorry."

She breathed out in exasperation, annoyed to be stopped so abruptly. The aura of longing coming from him was still strong, so the problem lay elsewhere. Wherever it was, she didn't care. She desired him so much it almost physically hurt, and it wasn't fair to have this taken away like that.

"I'm a consenting adult, Eric. I can make up my own mind," she said, gauging his reaction. As she expected, he reacted with a smile, and his fingers followed the outline of her face down to her chin, stopping just before touching her neck. Being deprived of his touch was unbearable.

"Are you sure you're already eighteen?" he chuckled, continuing the joke.

"I'm twenty-two as you well know! I might look younger but I'm quite confident I'm old enough to make my own decisions. To be with whomever I like, to do whatever I want."

Aware that it was a set-up to distract her, Ayla shifted towards him, swiftly covering the distance, and sat up on her legs to be at the same level as him. Plunging her eyes into his again, she gathered her strength. Having to make the first move had never happened to her before, but in this instance, it was what it took to push things further.

"I really like you," she whispered almost inaudibly, bringing her face closer. Her breath warmed his cleanly shaven cheek as she brushed her nose against his skin ever so slightly. A tiny shiver that went through his body told her she was on the right track.

Ayla pulled away, giving him a chance to catch up, and glanced at his full lips, then up into his eyes, then down again. Eric didn't push her away this time when she moved closer again. It was clear now that he was only holding back by choice, not for a lack of desire. She closed her eyes and finally touched his lips with hers.

A whirlwind of emotions descended upon her like a tsunami. It had been a long time since she'd been with someone, but this felt much more intense. There was no time to wonder if this was due to Eric's incubus blood or the suppressed passion they had been keeping hidden. Once the barrier was broken, all things happened at once.

The air in the room was no longer cold, heated up by their accelerating breaths. His hands, his lips—soft, wet lips on her skin—were all over her body, lighting up fires everywhere they touched. Eric was gentle, yet passionate, keeping the perfect balance of his actions. His kisses showered her with an affection that she had been longing for, making her crave more.

Eric's jacket fell on the carpet, and soon other garments joined it as there was no longer any need for them. The moment they had both been dreaming of finally arrived, and there was no remorse. Only the two of them mattered, and the rest of the world could wait.

Catching her breath, Ayla snuggled into his bare chest as his arms pulled her close. It was still dark outside, although it felt like the night was already over.

Eric caressed her hair, and everything was peaceful and quiet. She allowed herself to savour this moment of pure bliss, listening to his heartbeat, as the warm embrace of sleep gently carried her into darkness.

The first shy rays of sun made a slow appearance over the horizon when Ayla opened her eyes again. The room was getting lighter by the minute, outlining the scattered clothes on the floor from the night before. She gasped, gauging the mess. Everything needed to be fixed before it was time to leave for the Academy, and it needed to seem normal to Dolores's watchful eye.

Eric sat up too, rubbing his eyes and yawning. He looked around sleepily for a moment before snapping straight into action. "Oh my God! I'm sorry, Ayla, can't believe I fell asleep!" He jumped off the bed and started pulling his clothes together, throwing on the jacket and pants, and shoving the rest into the bag.

Ayla rushed to fix up her own clothes and made the bed. The sun rose higher with every passing moment. "It's okay, I'll deal with the rest. Quick, you have to go before anyone sees you!"

Ayla swung the window open and helped him out. With a cheeky grin, Eric stole a fleeting kiss before beginning his descent down the mansion's wall. She shook her head, watching him disappear into the surrounding bushes. He was really something.

It didn't take long to finish tidying up the place. Ayla pushed her clothes into the laundry basket and left the window open to let fresh air in. As thorough as Eric was, she could be sure there was no trace of his presence left behind.

A knock on the door. Ayla startled.

Without waiting for permission to enter, Dolores walked in with the usual distasteful expression on her face. She threw a suspicious look at the open window and turned her head around, slowly studying the room. Ayla sighed and crossed her arms over her chest.

"Good morning to you too," she said sarcastically. There was no point in pretending to be sweet to this maid. No matter what she did, it was never good enough.

"You shouldn't be sleeping with your window open. If you catch a cold, Master won't be happy," Dolores replied through clenched teeth as she closed the window and automatically swiped her hand on the windowsill to check for dust.

"So what? He's never here anyway," Ayla noted bitterly.

Dolores threw a cold glance at her and shook her head. "Well, he's here now. It's time for breakfast. Small dining room, as always."

She stormed out of the room, leaving Ayla in dismay. Corbin was back home, and she didn't hear his car pull over. When did he come back? And more importantly, had he noticed anything?

CHAPTER II. AYLA

For breakfast, Dolores served toasted fruit loaf with whipped butter and black coffee without milk or sugar anywhere in sight. Ayla rolled her eyes at the passive-aggressive maid.

Corbin walked into the dining room, and the atmosphere changed, as always. Dolores started fussing, bringing in fresh linen napkins. All of a sudden, a tiny milk jug appeared, just for his coffee, and two sugar cubes on a fancy saucer. Ayla learned he took his coffee exactly like that, while she enjoyed a spoonful of fine white sugar for hers. On those lucky days when she managed to get a coffee at the house, Dolores intentionally served it black without any lemon or milk to annoy her as she couldn't stand it that way. Today things were different.

"I believe Ayla prefers to have fine sugar with her coffee." Corbin's voice was smooth as ever.

Ayla froze in her seat. She didn't think he would remember, let alone care.

The young maid bowed her respect and flashed him a dazzling smile. "I'm sorry Master. She changes her mind every day. I'll bring it right away." She rushed off to the kitchen.

Corbin picked up his milk jug and put it next to Ayla's cup. "Here, take mine. I'm not hungry anyway."

Astonished by this sudden act of kindness, Ayla awkwardly thanked him. The usual silence between them was interrupted by Dolores nearly running with a sugar pot. With exaggerated care, she put it down near Ayla and her eyes popped at the view of Corbin's milk jug next to her cup. Enjoying the moment of triumph, Ayla picked it up and slowly poured the milk into her coffee, staring straight into the maid's eyes.

"I'm so sorry Master, your milk is coming up," Dolores mumbled, throwing a burning glance Ayla's way.

Corbin dismissed her with a careless gesture. "Leave it. Next time, please remember that she needs milk and sugar with her coffee. It's not that hard," he responded calmly.

Her cheeks a beetroot red, Dolores bowed once again and left the room. Ayla closed her eyes, savouring this moment. She didn't even have to tell him about the maid's arrogant behaviour!

"How is school?"

His question caught her unawares. She opened her eyes wide, thoughts frantically jumping in her head. Ever since the gala, he hardly spoke to her. On her first day at the

Academy, he wasn't at home. In fact, today was the first day he'd been back from his trip, and it had been a few weeks. "It's good," she confessed the half-truth.

The short answer didn't satisfy him. "Any luck with the magic yet?"

Ayla averted her eyes. It wasn't hard to predict this question was coming, yet she was still unprepared. Tucking a stubborn strand of hair behind her ear, she cleared her throat in a desperate attempt to waste time so she didn't have to answer. He was patient though, and the silence grew deeper until she could no longer stall.

"Not yet. But I'm trying my hardest," she squeaked, pretending that something caught her attention on the table in front of her.

He paused again as if trying to figure out whether to push the matter further or let it go. "I'm sure it will come, just give it time," Corbin decided at last. He drummed his fingers on the smooth surface of the table in a steady impatient rhythm. "Have you made any friends?"

Now, this was a question she could answer. Careful not to show too much enthusiasm, Ayla nodded. "Yes! A girl who goes to my class has been great at showing me around, and I also met a really nice Apprentice who's almost near graduation, Eric. He protected me from a bully and has been helping me with the lessons. He's been so kind!"

The drumming stopped. Corbin looked up, his expression as reserved as ever, however, Ayla could have sworn that a hint of irritation swept across his face. "Good, I'm glad."

Disappointment took over Ayla's mind. He didn't seem to care that she had been bullied at school, but at the mention of Eric, his attitude suddenly changed. All the questions she wanted to ask were on the tip of her tongue, but she was quiet in his presence, as always. Corbin stood up, showing that breakfast was over, and she followed his example, throwing a regretful look at her full plate. With his interrogation, she didn't get a chance to eat. Having breakfast served so beautifully and not being able to have any of it was frustrating beyond belief.

The door opened from the other side, revealing Dolores's arrogant face. She threw a smug look at Ayla, and a bad feeling stirred inside her.

"Someone's here to see you." The maid bowed to Corbin, a small smile dancing on her lips. "I believe it's Ayla's new *friend*."

Corbin nodded and Dolores stepped aside, giving way to the visitor. A beautiful face framed with perfectly styled braids swam into the doorway. Camilla stopped on the threshold, and Ayla waved at her. This was a perfect opportunity to show her Master that she was telling the truth. Camilla couldn't have arrived at a better time.

"Oh, hi! I didn't expect to see you here." Eager to see a friendly face, Ayla stepped closer and halted, realising that the girl wasn't paying her any attention. Her full attention was focused on Corbin, eyes pleading. Ayla frowned. She didn't like whatever was going on.

"Master." Camilla bowed to Corbin and then suddenly knelt in front of him.

Bewildered, Ayla studied the girl's frozen smile and submissive posture. Her desperation was almost palpable, and Ayla suddenly felt out of place. She made a move to leave but her feet were rooted to the spot.

"I told you last time that we're done." His voice was cold as ice.

Ayla shivered as if he poured that ice on her own head, but Camilla didn't budge. Instead, tears started rolling down her cheeks as she lowered her head and covered her face with her hands.

"It's really awful, Master, I can't handle it. Please, one more session! It will be the last time, I swear!"

"I have an arrangement with Tamil." His tone was still cold, with a hint of irritation. "He played his part, and I agreed to have no more sessions with you. It's time you learned how to face those fears on your own, as most other people do."

Camilla started sobbing louder. "I'll do anything, Master. Anything you want. Just one more time, I'm begging you!"

Corbin glanced in Ayla's direction and frowned as if he'd forgotten she was there. He nodded towards the door and she reluctantly took a couple of steps towards it and stopped again, unsure if she could leave her new friend all alone in this weird situation.

"You shouldn't be seeing this," Corbin said gently, covering the distance between them and giving Ayla a light push over the threshold. "Don't worry, she'll be fine. I promise, Ayla. Now, go!"

The door shut in front of her face. Ayla inhaled a full breath of air and slowly let it out. Her bewilderment knew no limits. So, Camilla only pretended to be her friend to have an excuse to come to the house and ask Corbin for whatever a 'session' was. Tamil was the nasty man who purchased her at the auction and brought her to Corbin's mansion. Did that mean she was the 'arrangement' he was talking about?

Another doorbell startled her like a deer on a deserted road. Her legs carried her towards the front entrance on their own accord. Anyone would suffice now, even if it was Sawyer. She needed a distraction from her strange thoughts. Rushing past Dolores, she pushed the door open and stopped on the threshold, a silly smile taking over her face.

"Hey. Long time no see." Eric's voice was like sweet summer honey, a symphony of joy and delight. Ayla giggled and jumped off the step to be closer to him. That would be the perfect thing now, getting lost in his charms and forgetting all about the troubled soul that had stayed behind in the fancy dining room.

"I'm so glad you're here! You can't imagine," she blurted and bit her tongue, realising she might have gone too far with her enthusiasm. The thought of her Master being home and the watchful Dolores tracking her every move brought concern to her thoughts. "Um, Corbin's returned."

"I noticed all the buzz here earlier so I thought I'd come and introduce myself. It's almost time for Halloween, and the Academy is closed. I was hoping he'd let me take you out to the markets."

"He hasn't seen you this morning, has he?"

"I don't think so. Did he say anything?"

"No. He hardly looked at me, as always. The only thing he wanted to know was if I had any success with my studies, and when I said no, he lost interest."

"It's okay then. I'm sure he'd have mentioned it if he noticed." Eric glanced above her head at the dark hallway. "If he's around, I can ask his permission to take you out now."

Ayla gulped, remembering the scene in the dining room and Corbin pushing her out. He wouldn't be in a good mood to grant any favours, and it would be a bad idea to interrupt whatever he was doing. Besides, she was no slave.

"He's busy. I'm sure he won't even notice. Let's just go."

Once the decision was made, a weight lifted off her shoulders. She glanced at the coat on the rack in the corridor, but decided to leave it as she ran down the steps to take Eric's hand. Dolores was nowhere to be seen, which was another blessing. The stars definitely aligned to make this trip possible.

The car whirred quietly and set off, leaving the dark mansion and her troubled thoughts behind. The small forest was quickly replaced by the spacious highway. It was still relatively early in the morning, but the road was already filling up. Watching the road signs speed by, Ayla breathed in the air of freedom and wondered what it would be like to be able to go anywhere she wanted. All the people in those cars had no idea how fortunate they were.

It didn't take long for them to get off the highway and follow the exit to a smaller road. Anticipation of the day's wonders filled Ayla's mind with delight and she closed her eyes to savour the moment. When she opened them, a tiny shriek escaped her lips as she saw what they were heading towards.

The whole side road was blocked by a strange shimmer curtain which was taking up all the space from the ground upwards. With a shaking finger, Ayla pointed at it. Did Eric see this?

"Eric, look!" she screamed, pushing her back into the leather seat.

Her companion briefly glanced at her but didn't slow down. "It's okay, Ayla. It's just a portal. Close your eyes if you're not comfortable, this will only be a moment."

His hand covered hers for some extra support. With a deep breath, she closed her eyes again. A silent prayer sounded loud in her mind when everything went dead quiet. An instant later, the air filled up with scents of flowers and fresh bread flowing through her open window. Ayla opened her eyes only to find out they were on a small road leading up to a colourful country market.

Ayla couldn't believe her eyes. A moment ago, they were on a completely different road, and now bright colours and laughter were all around, with a shimmer of the sea only a few hundred metres away. She gazed at Eric who was now smiling from ear to ear. He took her hand and placed it gently on his chest, looking deep into her eyes.

"I'm sorry I didn't tell you. I assumed you've seen a portal before, and I apologise for the fright it has caused you. Are you okay?"

"I am now." She forced a smile, trying to look like nothing major had happened. If something was wrong, he would have told her. There was no reason not to trust him, and she allowed herself to relax.

"Good. Let's go, there's so much to see!"

He jumped out of the car and gallantly opened the door for her. Ayla got out and stopped, breathing in the festive air of the bustling life unfolding in front of her.

Market tents were propped on strong metal poles, with merchants loudly praising their wares. Oh, the savoury scents that greeted her. Walking down the aisles, Ayla couldn't stop smiling at the variety of goods people were offering, at some of the outfits so bright and extraordinary they were almost blinding. The predominant colours were orange and black to welcome the upcoming Halloween. A couple of children in animal costumes were playing tag, swiftly moving through the crowd. Eric held her hand, a constant reminder of his sweet words and the night they had spent together. The thought of what was to come kept part of her mind busy, while she enjoyed the experience she hadn't had since Darren's death.

A shadow of sadness crossed her face at the memory of her life before, temporarily deafening the happy sounds of the market. Her lonely days at the mansion brought many of those moments back to her mind, making her time and time again regret not coming home earlier that fateful day. How things might have been different then.

"Do you like this one?"

She snapped out of the haze, struggling to focus on the silver bracelet Eric was showing her. It had a couple of small charms dangling from it, the first of which resembled a miniature tiger, and second a ball with tiny spikes.

The merchant, with his tray of similar trinkets, flashed a toothless grin. "Two layers of protection for the price of one! The ball will reflect a magic attack, and the tiger will keep you safe from mind spells," he announced.

Ayla reached for her pockets. This was her first time out since she'd been kidnapped. Busy with basic survival, she never thought about the money that had stayed behind in her old house. Her hands dipped in and out of her pockets, hoping despite all logic money would appear.

Eric gently squeezed her hand. "My treat, of course," he reassured her in his mellow voice.

Another dreamy smile emerged on her face. "Thank you," she purred.

He wrapped the cool metal bracelet around her left wrist. "There. This will protect you from Julian when I'm not around," he whispered in her ear. His fingers lingered on her wrist for a few more seconds before he stepped back to pay the merchant.

Something dark moved in the corner of her eye and she automatically glanced at the movement. The market seemed as bustling as before, yet goosebumps bloomed up her arms. She shivered and took Eric's hand to help steady herself. He seemed none the wiser and she comforted herself with the thought that she must have imagined it. There was no danger for her when he was around. Nothing could hurt her.

CHAPTER 12. AYLA

Walking past multiple stands, Ayla couldn't help but wonder about the history behind them. Most of the merchants seemed exactly like the ones she used to see at regular markets. She soaked everything in—piles of fresh fruit, fragrant candles, sweet and savoury pies straight out of the oven, children's toys, Halloween decorations, a small tent with darts and soft toy prizes. Of course, Eric dragged her to partake in all the entertainment. Ayla giggled when he won the biggest teddy bear with his precise skills of throwing darts into a range of pink balloons. She was cuddling the bear in her arm, while her other hand was holding onto Eric's. Today was the day all her worries fleeted away. She felt like a happy child, open for adventures and new impressions that were waiting for her at every turn.

"Is anything here magic?" she asked when they stopped to watch a street musician setting up his wares.

Eric smiled mischievously. "Most people here haven't heard anything about it. I brought you here because it's one of the biggest markets in the country and I assumed you haven't been here yet. However, some people here do use magic. The bracelet I got you? It's a real charm, possessing true properties. I gave it as a gift to you, so it will protect you for as long as I live."

Ayla nodded, her eyes fixed on the musician's guitar. The artist had finished his setup and gave her a light bow. His tall slender figure wore a short-sleeved shirt with frills, tight pants, and a strange hat that fit perfectly into this diverse crowd. Intricate tattoos covered both his arms from his wrists to the elbows.

All her thoughts disappeared when the musician lay a few practice strokes of his instrument. She stood still, staring at the polished body of the guitar in black and red, sparkling in the sun. The musician started singing a ballad about a princess and a vagabond—two star-crossed lovers—whose unfortunate circumstances kept them apart. Tears wet Ayla's cheeks when the song changed key and tempo, revealing a happy ending where the characters found a way around the king's law and got married. She was elated by the time the song finished.

The musician lifted his hat to her and winked. Ayla blinked at the crowd that had formed all around them, at their happy tear-tracked faces. Her shoes were covered by a thin layer of dirt that had been stirred up by strangers as they had danced around her. Eric pulled at her hand to keep moving.

"That song..." Ayla started and stopped, unable to describe what she wanted to say.

"Yes, Ayla. That was magic, bonded to that guitar. You felt it!" Eric's eyes sparkled with pride.

Thinking about all the other people who had listened to the song, she shook her head. "Everyone else did, too."

Eric didn't reply, his gaze searching the stalls for something else. Ayla suddenly felt ashamed of her remark. She was so tired of everyone being disappointed in her that she no longer felt like she could really feel anything special. Eric's trust in her was something different, and she needed to gather more optimism, though the how was still obscure to her. After all, if he didn't lose hope in her by now, she shouldn't either.

"How about this?" His finger pointed at a tent made from dark blue material, adorned with silver stars and moon crescents all over.

Despite her thoughts, she chuckled at the exaggerated insignia that would appeal to the general public, from children to the elderly. Magic or not, those merchants were always popular at any gathering. "Fortune telling?"

"Why not?" He shrugged and pulled her inside. "Let's see what the future holds!"

They walked into the tent, the entrance flap snapping back into place behind them. Complete silence enveloped their bodies. Ayla felt dozens of eyes studying her—judging, probing—and she instinctively stepped closer to Eric.

Only a few candles were breaking through the thick layer of darkness, sending her hair on edge. She smelled nothing but smoke and incense.

"Hello?" Eric's voice didn't betray any emotion, as if he felt completely at ease here. His hand was warm and strong, giving Ayla the comfort that she needed. But something was in this tent, and this something was up to no good. There was no reply, only a ghostly chuckle in those dark corners.

Eric squeezed her hand, reminding her of his presence. "Hey, it's okay. It's meant to be spooky, Ayla. This Sorceress possesses the great gift of reading people's futures. She should be free soon."

A rectangle of light appeared on the other side of the tent, revealing a man with a happy smile. He was clutching his hat in his hands, eyes reflecting the unsteady light of the candles. He declared his gratitude through earnest praise. After a deep bow, he made his way through the dark antechamber and out into the market's crowd.

Ayla's fears eased. The place didn't seem as dark and scary as before. Seeing this man getting a good reading, she relaxed and took a brave step into the next room.

Dozens of candles blinded. They were burning everywhere, floor to ceiling, on the cabinets and shelves, their glare chasing away the dark. There was a large one on the massive, centred table, right next to a crystal ball that was empty and white.

"Welcome, young lovers," a quiet voice released between crooked, yellow teeth. The Sorceress was a small, withered woman with a mane of straight grey hair. Her exaggerated makeup created the visage of a regular market fortune teller, along with tinkling trinkets decorating her neck and wrists, and a shawl with tiny coins she wore over her shoulders. Her dark blue colouring matched the outside of the tent.

"Who wants to go first?" she asked, pointing at the chair in front of her.

Ayla felt a gentle nudge and threw a playful look at Eric. He poked his tongue out at her, nodding at the chair. Encouraged by his confidence, she took the seat and straightened her back.

The Sorceress motioned for her to put her hands on the table, palms down. Cloudy air filled the crystal ball, mixing and rising to the top before slowly descending to the bottom, only to repeat again and again. The ball changed its colour from white to dark green, reflecting in the fortune teller's eyes.

"Look deep into the ball, my dear. Imagine your question and you will find the answer."

Ayla looked into the sphere, following the old woman's instructions. With a deep breath, she wondered if she possessed any magic or if she was indeed a fake. She thought about Eric and his warm hands, and all the touches they shared the night before. Corbin's face popped into her mind and she cringed, remembering the ugly scene from this morning.

The ball started spinning, and Corbin's face stuck before her. His expression changed from a smile to a frown, and a cloak of darkness slowly engulfed it.

"Your Master is not who he says he is," the quiet voice said deep in her head. "You are not safe with him, but you're in a bigger peril without him. Your destiny is to be with another. The white-haired warrior."

Ayla leaned closer to the ball, searching its depths. "Eric?"

"No, Ayla. Eric won't even last a month. You bear your father's curse, and those around you will suffer. One by one they will fall until you face your destiny."

Ayla stifled a scream when she saw Darren lying on the floor in a pool of blood. Eric lying on the cold ground, with his eyes staring into nothingness. Her own reflection smiling, with a strange blue light in her eyes. And a young man with a ball of bright light hovering over his hand, his hair white as snow, beckoning her to follow him.

"My father's curse?" she asked, but the clouds in the crystal ball evaporated. She glanced at Eric, wondering if he heard anything.

His face was pale, eyes wide open. He shook his head in disbelief and stood up. "This is wrong. I'll stand by your side, Ayla, and I will protect you from whatever peril you might encounter."

The hands of the Sorceress flew above the ball as it grew dark. The candles in the tent dimmed, with only a faint flicker sending dancing shadows on the walls. Her eyes sparkled a sickly green as she spoke again. "Young Apprentice," she addressed Eric, who took Ayla's hand to leave.

"I don't want to hear any more of these lies," he snapped, but that didn't stop the flow of her words.

The Sorceress paid no heed to him as if he were nothing but a nuisance. "You won't be able to protect her. The curse will follow her everywhere she goes until she accepts her destiny. You, however, might need protection of your own. Dark forces are set in motion, and if you stay by her side, they will crush your life. It won't be long before you realise it, but it will be too late for you then."

The candles sparkled bright and cheerful again as the crystal ball cleared out from the dark smoke. The Sorceress rearranged the candles on the shelf next to her, avoiding the couple. "No need to pay," she dismissed.

Eric scoffed and pulled Ayla out of the tent and into the antechamber. People always seemed to be pulling her around these days. "Right, like I was going to anyway," Eric said. "I've never heard a worse reading in my life. Sorry, Ayla, I was hoping this would be fun."

He looked at her apologetically, and she managed a forced smile. As he opened the outside flap of the tent, she was surprised to see that twilight had descended onto the market's increasingly busy aisles. A plethora of fairy lights and candles on every stall showed the way through the evening crowd. She searched the area with an intent stare, but nothing seemed out of the ordinary.

"I can't believe we spent so much time there," she admitted, shivering as the chilly autumn wind brushed her skin. Somehow evening had crept up. Eric wrapped his arm around her and pulled her close to him. This gesture of affection would have sent her over the moon with joy under any normal circumstances. After the odd events in the fortune teller's tent, however, she was feeling tense and uneasy.

"I think we should go. Corbin won't be happy that I'm out so late." She thought again about the morning scene, surprised at how it faded in comparison to what she'd just experienced.

Eric agreed.

Ayla didn't feel hungry, even though she hadn't had any food since the dinner Eric had brought her the night before. The smells of freshly cooked sausages, pies and baking goods were everywhere. Ayla quickened her step. Regardless of this abundance and the potential of a whole lot of nothing at home, she felt that she had to hurry back. Something was wrong. There was danger in the air, and it was driving her crazy not knowing what to expect and where it was coming from.

They left the joyful bustle of the evening crowd. The wind breathed an icy chill.

Ayla stopped, snapping her head in all directions. Eric felt something too, taking a swift turn and pulling her close. Ayla kept playing the words of the Sorceress in her head. Eric was neither white-haired nor a warrior.

The air cooled even more. Darkness slowly rose around them, unfolding like the petals of a dreadful flower. The same kind she had felt back at home when she'd returned to collect her clothes after Darren's death. Whatever its nature, its time had come now. Carnivorous, cannibalistic, angry.

Two shadowy figures stepped out behind them. "There you are, devil's spawn," one figure hissed, bony finger pointed in her direction. Their skin was withered and sickly white, reminding her of those pharaohs she saw in the movies a long time ago. This was how she imagined dead people. The figures advanced. Underneath their cloaks and hoods, their faceless silhouettes seemed ever-moving, changing their outline while keeping the solid basis intact.

Ayla yelped, jerking away from them. A sharp desire to live clouded her mind. Eric stepped in front of her in a protective gesture. The figures burst out in a dreadful laughter that sent shivers down her spine.

"You can't protect her, Apprentice. She is a misfit, out of this world. Her existence is an abomination. A spit onto the face of destiny! The curse she bears is destroying everything around her, and everyone will suffer the consequences."

"So, your solution is to do what? To kill her?" Eric held his head high.

The shadows didn't bother to reply. With a terrifying speed, one of them lunged forwards. Bony fingers swiped at Ayla but clipped Eric instead, their sharp claws ripping the sleeve of his jacket. The other shadow crept around them, looking to strike from behind.

A barely feasible change in the air alerted Ayla of another presence, and she turned her head to face it.

"What's going on here?" Corbin emerged from a shimmering portal that appeared in the middle of the second shadow, seemingly absorbing it.

"This isn't your fight, Sorcerer," the first shadow hissed, stepping around Eric to face Corbin.

He stood still, demeanour deceitfully relaxed. His eyes tracked the shadow's every movement, calculating all possibilities. Clinging onto Eric's arm, Ayla watched him wide-eyed. She wondered how he knew where to find her and how he appeared just at the right time. Whatever the answer, she was sure she wouldn't like it. If she survived long enough to receive an answer.

"This Apprentice is under my protection," Corbin explained calmly. "By trying to harm her, you are insulting me as her Master. Is this what you're trying to do? To challenge *me*?"

When Corbin glided forward, the shadow glided back. Its shape cycled from humanoid to beast, bloating and growing, heaving in the air. Its arms elongated, resembling branches of a bare tree, as it grew towards the sky.

A deep chill crept on Ayla's skin, and her heart stopped in her chest.

But Corbin just stopped and shook his head. "What's with the theatrics? Are you too scared to show your face to a little girl? Or do you think that cheap illusions are going to work on *me*? Pathetic!" His gold ring flashed bright green.

The shadow lost its volume, deflating back into a human silhouette. In the darkening twilight, it held the ordinary figure of a hooded man. Corbin waved his finger and the hood fell off, revealing a pale face that seemed vaguely familiar. Ayla could have sworn she'd seen this person before but under different circumstances. One of her neighbours from her old life or someone from university?

"That's better. Now you will tell me who sent you and what your deal with my Apprentice is," Corbin demanded.

The man gulped and raised his hands. "I can't. I just..."

With a light pop, he disappeared in the air, leaving nothing but a tiny puff of smoke in his place.

A sudden movement caught Ayla's attention. The second figure fled from wherever it was hiding and stepped through a dark portal. Corbin followed Ayla's eyes, but his reaction was too late. There was nothing else to do.

Ayla squeezed Eric's hand tighter as her Master's gaze fell upon her.

"You have some explaining to do," Corbin stated in his calm voice. Tiny sparks of discontent floated around his eyes like the undertow in a peaceful sea. Ayla stifled the terror of being in trouble with him. She had never seen him do any magic, even though she knew he was perfectly capable. Mercy was not in his deck of cards. He quickly scanned the scene for any more threats before turning to Eric. "Your Master's name, please."

"Um, it's Master Boreus. This isn't Ayla's fault. I should have asked for your—"

"—I don't want to hear it, boy. Stay away from her." Corbin shook his head and grabbed Ayla by the arm, dragging her towards his shimmering portal.

Ayla let go of Eric's hand, realising that by staying too close to him she revealed their relationship to Corbin. No doubt, this would anger him even more. In an instant, she was manhandled through the portal. She wrapped her arms around her shoulders and tried to think of something warm and safe to stop herself from shivering. Her Master stopped in front of her, and she looked up at his face, seeking words of comfort.

"What were you thinking?" He didn't bother to cover his displeasure, raising his voice straight off the bat. Ayla stood frozen, too afraid of his anger to move. Nobody had ever yelled at her, let alone someone like Corbin. Someone who held her life in his hands.

"I'm sorry, I just went out with a friend. I didn't know it wasn't allowed." She sniffled, shaking all over and wishing for Eric to be there to support her.

Corbin sighed. After a lengthy pause, he spoke again in a much calmer voice. "What shall I do with you? Ayla, you can't risk yourself like that, you should know better."

Ayla stepped back to restore the distance between them, but he didn't pay attention to it. Instead, he approached her again. Ignoring her discomfort, he stood in her personal space. She looked to the side to avoid his direct gaze. His behaviour unnerved her, and she didn't know what to expect.

Corbin reached for her shoulders and pulled her close, wrapping her rigid body in his arms. He cooed her name as he circled his thumbs against her hair. Shocked by this strange display of affection, she couldn't move a muscle. After a few tormenting minutes, he spoke again. "Isn't it enough that Darren was killed because of you? Are you trying to get some sort of penance by inviting even more danger into your life? What's wrong with you?"

His harsh words were uttered in a soft, soothing voice. Ayla didn't register their meaning at first. When realisation finally hit, she tried to break free, but there was no way out of his iron clutches. This made no sense at all. Hugs were supposed to be followed by consolation, not a reprimand. Corbin squeezed her tighter, killing any hope to escape unless he chose to let her go. Her body fought it for a few moments until there was no more strength left. Ayla gulped down her tears, guilt blooming in her throat. Her head dug into Corbin's chest. She suspected that she might have been the reason why Darren got murdered, and it became clear now that Corbin believed that as well. Did it mean that by taking her in he made himself a target too? Was it because she was cursed, like the fortune-teller said?

Corbin planted a kiss on Ayla's forehead and lifted her chin, forcing her to return the gaze of his dark eyes. There was no understanding in them, no sign of yielding. Just a stone-cold calculation. "I've been informed that the boy has been visiting you here. Is that true?"

There was no way to hide from his penetrating stare. His face was so close she could feel the warmth of his breath caressing her skin. Ayla squirmed, uncomfortable, knowing that he would find out regardless once he set his mind to it. Maybe he did notice Eric leave that morning. Her voice broke when she replied. "Yes, Corbin. I have been struggling with my studies and Eric has been teaching me after lessons, too."

Though Corbin only had one cold finger on her chin, Ayla felt locked into place. "Is that all?"

With a violent heartbeat, she mustered up the courage to respond. She whispered, "He's been bringing me food."

Corbin's expression changed, unreadable. He stepped back, finally giving her space to breathe. The air of an unforgiving authoritarian disappeared, but Ayla still flinched when his hands lifted. They didn't strike, coming to rest on her shoulders. The person standing in front of her was the same man who took off her chains on the night she was brought to his house. The man who told her she wasn't a slave. "Why would he bring you food?"

Ashamed, Ayla averted her eyes and hoped he would let it go. She knew better, though. He wasn't going to stop until he got to the bottom of this, and now was the time to confess. "I'm just so hungry," she murmured, as her cheeks grew hot with embarrassment.

Corbin stepped further back, looking her up and down as if it was the first time he'd seen her. "You did lose some weight," he remarked, rubbing his chin. "What's going on?"

She shook her head, unable to talk any more. Bitter tears flowed down her face, cooling down the merciless blush. There was nothing she wished for more than being anywhere else but here. Having to admit her weakness was humiliating.

Thankfully, Corbin didn't need an explanation. "You haven't been fed here, have you? I'm so sorry, Ayla. I didn't realise how you were treated in my absence. No wonder you're acting up."

A hint of irritation sparked in her mind at his comment. Though she struggled to keep her balance, she had to remain strong until she was alone.

Corbin straightened his back and snapped his fingers, the sound sending an echo against the cold stone walls.

The door opened, and Dolores swam into the room. "Did you call me, Master?" She bowed and looked at him quizzically, ignoring Ayla's presence.

Corbin shook his head in disappointment. "Please remind me what your duties are," he said calmly.

Ayla suppressed a smile when she saw the maid's face drop in concern. No doubt she knew this was trouble.

"To serve you and take care of the household in your absence." She bowed again, hiding her eyes. "Have I done something to displease you, Master?"

For a moment, Ayla thought he was going to lose his temper. Corbin pulled in a long breath as if he was going to yell, but nothing happened. He spoke in an even voice, and she wasn't sure if this was better. No matter what he did, whenever he was upset, he was scary.

"I'd like you to have a look here." He pointed at Ayla, and Dolores politely glanced at her. Corbin nearly poked Ayla's chest as he raised his voice in annoyance. "Look at this! I'm really struggling to understand why my Apprentice is so malnourished she can hardly function! I am very disappointed with your service. You should know better."

Ayla stayed quiet during the exchange, too afraid to move or make any noise. He seemed to be getting angrier and she hoped he'd forget about her. Ugly feelings swirled around her mind, how she so desired punitive action against the maid to take the attention off her. Would the maid last twenty lashes?

Corbin turned towards Ayla, and she stiffened her back. Once again, she was forced to look into his eyes. He had made a decision, and Ayla knew she wasn't going to like it. Words like the crack of a whip, he said, "Now, you. From now on, you're not allowed to leave the house without my explicit permission. The only other place you'll be safe is the Academy. My driver and a bodyguard will drive you there and pick you up after classes. No exceptions. There will be no visitors, either. Do you understand?"

Ayla lowered her head in defeat. Her tears were now falling freely on the floor, and she wondered for a second if she could dive into them if she cried long enough. "Yes... Master," she whimpered.

Corbin sighed and gently pushed her towards the door. "Good. Now, go to your room and think about your risk-taking behaviour. I need to figure out how to undo the damage you've done."

CHAPTER 13. AYLA

Thick, metal bars filtered the gloomy morning light onto her skin. How were these installed while she slept? Ayla wrapped her fingers around the silver and rattled, but no budge. Prison. *There will be no visitors.*

Corbin's words from the night before resonated within her mind and she sank back into the bed, clutching her head to keep it from splitting. He trusted her so little, then. Or maybe he thought of her as nothing more than a stupid, disobedient child who would jump into the same trap again and again.

The skin on Ayla's neck pulled taut. She ran to her bedroom door and turned the knob to leave. Nothing happened.

She paused for a deep breath. Her throat constricted. The harder she breathed, the less air came in. It wasn't as if someone was going to lock her inside the room with no way out, especially knowing about her claustrophobia. Ayla was confident she had mentioned her fears to Corbin before. There was nothing for her to worry about. He wouldn't do this.

She tried the door again. The knob remained unyielding.

Calm down, she told herself. *It's not the end of the world. The door just jammed, it happens. Someone is going to come in sooner or later.*

Cold sweat descended upon her as she stewed in her thoughts. All the things about Corbin's ruthlessness that Eric and Camilla had told her and she didn't want to believe. Realising that in this society, she was owned property without any rights until proven worthy, even though Corbin had told her she wasn't a slave. Knowing that as her Master, he had the right to do with her as he pleased. The fact that he hadn't used his power until now didn't mean that he couldn't change his mind at any time.

In the corner of her eye, the walls trembled as if they were about to crumble. Ayla jerked, heart racing. The room looked unchanged, with all her things exactly where she had left them. The ceiling was as high as always, and the door to the bathroom was still open. There was nothing in the whole room to threaten her.

This is a big room, she reassured herself, taking a deep breath. *I'm not afraid. Breakfast will be served soon and Dolores will open the door because Corbin is in the house and she has to be nice. It won't be long. There's nothing scary here. Lots of space. Lots of air.*

The feeling of dread intensified as her vision grew blurry. The walls seemed to move ever so slightly, making the room close in around her, drawing the oxygen out. Closing her eyes to chase the image away didn't help. On the contrary, it made her feel dizzy as if the room was spinning around her, getting smaller with every turn. The room was going to crush her unless the air ran out first. One of them was going to kill her.

Terrified, Ayla started pulling and twisting the knob with all her might as panic rushed through her mind. She pounded the engraved wood with her fists without feeling the pain of impact, even though the sensitive skin on her hands quickly bruised and broke, letting the blood out in a bright red mess.

"Somebody help! Get me out of here!" she screamed between breaths as the panic was driving her to throw the weight of her whole body against the door. No sounds were coming from outside as if the house was completely deserted and she was the only living soul left behind, alone, trapped in a tiny cage, unable to breathe. Nobody was going to hear her.

The barely audible click of the lock was the most beautiful sound in the world. As soon as the door inched inward, Ayla grabbed onto the edge and pulled it open, ready to push the spiteful maid out of the way and run as far away as she could. There seemed to be no force in existence that could keep her inside. Nobody could push her back into that trap.

Unless it was Corbin.

He stood in the doorway as composed as ever, blocking the only way out of the room. His expressionless face made her stop in her tracks. Still hyperventilating, Ayla looked up at him, desperate for even a tiny spark of compassion in his dark eyes.

"Please," she breathed out, hoping he would step aside and let her out. The room behind her retreated to its original shape, but she couldn't be sure how long that would last.

"What's going on?" he asked calmly, and Ayla stared at him in disbelief. He was aware of her claustrophobia, she was sure of it. Why would he sentence her to this kind of punishment? Anything was better than this.

"I'm afraid of confined spaces," she gulped, trying to regain her composure. She thought that he might react better if she stayed level-headed like him and could explain things logically. With adrenaline still pulsing in her veins, it wasn't an easy task.

Corbin didn't respond, studying her with a tired look as if she was an annoying issue he wanted to have resolved so he could go back to something more interesting. Ayla took another breath and tried again. "There are bars on my windows and the door was locked. I had a panic attack because I'm very scared of being restrained like this."

There was no sympathy in his midnight eyes as he kept silent. Ayla shuddered, realising she had to plead her cause if she ever wanted a chance of redemption. "Please, Corbin. This is unnecessary. I promise there will be no visitors, there's no need to lock me in. I swear I won't set foot outside of the room without your permission. Please, I'm begging you!"

"You brought this upon yourself," he finally replied, his voice devoid of all emotion. His dark eyes were cold as ice, and Ayla shivered, wishing for Eric's presence. How much would she give to be with him again!

"I'm sorry I left without asking permission. I'm sorry I allowed my friend to visit me here. I promise I'll be good, I'll obey everything you say, I'll do anything you want. Just don't confine me to the room, please, Corbin!"

He shook his head with a terrifying look that told her he had made his decision. The stone walls radiated the winter chill that she was finally starting to feel again after all the adrenaline rush. The soft carpet was absorbing some of it, yet her feet were cold. The stinging feel of icy fingers crept along her body, making her tremble with fear of the worst outcome. She was dreading his words, and the wait was unbearable.

"You put your life at risk one too many times. You endangered other people's lives, too. I don't know if you realise it but your careless behaviour is unacceptable. I've been very soft with you, and it shows. All of this comes from a lack of discipline. You need to understand that actions have consequences. Last night, you had a great time out, and now you'll be staying in your room until I see that you've learned the lesson."

"No! Please, don't leave me! Please, Corbin! Don't lock me in, don't go!"

Ayla tried pushing out of the room, accidentally grabbing onto his hand to squeeze past him. She immediately understood it was a mistake. Corbin frowned as if she committed another offence, and she unclenched her bloodied fingers and stepped back. The fear of being alone was so intense she couldn't think straight. The only thing that mattered was to keep the door open. If that meant she had to overstep the boundaries, she was willing to do it.

"You're forgetting your place." With a disappointed sigh, he lifted his arm and struck her with a swift slap on the face. Ayla wavered on her feet but managed to stay up. The hit wasn't a strong one but it stung. She pressed her cold hand to the cheek to cool it down. He was right, she wasn't allowed to misbehave. By trying to defy him, she doomed herself to a bigger punishment. Tears welled up in her eyes but she knew it wouldn't move him. Nothing seemed to be able to melt the ice in his heart.

"I'm so sorry! I didn't mean any disrespect. I'm just so scared to be locked here, please, Corbin, I'm begging you! There must be something else you can think of. Anything is better than this," she rambled, wiping her cheeks with her sleeve and trying to think of a way to convince him. Maybe if she knelt she'd have a better chance? There was no more pride left in her. She was prepared to do whatever it took to change his mind about the punishment, even if it was something like being lashed in front of the whole town again.

For an instant, there was a hint of compassion in his eyes which went away as quickly as it appeared. With a practised move, he took her by the arm and walked her back into the room. Ayla didn't have a chance to say a word when he lifted her effortlessly as if she weighed nothing more than a feather and carefully put her down on the bed.

"*Cálmate*, Ayla."

The familiar spell jolted her memory of the day she was bought at the auction. It felt like that happened years ago, though she knew it had only been a few weeks. She didn't get to ponder too much as his power crept around her consciousness, relieving her of the panic. He didn't take the fear though, leaving it subdued but still running in the background. Her eyelids growing heavy, Ayla struggled to keep her focus as he leaned closer to her.

"You must learn to obey me, darling. This might take a little while but trust me when I say that everything I do is for your own good. I don't want to hurt you and I certainly don't want to break you. Deep down, you are fighting, and might still have the illusion that I can't see it. You have to learn to let go and give up control. Please don't make me take it from you by force."

He gently kissed her on the forehead as if she were a child he was tucking in to sleep. She hardly remembered having the warm blanket pulled over her and the door closing with a quiet click of the lock as her consciousness slipped away into the fuzzy grey fog.

It swirled around her ankles as she followed an invisible path. It didn't feel like walking without a direction; Ayla knew this was a way leading her somewhere, and she wanted to know what was waiting for her at the end of it. The grey fog seemed to be a living organism, ever-changing, its colours varying from almost black to the lightest grey. The further away she moved, the higher it went, giving way and closing up behind. It only lay low by her feet as if obeying her movement, and it felt bizarre and thrilling at the same time.

The pathway gradually got lighter as she approached her destination. Someone was there, expecting her arrival. Ayla stepped closer and stopped at the edge of the soft cloudy wall.

It was an illusion, or perhaps a strange dream. The young man she saw wasn't waiting for her. He was in the middle of a conversation with a stocky middle-aged woman and a lanky teenage boy who was leaning on a wooden staff. Curious, Ayla strained her ears to find out if she could hear what they were talking about. It didn't take much effort on her part, as everyone was speaking clearly.

"Thank you so much for the lesson, especially considering how busy you are, Blaze. It's an honour." The woman bowed to the man, pressing her hand to her heart. The teenager awkwardly repeated her gesture. Despite their age difference, it was clear the two were somehow related. They had the same brown eyes and honey-hued skin, and their clothes were made of the same light cotton material in a shade of beige. *Mother and son*, Ayla thought before glancing at the third member of the conversation who was the one to draw her attention originally.

"No trouble at all." He gracefully returned the bow and nodded at the wooden staff the teenager was clinging to. "You'll need to keep practising daily just like I showed you, okay? Only discipline and perseverance can make you a true warrior."

Ayla couldn't take her eyes off him. Even if it wasn't for his exceptional looks, there was something about him she couldn't quite figure out. His hair was white like the pure snow covering mountain tops she had always dreamed of visiting. His eyes shone a bright emerald green that she'd never seen before. The athletic masculine figure, the perfect posture, the smooth movements all painted a dream picture of any teenage girl or young woman. Or *any* woman. She didn't think anyone would be able to turn him away, were he to lay his eyes on them.

She felt her cheeks grow red as she considered it. He was handsome, yes. But she already had an amazing boyfriend who doted on her. There was nothing else she needed, apart from sorting things out with Corbin so she could see Eric more. The thought conjured darkness in her mind and she stopped smiling. No matter what, the situation needed to be fixed.

The white-haired man replied to some questions of his two companions and looked around, his gaze lingering a little longer in Ayla's direction. *He can't see me*, she realised with relief and allowed herself to relax. *This is just a dream anyway. He isn't real*. Her heart skipped a beat when she focused on their conversation again.

"Is everything okay?" The middle-aged woman asked, an expression of concern crossing her round face.

The man called Blaze nodded in reassurance as he kept studying his surroundings. "There's a presence here I can't figure out yet. Not an evil one, don't worry. More of a curious being. Something I have encountered before, but so far only in dreams."

Perplexed, he looked again to where Ayla was standing, as if he knew she was there. The fog rose higher as if warning her of potential exposure, and she stepped back to hide behind it. *How odd*, she thought as the path led her into a darker area, submerging her into a deeper sleep. *I wonder what this dream can mean. Maybe I can find the answer in one of the library books.*

The fog made her feel safe as she walked and walked until it started carrying her in a soft embrace. This strange place between dream and reality gave her much-needed reassurance. Ayla smiled, letting go of her worries. She only wished she could visit this place more. It was almost like home, and it was beautiful.

CHAPTER 14. AYLA

Monday morning was a fresh start. After Corbin had confined Ayla to her quarters, she spent the weekend trying to figure out a way to his forgiveness. He had to use the *cálma* spell a few times to relieve her panic but keep her scared enough to feel the full extent of her punishment. Once the weekend was over, things went back to normal. Breakfast of French toast with whipped cream and raspberry conserve was served for two but Corbin didn't show up, and Ayla felt relieved she didn't have to talk to him.

The stone-cold face of the unsmiling driver was the most welcome sight. He seemed startled by Ayla's warm greeting as she flew out of the door, enjoying the cool fresh air on her short walk from the mansion's door to the car that was taking her to the Academy.

"Good morning! What a beautiful day!" she sang with a gracious smile, latching her fingers over the handle of the car door. With the enchanted fabric of her school uniform adjusting to keep her warm, she didn't have to wear a jacket in this cold weather. The only items she needed to add were a pair of stockings and leather gloves that were delivered that morning in a velvet box from a fancy store in town. She hoped with all her heart that this kind gesture meant Corbin finally forgave her and she could at least move around the house freely again.

"Hurry up. Master won't be happy if you're late," the driver mumbled, slamming the car door shut after she climbed onto the back seat. The drive to the dreaded school had never been better. Ayla enjoyed every moment of the journey, looking out the window at the bare trees of the forest and the messy brown leaves lying in the mud from the recent rains. She smiled at the change of scenery as the car entered the highway and rushed past the road signs. Each of them had a place in her memory, and each of them was precious in its own way. The sudden sting of the cold wind attacked her once she got out of the car, but that made her happy too. Fresh, clean air was a symbol of freedom, even though it was still under restrictions. It was better than staying in the same room for days.

The Academy was almost unrecognisable under layers of Halloween decorations. Orange so bright it was melting her eyes, and black so deep one could drown in it. Moving skeletons, talking pumpkins, and screeching banshees at each door filled the air with so much racket her ears nearly popped. Ayla wondered if there was anything here that wasn't enchanted to do one thing or another, and her mind automatically went to Julian. This would be the perfect time to set up a prank. She looked around carefully and touched the bracelet Eric had bought her. It felt warm, and she wondered if it was fighting off a spell or just reflecting the heat of her body.

Another student stopped in her personal space and Ayla automatically stepped back. Julian's handsome face hovered in front of her. "Hey, little bunny. You're so brave, coming here on Halloween."

"Why's that?" Ayla kept her eyes on him, thinking of a way to get out. She had no time for his games.

He flashed his impeccable smile. "It's Halloween. The one day—and night!—when Apprentices can do whatever they want, without any consequences. Imagine all the things we can do." He moved closer, and Ayla's back felt the cold stone wall. The bracelet felt warmer on her wrist, alerting her. Julian leaned in, his breath brushing the sensitive skin on her neck up to her ear. "Got yourself some protection, I see? Oh sweetie, you will never bore me. A bunny with a bite! I can't wait to properly get my hands on you. I think I'll ask my Master to have you as a gift."

"What?" Ayla tried to sound indignant, fighting off the sick feeling in her stomach. Dread locked her in place as she waited for the answer like a mouse in a trap.

A smug expression crossed Julian's face. "Masters can arrange to swap Apprentices, or lend them to one another. I've been exceptionally good with my studies and made my

Master proud. He'll undoubtedly get me a sweet reward. How about you, bunny? Do you think Corbin will reward you? Or have you done something to displease him so he'll seek a punishment instead?"

"None of your business. Leave me alone!" Ayla pushed him away and sprinted down the corridor, adrenaline clouding her mind. Julian's laughter echoed in her ears even after he was long gone. His words pulsed in her brain. She didn't want to believe it, yet she knew it was true. She had to make sure Corbin was never unhappy with her again. If life at his mansion wasn't great, she was too terrified to imagine what it would be like if she was traded in like a toy for Julian's sick games. One thing was for sure, though. No matter how much turmoil she was in, she couldn't tell Eric. He would undoubtedly try to step in. She couldn't get him in trouble again.

The halls were buzzing with activity, full of students scurrying along to have a quick catch-up after the weekend and discuss plans for the night before it was time to go to class. Ayla squeezed past the crowds to the usual spot at the library but it was taken up by others. Frowning, she walked around the school grounds, checking the corridors, the canteen, the outdoor picnic area. Eric was nowhere to be seen.

It wasn't until lunchtime that he finally showed up. Before joining her at the cosy corner table, Eric moved his hand around them, pronouncing a quiet spell. The purple gem he was holding in his open palm sparkled as the magic took hold, surrounding the table with a semi-transparent veil.

"Invisibility," he explained to wide-eyed Ayla. "We're not allowed to be together and I don't want to get you in more trouble."

"Are you okay?" Ayla touched his hand, half expecting him to pull away. She felt guilty about putting him in danger and causing unnecessary conflict with Corbin. Boys' egos were fragile, and being put down in front of the girl he liked would have been awful. Eric placed his hand on hers and looked her in the eye.

"I'm sorry, Ayla, I didn't mean to appear distant. The weekend was a bit odd. On Saturday, Corbin paid a visit to my Master and they had a long chat about our Friday trip to the markets. I believe he mainly wanted me not to spend time with you anymore, in or out of school. Apparently, I'm a bad influence." He winked, and she forced a smile. This wasn't what she expected, but it was no surprise. Corbin was thorough in everything he did, and it was starting to get to her.

Squeezing her hand in a comforting gesture, Eric continued. "My Master told him he'd keep an eye on it. Once the drama was over, Master spoke to me as well. Looks like Corbin is serious about this issue, so there might be some nasty spells around your house now, to repel any uninvited guests. However..."

"What?" Ayla couldn't stand theatrical pauses, having had her fill with Corbin's.

Eric chuckled and moved closer to her, wrapping his arm around her shoulders. "My Master, Boreus, has an excellent sense of humour. He's too old for these tricks. So, I have this bracelet that I have to wear now, to keep me away from you, for Corbin's peace of mind. Quite annoyed at the amount of power he has, to be honest." Eric wrinkled his nose as if he smelled something foul. "Anyway, Master said it would be great if I followed the advice not to hang out with you at the Academy but the bracelet has this little lock that might be opened with a little incantation that was written down and accidentally forgotten on the kitchen bench after dinner. Enough about me, though. How was your weekend?"

Ayla shrugged, trying to make it look insignificant, before reminding herself that Eric would be the one person she could be vulnerable with. It would have been a disaster to have her last friend taken away, and she was glad he managed to find a way around Corbin's orders.

"He locked me in my room and put bars on the windows, knowing that I'm claustrophobic. It was horrible!" She shivered, remembering the suffocating feeling of being trapped that kept her terrified every moment of her confinement.

"I'm so sorry, Ayla. It's all my fault. I should have never taken you out without asking him," Eric responded sadly. "He didn't... hurt you though, did he?"

Startled, Ayla jerked her head. "No. Was he supposed to?" She thought about Corbin's strange hug and his mean words. A chill crept up her spine. That was wrong in so many ways, but somehow, she didn't want to tell Eric, as if it was something to be ashamed of. Something that was her fault.

"He could have, but I'm glad he didn't." Eric pushed his plate aside and tapped on the table again. A small porcelain bowl that appeared in front of him held a beautifully decorated blueberry muffin. Eric placed it next to Ayla.

"I don't understand," she said, enjoying the sweet smell of freshly baked pastry and the warmth of Eric's arm around her. "Why is Corbin being so controlling? He's not my father, after all. I just don't get it."

A small cloud of darkness crossed Eric's handsome face.

"You know, Ayla, he might seem older because of the extent of his power in society. However, there isn't that much of an age difference between you and him. It's only about ten years if not less. He's too young to be your father. Way too young."

This wasn't something she had ever thought about. Ayla frowned too, as the air of intimacy between her and Eric disappeared at her Master's mention. Inexplicable dread gripped her heart and she had to stop and silently count to ten and back to clear her head.

Eric reached out for her and held her tight, his heart beating next to hers. She closed her eyes, slowly relaxing against him. Maybe they belonged together regardless of all the obstacles that fate seemed to throw their way. That despite all odds, they could still be a couple. At least, while Eric remained an Apprentice.

"Once I ascend to a Sorcerer, I'm going to marry you and take you far, far away." His words startled her. With her eyes wide open, Ayla stared at him until he laughed. "Unless you say no, of course."

"But what about Corbin?" she asked meekly, unable to believe her ears.

"If we get married, I'll become your primary caretaker instead of him. And then, we'll go as far away as we can, somewhere safe from those murderers. You'll finally be free to live without fear and I'll help you learn about magic once it manifests."

His confident smile gave her hope. A loophole in the agreement that she didn't see? What if it was indeed as simple as that?

Ayla snuggled closer to him and let out a content sigh. At least that was going well, which couldn't be said about her studies.

The runes seemed to be a fail, and with them, the spells. Not being able to manage spells made it impossible for her to create potions and enchantments, or even read the spell books. No matter how hard she tried, she couldn't feel any difference between charmed and regular objects. Thankfully, the teachers only asked those students who wanted to answer any questions during lessons. She was aware, though, that there would be no such luck during exams.

I'm nothing but a null, she thought bitterly to herself. As she learned fairly quickly, a *null* was a person who didn't possess any magic. Julian made sure she heard plenty of the word to learn. He passed his first exam ahead of time and was rubbing his success in her face every time they met.

Eric's warm embrace once again carried her away from negative thoughts. She breathed in his smell, the beautiful fragrance of mint and driftwood, that became so much like home that it hurt. The gentle strokes of his hand on her hair, his steady heartbeat and the quiet of their surroundings gave off an illusion of complete safety. There was no threatening world around, no murderers, no nasty bullies. Only this bliss and the person she loved next to her.

The sharp ring of the bell broke the spell. Eric got up and gave her a hand. As she rose from her cosy seat, she picked up her school bag and straightened the wrinkles on her skirt. It was time to go to class.

"It's going to be okay. The charms will protect you from any magic trouble," he gently reminded her to ease her anxiety.

Ayla pressed her head against Eric's chest one last time and exhaled sharply. "I'll see you soon!"

No pranks were waiting for her in the hallway. Confident and cheerful, she walked into the classroom, and the student chatter suddenly stopped. Walking past chairs, she shuddered, feeling everyone's eyes on her.

She found her seat in the back of the room. Silence and strange anticipation filled the air. Ayla felt a little hazy as she looked around, trying to pinpoint the trap but as always she couldn't see it. She carefully lowered herself to her seat, listening for any strange sounds. And there it was, a faint squeak. In slow motion, Ayla raised her eyes to the ceiling and saw a bucket of water slowly turning upside down, triggered by an invisible rope that was activated when she sat down. She jumped off the seat but it was too late. Water gushed down, soaking her through. The silence burst into laughter, and through her tears, she saw Julian's face. A smug grin flashed at her, challenging, provoking. He wanted a fight, knowing that he would win and humiliate her in front of everyone again—but he wasn't getting one.

Shivering from the draft, Ayla wiped the water off her face and looked at the damage that was done. Her uniform was soaking wet but drying fast thanks to the enchanted fabric. Her bag was full of water, and that wasn't going away. The area around her desk was a puddle.

The teacher walked in. Ayla cringed. Of course, it had to be Sawyer. They were getting ready for the exams, and the class was bigger than usual. Students from higher levels were joining them. And Sawyer, being one of the senior teachers of the school, probably wanted to pop in to check on them.

He looked straight at her, and a grimace of disgust crossed his face as he observed the water damage.

"What's this? Are you trying to interfere with the lesson?" His sharp tone left no illusion he blamed it on her.

Ayla's lower lip trembled but she contained her urge to cry again. She wasn't going to give him the pleasure of seeing how his words hurt her. "No, Master. This was a prank set up by another student. I apologise that I didn't notice it sooner," she said, lowering her head in a respectful bow and struggling hard to keep her dignity. This was no easy task for someone standing in a pool of now muddy water.

Sawyer cocked his head to the side, studying her as if she was a curious bug. Other students started to chuckle again, and he raised his hand to restore silence. Once everyone was quiet, he spoke again.

"You need to clean up this mess, girl. Use magic if you want." A wicked smile touched his lips, and Ayla once again wondered if he lied about her having any talent at all. It was as if he were taunting her to see what she would do.

"Everyone else, open your books and let's see the recap of chapter twenty-three."

Stifling a cry, she picked up the books and looked under the desk. There was even more water there. How was she going to get rid of it without magic?

"Here, this may help." She heard a whisper, and a bucket with a large rag appeared next to her. Ayla looked in the direction of the voice. Camilla's eyes were wide with sadness and pity, and she silently nodded. Ayla returned a thankful nod and turned back to her puddle. Even though Camilla hadn't said a word to her since the unfortunate situation at Corbin's house, she still seemed to sympathise. This small gesture of goodwill told Ayla she was secretly on her side. Camilla seemed to understand what it was like to be a target.

Feeling others' eyes on her, Ayla got down to work. It wasn't until after the bell rang and all students left that she finished cleaning the puddle. Gulping down angry tears, she pictured in her mind all the things she would do to all the bullies in her life if only she had even a tiny shred of power. *One day they'll get what they deserve. They have to.*

CHAPTER 15. AYLA

Despite her situation and fear of coming exams, the small joy of seeing first snow overcame Ayla's troubles. Winter had finally arrived. For a couple of minutes, she stood by the window, enjoying the view through the bars. Even though she was a prisoner in the house, nobody could deny her the aesthetic pleasure of observing the beauty of nature.

Ayla splashed cold water on her face and gently dabbed it with a feather-soft towel. A bit of fragrant hand cream glided smoothly over her skin, leaving the scent of rose petals and lavender. Ayla normally used the cream before bedtime, but she felt like it was needed today. Something strange was in the air, and now that she was fully awake, it resonated within her.

Pushing bad thoughts aside, she tried to ignore the unfriendly gaze of the maid as she passed her on the way to the small dining room. The mansion's walls were colder than usual now that winter was there. Ayla wondered what it was like when snow properly settled and whether they had snowstorms here. Back home, the weather was mostly mud and a bit of snow every now and then. She knew, however, that only a few hours away the winters were full of sunshine and fluffy white covering the ground all through the season, with only a flash of mud when it melted and gave way to nature's great awakening.

Out in the hallway, the strange feeling intensified, and she slowed her pace, listening for anything that might identify its source. The door to the study was slightly open and a strip of artificial light coloured the tiles of the corridor a soft yellow. Ayla approached and held her breath as she gently pushed the door.

She stopped on the threshold, taking in the picture in front of her. Corbin had his back to her, and an unfamiliar woman was sitting on the chair facing him and the door. Her face was vacant, unconscious. Her pale blue eyes were fixed on Corbin who sat still, softly speaking to her. Ayla couldn't hear a word he was saying, but the air in the room was stuffy and odd. He was doing something wrong, she realised. This was what Camilla wanted, whatever this was. Ayla stepped back quietly until she was safe outside of the study. Only when she was well out of the room's earshot did she allow herself to lean against the cold wall and let out a pent-up breath.

What was he doing? The thought was bothering her all morning after she had her breakfast in solitude, and all the way to the Academy. There was nobody she could ask, except maybe Melody or Eric. She was sure Camilla wouldn't share, but other people might know.

A bitter smile crossed her face as she unloaded the books on her desk at the dreaded runes class. Melody recently left to travel around the world and study other Sorcerers' practices before settling down, and Ayla couldn't blame her. She would probably do the same if only she could master her alleged power. As days went on without any success, she lost her hopes of ever getting a spark of what everybody else seemed to have in abundance. She had become her own amorphous bogeyman, unable to contain anything within the undefinable lines of her body.

"Ayla!"

The sharp tone of Sawyer's remark dragged her out of her thoughts. She blinked, returning to the bleak reality of the boring class that was now doing final rounds of exam preparations. All the students were quiet, observing her with judging eyes. Ayla realised he must have asked her something and she didn't answer. Her cheeks burned hot as she stood up and slightly bowed to show respect to the teacher.

"My apologies, Master Sawyer. I'm not feeling well."

The words she said were the usually expected answer, though she clenched her teeth so hard it hurt. Not a single lesson these days went by without him asking her something she couldn't give an answer to, which was anything. Sawyer scoffed, his attitude towards her clear.

"Well, I'll say it once again for you. What rune starts all incantations for the new harvest and soil fertility?"

She must know this. They've been over these runes a hundred times with Eric. Ayla squeezed her eyes shut, trying to remember the multiple hooks and sharp angles of the runes. Was it the stick figure? Or a circle of some sort? All the images of the runes, so carefully studied, were gone from her mind.

After what seemed like an eternity, she shook her head. "I'm sorry, Master. I don't remember."

He let out an exaggerated sigh and nodded at a ginger-haired girl from the front desk who held her hand high the moment he asked the question.

"Jacinta."

"Thank you, Master," the girl rambled, happy to be asked. "Dagaz, the rune of dawn, in its meaning of hope and awakening will start all the spells for fertility, be it for nature's resources or human's. Dagaz will end the ones that expect a result in the far future for the long-lasting results, whereas short-term spells will start and end with Wunjo, the rune of joy, for reward and success."

Sawyer lifted his hand to stop her and turned to Ayla. "Is it so hard? You've been here for a couple of months now. Even considering that you started after the beginning of the term you should have learned at least something. Can you write Dagaz for us or is that too complicated, too?"

Face scorching hot, Ayla shook her head again. She was biting back tears of helplessness and disappointment in herself. It was as if this wasn't meant for her. No matter how hard she studied, she couldn't remember anything. The only thing she could do was recite the logic of the rules, but nothing practical stayed in her mind once the book was closed.

With a dismissive gesture, Sawyer let her take her seat and turned his attention to the rest of the class. "Your Masters will be receiving your report cards shortly. Let's just hope nobody gets in trouble." He shot a sharp glance at Ayla. "Apart from that, keep studying and good luck with the exams!"

The bell rang as he finished his sentence, and Ayla was among the first students to be out of the classroom. As she made it to the door of the cafeteria, she realised she had left her book of runes on her desk in the rush to get away. Hoping Sawyer had gone, she went back, cutting through the crowd of hungry scholars.

She stopped in front of the door, picking up Sawyer's elevated voice. It sounded as if he was reprimanding some-one, and Ayla decided to wait until he was done to walk in. Unable to beat her curiosity, she moved a little closer to be able to hear. It was the first time she had ever heard him angry at someone other than her, and it was too interesting to miss.

"...like nothing is good enough for you! Are there really no other things you can do with your life?"

"I'm sorry, Dad. I promise it was the last time." Camilla's voice trembled as if she was crying.

Ayla placed cupped hands over her mouth.

Sawyer started pacing around the room, his angry steps resonating within the walls. "After all the things Tamil and I do for you. Giving you all the freedom in the world to go out and entertain yourself with anything your heart desires. Parties, shopping, travelling, any hobby you like. We jump out of our skins to help you, and yet you are still going back to him. Tamil paid off our debt by bringing him that useless *null* that he wanted so badly. Corbin wasn't supposed to give you any more 'fixes'. He agreed to it! Why did he still see you? Why am I just finding out about it now?"

"He didn't want to see me. I'm sorry Dad, I went there pretending like I wanted to visit Ayla. I couldn't help it when I saw him, I needed just one more session! He didn't do it though. We only talked and he said I wasn't allowed to come to his place anymore. I'm so sorry!"

Ayla slowly backed away from the room until she was out of their earshot and lowered herself to the floor. She wrapped her arms around her to keep the sudden chill away. It wasn't the cold air that was bothering her. The cold came from inside, shaking her whole body. There was no escape from it, no remedy. She was right in her suspicion that she had no powers. Why did Sawyer lie then? This piece of the puzzle didn't fit, and she played Sawyer's words over and over again until her head hurt. Why keep the ruse and let her come to the Academy?

"You look like you need a hug." Eric's gentle touch startled her. "What happened?"

Ayla took a full breath, forcing herself to keep a calm face when all she wanted to do was burst out crying. Certain thoughts about Eric tore at her heart. If he was also a part of Sawyer's wicked plan she could not bear it.

"Sawyer admitted that I'm a *null*," she said firmly, looking straight into Eric's deep eyes. If there was any doubt in them, she didn't see anything that would tell her he knew. He seemed genuinely shaken.

"No, sweetheart. I'm sure he didn't mean that. You're just learning at your own pace and you'll get there one way or another."

Ayla shook her head. "He said it to someone behind my back, and I accidentally heard it. That would explain a lot though. How I can't remember the runes or feel any connection to enchanted objects. How I can't force the slightest spark of magic power of any kind. He's done it on purpose. The only thing I don't understand is why. Why would he lie to the whole community about me having potential? Does it have anything to do with Camilla?"

Eric stepped back and stared at her as if he'd seen her for the first time, his eyes filled with worry.

"You know about Camilla?" His hand gently squeezed her shoulder.

She shrugged impatiently, annoyed at him for keeping this from her. "Yes. On the day we went to the markets... I didn't tell you but I saw what she was like with Corbin. And today, I heard Sawyer's conversation with her. He was scolding her for that addiction... What exactly is it? What does she want so badly that she's willing to go against her father's word?"

With a sigh, Eric stood up and held his hand to her. "Let's find a more private place to talk."

The library was quiet during the lunch hour. All the students were at the dining hall, too busy catching up. It was hard not to build resentment towards others who didn't heed her any attention as if she didn't exist. Except for Julian. He seemed to always have his eyes on her, and an evil grin on his face reminded her every time that he was only staying away for as long as Eric was around. Ayla shuddered, thinking that Eric was going to graduate after the winter solstice celebrations. With him gone and things being strange with Camilla, there was nobody else she could rely on to help her at the Academy.

Eric motioned for her to sit next to him at a small table made from blackwood and put a shimmering curtain of invisibility around them.

Ayla took a deep breath and turned to him. "Tell me," she demanded.

Before uttering a word, Eric covered her hand with his, instantly warming her skin on the cold wood. Despite her anxiety, this small gesture helped her feel more secure. "I told you a little when we just met, but there is still so much you don't know. Corbin Blackbyrne keeps his matters private. I don't know anything about his family but he was off to a great start at the Academy. His gift was discovered by Master Darren, who was a wonderful scholar with the ability to see special talents in people. I believe this is the same Darren who raised you."

Ayla's eyes filled with tears as she thought about Darren's still body in the pool of blood on their living room floor. It was only a few months ago, but it felt like the wound in her heart was never going to heal. The people who killed him were looking for her, and he was only a casualty. What made them believe she was even worth anything?

"I'm not sure," Eric replied, and she realised she said her question out loud. "Darren being Corbin's old teacher, I believe there would have been some sort of correspondence between them. Maybe he told Corbin that you need protection, so he took you in."

"Looks like I need to ask him to find out the full picture." Ayla clenched her teeth, thinking about Corbin's strange behaviour towards her. After reprimanding her for disappearing to the markets and getting attacked as a result, he never said a word to her. In fact, she hardly saw him though she knew he was spending a lot of time in the house now.

Eric let out a sad sigh. "I think it's a bad idea. He's a very dangerous person, Ayla. The things that he's done... they're despicable."

"To Camilla?"

"It wasn't only her." Eric's eyes darted to the entrance to the library and Ayla followed his gaze. There was nothing there, but she felt uneasy as if someone was eavesdropping on their conversation. "I told you before about his success here at the Academy." Eric lowered his voice, and she moved closer to be able to hear him. "He learned about his power very quickly and started using it for profit. People were flocking to see him... those who had painful experiences and just wanted it to stop. Corbin knows how to remove those memories permanently, but he only uses the incantation at half-strength. The memories would eventually come back, but once a person knows they can see him to make them disappear, they get addicted and keep coming back for more."

"What happened to Camilla?" Ayla whispered, her eyes wide.

Eric squeezed her hand again. "She was only seven when her mother was killed trying to protect her. It happened right in front of Camilla, and she hasn't been able to recover from it."

Ayla shivered, realising how hard it must be to live in constant guilt. No wonder Camilla wanted to ease the pain, even if it was temporary. To have some time where she didn't have to blame herself for the death of the person who gave her life.

In a way, she knew that feeling all too well. She wiped tears off her cheeks and sniffled.

"Things became worse when she grew older and her father partnered with Tamil. They both tried to take good care of her but there is no replacement for a mother," Eric continued. "Once she learned about Corbin's talent, there was no hesitation. Her family is beyond wealthy, and she's spent a fortune seeing Corbin. Sawyer was furious but he couldn't do anything about it as she wasn't a minor anymore. The only way he could stop the sessions was if Corbin himself agreed to stop, and for that he needed to give him something valuable in return. Something other than money."

"Me," Ayla whispered.

Eric opened his mouth to continue but a sudden noise at the door cut him off. Corbin's driver walked into the room and checked his surroundings before proceeding to look among the bookshelves.

"See what he wants." Eric pointed at him and Ayla carefully walked through the shimmer.

The driver heard the noise and turned around.

"Master wants to see you."

"School isn't finished yet. I have one more lesson to go to," she replied in defiance. "Aren't I supposed to stay here till the end?"

The driver scoffed and beckoned Ayla to follow him. "He said *now*. I don't think it's a good idea to disobey a direct order, girl."

Ayla looked towards the seemingly empty table and mouthed a quick goodbye. There was no movement in the corner, but her imagination painted a sweet smile on Eric's lips and a promise of a better future. One that didn't seem so bright as she followed the driver to Corbin's luxurious black car and let it swallow her whole.

CHAPTER 16. AYLA

"I can't believe this! A whole term for nothing!"

Corbin shook a piece of paper in front of Ayla's face, and she flinched. Ignoring her discomfort, he started pacing the room with large angry steps. Ayla muttered an apology, her breath caught in her lungs. He stopped, pivoting towards her. The rage in his eyes sent her backwards. Black dread seized her heart. He had never been that angry before, and after Eric's revelation about his power, she wasn't sure she ever wanted to see him like this again.

"You're sorry? That's all you've got? After all that I've done for you?" He threw the paper at her and she automatically caught it. The bold red words on it read: *No progress this term; unfit for exams; check for potential null abilities.*

Her eyes widened at the realisation that this was real. That the teachers at the Academy deemed her useless—and even worse, that Julian's hurtful remarks might have been true.

Corbin took a deep breath and threaded his fingers through his hair. Ayla cowered as his dark eyes pierced hers. "*Sorry* doesn't cut it, darling. Do you know what happens if you are a confirmed *null*?" Without waiting for her answer, he continued, "This means you'll never be able to attend the Academy again, and you'll never ascend to a Sorcerer. You'll be a slave for the rest of your life, and will be treated as such. Have you seen slaves at those functions? Of course you didn't, being too busy getting in trouble." He lifted a hand when she was about to mutter something in her defence. "Well, the Winter Solstice gala is coming up and we'll have to attend. I'm going to pull some strings and get you to stay at the Academy for one more term, with an exemption from exams this one time."

"Why do I have to go back there?" she sobbed, finally having an opportunity to say something.

Corbin stepped closer to her, and the aura of danger coming from him came upon her like a storm wave. "Surely, you can't be that dumb. You being a *null* will seriously impact my reputation in society after taking you in as a promising Apprentice. You'll ruin everything I worked so hard to achieve, and I won't tolerate any more failure. Darren saw something in you, so you better work it out quickly. Or else."

Bitter tears running down her cheeks, Ayla didn't dare take a look away from his penetrating gaze. Wet hairs stuck to her face, but she was too scared to push them away.

Her heart was beating violently, almost jumping out of her chest. All she wanted was to run far, far away. To have Eric's loving arms around her, and to hear him tell her she was safe. Where was he when she needed him so much?

"I tried my best, Corbin. Everything I could think of, any help I could get. I just can't," she mumbled, too afraid to move.

He raised his hand and before she could react, a heavy slap stung her face, sending her against the wall. Ayla fell to her knees, hard against the solid oak floorboards. She felt the back of her head for a bump before wiping the hot liquid under her nose. Staring blankly at the sticky red dripping off her trembling hand, she struggled to process what she was seeing.

Corbin was supposed to take care of her, not hit her. She could justify him doing it to discipline her when she overstepped the boundaries, trying to avoid punishment for the incident at the markets. Getting a bloodied nose over school grades was something else entirely. Did it mean so much to him that he was willing to hurt her? Ayla's stomach curled into a tight ball. She signed the Apprentice agreement herself. Now, her life belonged to him until she ascended to a Sorceress. Until then, he could do whatever he wanted. Without any consequences.

She started hyperventilating, her imagination painting pictures of things he could do. Hot blood gushed from her nose and she had to wipe it off again, this time with her other hand. Shaking all over, she pressed her back against the wall as if it could protect her, and squeezed her eyes shut, hoping this was just a nightmare.

A strong hand gripped her neck and forced her body to her toes. Ayla opened her eyes, squirming under his terrifying gaze. Corbin shook her as if making sure she was awake.

"You have to try harder! If you spent less time fooling around with your little boyfriend, you might have learned something to help you pass at least one of the exams. You'll have three more months to prove that you're worth something, do you understand? If you show no progress again, I swear you'll wish you were never born!"

Ayla pulled at the hand that was squeezing her throat so hard she could feel blood pulsing against his grip. She struggled to get a breath of air, ready to do anything to make it stop. He suddenly let her go and she plopped on the floor, gasping and fighting to regain her breathing.

Corbin stepped away and Ayla raised her head to see what distracted him. The doorway to the study outlined a familiar shape. Eric dropped something on the floor, and Ayla recognised her bag of school books that she must have left at the library when she had to go in such a rush. Grateful for his arrival, she couldn't chase away the bad thought. Was it for the better or the worse that he witnessed what happened?

Eric's nostrils flared as he took in the scene. His blue eyes slid across her bloodied face soaked in tears and her trembling body cowering on the floor, before turning to Corbin.

"You can't just hit her like that, she hasn't done anything wrong." His voice shook as he took a brave look at the dark-haired Master.

Corbin cocked his head to one side, studying him with disdain. "If it isn't the knight in shining armour," he mocked, and a crooked smile crossed his lips. Ayla watched him take a deliberately slow step towards Eric. Somehow, the movement reminded her of the game that cats played with caught mice before killing them.

The mansion was empty and cold, and nobody was there to bear witness. Eric was still only an Apprentice himself, and even being close to graduation he had nothing against one of the most powerful Sorcerers in society. But he was still standing up for her, even though he was most likely to lose a direct challenge—and he didn't have his graduation ring yet. Which meant he wouldn't be able to use magic if Corbin were to attack him.

"I'm going to marry her, Master Corbin. You won't have to worry about your reputation anymore. I'll take full responsibility for Ayla, and we'll travel as far as we can to never have to face any of this. I can't believe you beat her up like that, especially considering that she can't defend herself. You should be ashamed of what you've done."

Ayla shrivelled on the floor as Corbin's aura became palpably black. He threw a quick glance at her and flicked his hand towards the door.

"Get out. Go clean yourself up and I'll deal with you later."

Ayla stayed frozen until he grabbed her arm, yanking her off the floor, and dragged her across the room, painfully digging his fingers into the tender flesh. He nearly threw her out and slammed the door shut in front of her face. She heard Eric's angry voice and Corbin's reply as smooth as a snake gliding in the grass. The exchange of elevated sentences that were rising in tonality. Unable to move, she stood leaning on the cool wooden door, struggling to make out what they were saying.

There was a brief swooshing sound followed by a stump, and an eerie silence settled in. Ayla counted to ten and backwards, but no more noise came from the study. Unable to contain her anxiety, she pushed the door open and stopped in her tracks.

Eric was lying face down on the floor, his body unnaturally still, just like in the vision she saw in the crystal ball. Ayla rushed towards him, already knowing what that meant. Blood was pooling under his chin and onto the oak floorboards. His shape was getting rigid, reminding her of Darren's body. The fortune-teller's words resonated in her ears. The curse of her biological father that destroyed everyone around her.

Desperate hope pushed her forward. Maybe she could still help. Chasing away the déjà vu of finding yet another person she loved dead, Ayla dropped on the floor next to him. It couldn't be the end, not when things were starting to seem better for Eric and her. Maybe she could somehow share her life force with him. He was going to be okay. He would take her away from here, and no Master would ever find her.

She gasped when Corbin grabbed her by the arm and turned her around in one swift move. His eyes were cold, devoid of the anger from before, and he studied her face for a long second before making a decision.

"You killed him," she whispered, unable to believe the harsh truth. "He wanted to help me, and you killed him."

Without a word, he dragged her into the small room next door. A small powder room that she never used as it never felt right to be there, so close to Corbin's private study. Two velvet ottomans on solid bases stood next to each other, and Corbin sat her on one of them.

"Look at me, darling." His voice was unexpectedly soft, and she was awed by this sudden change.

She hesitantly looked into his eyes and froze. His gaze was captivating, luring her in like a siren's call—there was no hint of his previous anger or disappointment. Soft and welcoming, it was calling her further into the darkness.

"I'm sorry you got scared." His voice mellowed her ears and she felt her muscles slowly letting go of the tension that had been building up ever since she moved into this tomb-mansion. "Show me what you think happened."

His words sounded wrong, but his eyes gave off a feeling of security. Ayla felt a gentle pressure that seemed to be coming from inside her brain. She frowned, puzzled at the strange sensation. Corbin's hand was on her shoulder, and his face very close to hers. When did this happen?

"I'm not going to hurt you, Ayla. I just want to help. Let me take the pain away," he purred so close she shivered. The two pools of living darkness were dangerously close, and the pressure in her brain grew stronger. She suddenly saw the image of Eric's body lying on the floor, but before she felt overwhelmed again, it started fading. It frayed at the edges at first, losing pieces thread by thread, as if it were an embroidered picture. She exhaled as the last thread dissolved in her mind and blinked as the darkness pulled away.

The room was dimly lit by the small button lamps scattered on the ceiling. Hazily, as if waking up from a dream, Ayla looked around. It was twilight now, the time between day and night—the gateway to other worlds, as Darren used to say jokingly. The light curtain on the window was still open, and a gentle breeze rocked it back and forth.

The feeling of someone's presence made her look closer and she frowned, seeing Corbin next to her, holding her hand. He looked concerned, studying her face for something. Noticing her gaze, he smiled and carefully traced her face with his other hand. "How are you feeling?"

Grateful for his touch, Ayla closed her eyes for a moment before replying. "A little light-headed. Did I faint?"

His hand felt warm and safe holding hers. The twilight made his eyes seem even darker and exacerbated the sharp features of his face. Somehow, Ayla felt fragile and fought the urge to cry. There was nothing for her to be upset about, though. She wasn't alone, and everything was okay.

"Yes, darling. I think you've been pushing yourself too hard. What's the last thing you remember?"

There it was, that almost unnoticeable strain in his voice. She tensed up, trying to work it out. Was this another test?

"I think Eric came to visit me," she said uncertainly. Her brain was like mush, and getting anything out of it was like pulling teeth. She could remember her day at the Academy, but not much after the driver took her home. There was something about Eric though... he said he was going to marry her?

She carefully touched the back of her head, surprised to find a bump. Her fingers studied her aching face, wiping sticky blood off her skin. Ayla frowned, trying to make sense of it.

"You two had a big fight," Corbin replied softly, his eyes never leaving hers. "A few strong words were exchanged, and it escalated to the point that I could hear you all the way from the front door. I walked in on you lying on the floor here as he left. I believe he said he was leaving without you. Ayla, I'm so sorry this happened, but I did warn you to stay away from him. I wish you had listened."

She shook her head in disbelief. They hadn't fought before, and she couldn't think of a reason why they would now. But if Eric left...

The thought brought back the insecurities she had been battling with all her life. The mystery of her childhood that was never resolved. She could only think that her family abandoned her and never wanted to look for her when she was left all alone in the park where Darren found her. Darren passing away, leaving her at the mercy of the likes of Asher and all those vultures betting on her at the auction. And now, Eric leaving her, only to prove that this was where the vicious circle cycled on and on.

"Everybody leaves me." She shivered as a gust of wind brushed against her skin. "It's always going to happen, isn't it?"

"No," Corbin said firmly and gently lifted her chin.

Ayla slowly blinked, starting to sink into the darkness of his eyes. It was safe here with him. She was silly to doubt it. Of course he wouldn't leave her. He was her Master, after all, and he took her in and cared for her when nobody else believed she was worth anything.

Corbin carried her in his arms. He brought her to the small living room and settled her on large cushions. He waved his hand, and Dolores rushed in with a cosy throw and a mug of hot chocolate that she set on the glass coffee table next to them. She disappeared just as quickly, making Ayla wonder if she was ever there or if Corbin did some magic to make things appear.

"This will help after your... dizzy spell." He wrapped the soft wool of the throw around her, spreading it gently all over her body and tucking it under her freezing feet. She gratefully accepted the warm mug from his hands and took a sip of the delightfully frothy drink. The sweet rush made her feel better, and she sighed, finally relaxing.

"Thank you, Corbin. I'm so sorry about the inconvenience I caused," she muttered, as her muscles weakened. Warmth flowed through her body, lulling her to sleep. Her eyes struggled to stay open for a little longer, but exhaustion took over with an overwhelming force. The half-empty cup slid from her fingers and her head rolled back. Darkness descended upon her again, a beautiful numbness leaving nothing but peace.

CHAPTER 17. AYLA

P air after pair of swallows swept their forked tails across Ayla's line of sight. The sky was the happy blue of summertime, with only a couple of feathery clouds tattered across it. Light wind rustled the lush green leaves and the emerald grass Ayla was lying on.

She propped herself up on her elbow and looked around in surprise. It was warm, and she was wearing a pair of jean shorts and an off-shoulder cotton shirt in pale green. Threading her fingers through her hair, she smiled at the feeling of silken waves. It felt the same way it did many years ago when she used to wash it with camomile water. She got up, surprising herself with the lightness she felt.

A branch cracked. Ayla turned in the direction of the sound. A young man was standing a few metres away from her, and she wondered how he turned up there. After all, she did look around when she woke up and there was nobody else there.

The man seemed as puzzled as she was. While he was deciding what to do, she took the chance to look at him properly. He was dressed in light cotton too, a dark green T-shirt bringing out his surprisingly bright green eyes. Ayla had never seen anyone with such eye colour. In fact, she wouldn't have thought it was even possible in nature. His face with a strong chin and chiselled cheekbones was perfectly shaven, highlighting his friendly expression. Two ugly scars crossed his left cheek, but they only added charm to his image. His hair was another thing that stood out in his appearance.

It was white like fresh Christmas snow, like the tops of fluffy summer clouds, like the distant icy mountaintops. It was cut in layers to flatter his face shape, and created a gentle wave around his head. Ayla frowned, realising that she *had* seen him before, in the strange vision in the fog. His looks were still dazzling but not as memorable as now. He was talking to someone back then and didn't see her. In this dream, things were different.

Ayla blinked and averted her eyes, realising that she was staring.

"It's okay, you don't have to look away," he said, voice a pleasant baritone, reminiscent of the perfectly trained pitches of theatre actors.

She smiled back as they both simultaneously made a few steps towards each other and stopped at the same time.

"How are you doing this?" their voices sounded in unison, leading to an equally mirrored rupture of laughter.

The young man covered the remaining distance between them and extended his arm towards her. "My name is Blaze."

"I'm Ayla. Nice to meet you, Blaze." She shook his warm hand and gestured around. "Do you know where we are?"

She felt inexplicably calm and relaxed, as if the pure air here was weaved from peace and happiness. Light and free, it seemed that she could stay forever. For a moment, Ayla wondered if that was possible.

"I think this is a dream. This meadow is my happy place, just like the one I used to roam when I was a child," Blaze replied. "I sometimes get here after my meditation if I manage to clear my mind enough. It's the first time I've seen anyone else here, though."

"So I'm in your dream?" She asked and immediately shook her head. "No, it can't be. If I think I'm real, I must be real and this means you're in *my* dream."

"If it's your dream, why are you in *my* happy place then?" He stuck his tongue at her and she wrinkled her nose in slight annoyance. This teasing felt so familiar it nearly crawled under her skin, though she couldn't remember why she would know it. She had only seen him once in that vision, or someone very much like him. Yet, it felt like she had known him for years.

"No idea. Tell me what though... have we met before?" She decided that if she voiced her concern it would be easier to get the answers. His grin grew wider.

"You feel it too, huh? Well, I'm glad you asked. As a matter of fact, I do see you in my dreams sometimes, but I've never actually spoken to you until now. It was always as if I saw you out the window, you know?"

"Doing what, for example?" Ayla was starting to like this game. Blaze seemed like an easy-going person, someone who would be fun to be around. This light-hearted chat made her happier than she'd felt for a very long time.

Blaze rolled his shoulders and looked at her sideways.

"Well, once I saw you in a little bakery. There was a middle-aged couple there, with the man busy baking and his wife giving you tiny pieces of different breads and buns to taste. Then, there was one of you having dinner with a grey-haired guy, who I thought was your father or something? In another dream, I saw you on a park bench with a leather notebook in your hands and you were crying. It was heartbreaking to watch, and it felt so real, too. I wish I could have helped you. Hey, are you okay?"

His expression quickly turned to concern as Ayla's head spun. She remembered all of the things he mentioned. The little bakery, the dinners with Darren. The night he was murdered when she was sitting on the bench in the park alone, sobbing over his notebook that left so many questions.

Blaze gently touched her shoulder. "I'm sorry I upset you. I didn't mean to."

Ayla forced a smile and he took his hand away. "I know. It's okay. Strange thing though, Blaze. All the things you spoke about actually happened to me. Those are some of my brightest memories... and I'm puzzled as to how you managed to see me. I only saw you once, for instance, and I'm not too sure if it was you or someone similar. However, I feel like I somehow know you. Why? Are you a Sorcerer?"

Blaze opened his mouth, but before he had a chance to speak Ayla's vision grew dark, carrying away the image of the lush meadow and the handsome stranger. She jolted awake when someone's hand roughly shook her.

"Wakey wakey, princess." Julian's voice startled her. Ayla pushed his fingers off her shoulders and tried to stand up, but black dots danced in her vision and her mind wavered between darkness and reality. Julian gave her a wicked grin. "Oh, I'm sorry. Too busy daydreaming, are we? I guess reality isn't that bright for you anymore. You know, with Eric dumping you and all that."

The laughter of other students struck her like lightning. Ayla carefully moved her head from side to side and pressed her cold fingers to her eyelids.

Eric left me and they all know.

Stifling a cry, she got up on her feet and faced him. Other people were watching her, but they didn't matter. Pushing back the tears that welled up in her eyes, she stared at Julian's detestable face. His expression never changed from amused when she jumped at him and punched him in the chest.

"I hate you! Why won't you leave me alone?" She kept on wriggling even after he twisted her in an iron grip, immobilising her arms. Ayla tried to kick him but quickly realised it was no easy task when she was held tight with only enough space to breathe. The chuckles from the growing crowd made her angrier still.

"But I like you too much." Julian's voice was smooth as honey. He held her still, making sure she heard every word. "You're so delicious to torment, little bunny. I would be happy to keep you in my dungeon, even if you are a *null*. Maybe your Master will let me have you once he finds out you're no use to him. That's right, sweetheart. Everybody knows you have no power of your own. You're only here because Corbin is still trying to convince himself you're not a useless piece of meat. Sooner or later, he will realise the harsh truth. Oh, poor little bunny. What's going to happen to you then?"

Julian suddenly released his grip and she nearly stumbled on the floor. Under the mocking stares of others, she got up and faced him again, fighting the urge to run away.

"Stay away from me!" This was all she could think of right now. With Eric gone, she wasn't sure how it would be possible for her to survive at the Academy. Julian's words hit home. So, everyone here believed she was worthless. They were just waiting for the show. Eager to see what

Corbin would do to her once her time ran out. Anxiety bloomed in her chest like poison hemlock, paralysing her will to fight.

Julian took a mocking bow and chuckled. "How cute. You still believe you can win. Oh well, I'll leave you to it. See if you can learn some spells, for Corbin will show you no mercy. Watch yourself, little bunny."

His boots clicked on the stone floor, followed by dozens of others as students left for their lessons. Ayla realised that she missed the sound of the school bell. She tried once again to make sense of Eric's sudden departure and what kind of argument they would have had, not coming up with anything. Without him, her chances of surviving school were slim.

She raised her head in sudden realisation. There was no future for her at the Academy, or in the Sorcerers' world altogether. Now that everyone was in the classrooms and there was still time before the driver came to pick her up... She could do whatever she wanted.

Unless the exit was enchanted, of course. Ayla carefully approached the tall door with iron embellishments and touched it. Nothing happened. Inspired by the idea of freedom, she pushed the door and it opened with surprising ease. She stepped out onto the porch and breathed in the sweet air of the winter chill.

It was another gloomy day, with heavy clouds hanging low in the sky. The green lawn in front of the Academy was tattered with patches of snow that appeared overnight. They crunched under her feet as she made haste to cross the open space. The tall trees of the forest were mostly pines, with a row of young undergrowth which pricked her skin with their sharp needles. Once she got through those, it was much easier to get further away.

Ayla ran for a minute and then stopped to catch her breath. She might only be a couple hundred metres from the Academy, but it felt like she was in this deep forest all by herself. As the chill of winter air made its way through the thin fabric, Ayla remembered Melody's words about the enchanted uniform. It only kept its magic properties as long as she was a student. Deciding to leave must have broken the spell. Her clothes were back to their original state, made from regular cotton material. Ayla blew a few warm breaths into her hands and shivered. She had to keep moving to stay warm.

After what felt like an eternity, she finally reached the road. It was empty at this hour, but sooner or later someone would drive past and hopefully stop to help her. She thought about hiding behind one of the trees if a car was approaching, to make sure it wasn't Corbin's, and see where she went from there.

The mud from the autumn rains had crystallised into icy puddles that broke with a gentle crack under her feet. It got colder as the sun went down, and there was still no one in sight. Maybe she was wrong, after all. Maybe there would be nobody here until she froze to death. Still a better outcome than being stuck at the Academy waiting for the inevitable.

The cold crept under her skin, draining her energy. Ayla struggled to keep her eyes open and thought about the road. It was going to end somewhere. Hopefully, she was walking in the direction of the highway and then it would be easier to get help. She wasn't tired, not at all! Not sleepy... not getting warm and comfortable to have just a little break from walking and close her eyes for a second. That wouldn't hurt, would it?

Someone stepped in front of her, and she didn't register a presence straight away. Only when she nearly bumped into the dark figure did she raise her eyes.

The shadowy figure slowly lowered its hood, revealing a vaguely familiar face. Ayla squinted, trying to remember where she saw him. It felt like an eternity away but it was definitely one of the people who had captured her at Darren's house. She jumped back, her heart suddenly pounding in her chest. There was no more cold. Adrenaline pulsed through her veins, jolting her awake.

"Asher's Apprentice," she pronounced through clenched teeth. This was one of the men who captured her at Darren's house, one of her father's murderers. There was nothing she could do against him, magic or not. He was a much taller man, who would easily overpower her.

In fact, most people would. The disadvantage of being a short girl who weighed next to nothing.

The figure studied her as she frantically thought of a way out of this. Was this the end of her here, on this cold deserted road?

"Kendall. At your service." He took a small bow, a content grin on his face.

Ayla looked at his broad face with distaste. "You killed Darren," she stated blandly. If this was the end of her life, she might as well get the answers to her burning questions.

"He wasn't giving you up, so regretfully I had to."

Ayla darted her eyes to one side, then another. She had to keep talking to distract him long enough until someone appeared. He easily spotted this and chuckled. "Don't think anybody's coming to the rescue this time. Sad, isn't it?"

"So it was you trying to kill me at the markets? You were the second shadow who disappeared?"

Kendall looked her in the eye and didn't reply. She already knew the answer, but stubbornly asked anyway. "Then why didn't you kill me when you and Asher found me in the house? Wouldn't it have been easier then?"

"I couldn't disobey a direct order from my Master." He sighed in annoyance. "Asher was keen on getting you out safely so he could claim the bounty that Corbin had on your head as long as you were delivered unharmed. He raised a hell of a lot more money by putting you up for an auction. I had other instructions, however. It wasn't easy to keep watching you. Corbin put a lot of thought into your protection. His house, an impenetrable fortress. The Academy, covered by some of the most powerful spells known to man. And then you ran away with your boyfriend... I couldn't miss the chance."

Ayla was silent, trying to process it. He killed Darren but Asher kept her alive. What was Kendall's game here? How would an Apprentice go against the word of the Master?

Unless there were other forces at play. He said he had other instructions. From whom?

Kendall's laughter echoed in the empty forest. "I am truly sorry, Ayla. It's nothing personal... in fact, if it was up to me, I'd let you go. If you were a simple *null* who would become nothing but a slave and live the rest of your life serving and obeying. But you are something different. You are dangerous because of what you are. And we can't let you live."

"Who's *we*?" Ayla asked, but the change in his eyes told her the time for talking was over. The road was still empty, and the chilly night slowly descended on them. Kendall quietly took a silver dagger out of his robe and it flashed like lightning in the calm skies.

"It will be quick, little one. I'm sorry it had to be this way."

The dagger lunged forward. Nothing happened. A soft blow under her ribs didn't hurt. Ayla cupped her side with her hand and looked at it in a dull haze. Hot liquid was gushing out of a wound and she remembered somewhere deep in her mind that it was important to keep pressure on something like this until help arrived. She slumped on the cold ground and rolled on her back, holding her hand over the pulsing flow.

CHAPTER 18. AYLA

The pain of Corbin's touch brought Ayla back into cruel reality.

He moved her head to the side and she saw the candles. The line of salt that enclosed them in a circle. Corbin deepened his pressure on her wound. She tried to close her eyes, but his free hand pinched at the sensitive skin on her neck. "Stay awake, darling."

The flames on the candles grew brighter until their colour changed to cold white. Through the haze, Ayla heard Corbin's voice speaking a language she didn't understand. The words were extended and it sounded almost like singing. An eerie feeling crept along her skin as she heard him switch to a regular tongue.

"Life for life is what I offer. Give me hers or take mine too."

He changed the language again, and she felt his hand getting warmer. The incantation took the form of a rhyme that kept going on and on. An invisible thread kept her chained to her body, forcing her to stay awake even without his help now.

"Life for life and blood for blood. This can never be undone." Under the blanket of a ghostly voice, a crowd of pale transparent figures huddled around the circle of candles. Their bony fingers reached for Ayla but never crossed the line. The faces of the ghosts were blurry and changed shape from young to old, from male to female, from regular to misshapen, stretching and falling apart until there was nothing left in their wake.

The flames roared towards the sky and extinguished in one solid blow.

Corbin took his hand off Ayla's wound. He wiped it carefully on a white cloth and she saw that his palm was sliced open too. He gave her a small smile and gently caressed her cheek. "It's going to be okay. You've lost a lot of blood though, so it might take some time before you're strong again. The worst of it is over, Ayla. You can go to sleep now."

Grateful for his permission, she closed her eyes and immediately fell into the peace of a deep slumber. It felt like only a minute passed when she opened her eyes and realised it was already a bright morning and the pool of sunlight was straight on her pillow.

She recoiled from the light, memories that passed flooded her mind. She felt for her wound. A clean dressing was on it, but it didn't hurt. She sat up in the bed and tried to steady herself when her head spun. From the haze in her brain, she remembered Corbin's words about her losing a lot of blood and wondered if this was why she felt light-headed and weak. The words of Kendall also surfaced in her mind. She frowned. He wanted to kill her for what she was, and she had no idea what that meant. Yet another mystery for her to solve.

She squeezed her eyes shut but no further recollection emerged. This sunlight was too bright for her. Far too bright for winter. Ayla looked around the room and gasped.

It was very different from any of the rooms in Corbin's mansion. The walls were a warm pastel beige, and a lone large picture to her left depicted a ship anchored near a jetty, under the light of a full moon sending its peaceful reflection upon the calm waters. Ayla folded herself into the image's soothing beauty for a minute or two, before switching her attention to other things around her.

There was a small nightstand next to the bed, with a bottle of water and a sparkling crystal glass. A white wooden chest of drawers to her right and a mirror above it. A tall hatstand by the door in the small hallway. A half-open door to the bathroom with tiles of azure.

Ayla sighed. She turned her head towards the source of light and her eyes widened.

Instead of mansion curtains, the window wore blinds, pulled away to welcome in the sunny day. The sky was impossibly high and joyfully blue, without a trace of any grey gloomy clouds. There was nothing else she could see from where she sat, which made no sense. Where were the gardens and the trees of the forest surrounding the mansion?

Ayla climbed out of bed, holding on to the railing as she carefully stepped closer to the window. She placed a hand to her chest and held her breath. The panorama of the city below sprawled to the heavens like a large anthill. Skyscrapers declared themselves, resolute, and the lower-standing buildings boasted rooftop gardens and flashes of sparkling blue swimming pools. A large body of water to the left of the buildings glimmered under the sun, and Ayla squinted, trying to make sense of it all. She must've been in a skyscraper herself, tall enough to see over others. She wondered what floor she was on, wondered how she ended up here and where exactly *here* was. The sheer atmosphere of this city was different from anything she had ever seen.

From the corner of her eye, she noticed someone walk into the room, and turned her head in his direction. Corbin's steps were soft on the thick carpet as he extended his arm towards her.

"You shouldn't be walking around yet. Come, I'll help you get back to bed."

She took his hand hesitantly and he gently guided her back, his other hand warm on her waist. Once near the bed, he picked her up and settled her on the pillows.

"I'll get them to bring you breakfast and then it will be time for another blood transfusion. You need to rest as much as possible in the next few days to make a full recovery. Then I'll show you around our new home. Please, stay in bed for now."

He patted her hand and left the room without another word. In less than a minute, Dolores rushed in with a tray that boasted a shiny silver dome, a cup of steamy drink and a small vase with a single crimson carnation on it. With a kick of her foot, she pushed out an overbed table and set the tray in front of Ayla. As always, her expression was cold and her smile smug. Ayla wished there someone else was here. Anybody would be better than this resentful maid. She wondered why Corbin had brought her here, but her thoughts were interrupted.

"Breakfast is served," Dolores pronounced through clenched teeth and took the cloche off the beautiful porcelain plate.

Despite herself, Ayla smiled at the skilful set-up of the traditional meal. Sausages and beans bathed in a rich sauce, sun-dried tomatoes, a generous piece of buttered toast and a fluffy omelette seemed just like the thing she needed. Inhaling the smell of freshly made food, she allowed herself to enjoy the moment. Everything was perfect. The only thing she was puzzled by was a small empty side plate and an extra fork near it.

Before she could question it, Dolores picked them up and quickly transferred a small piece of everything on Ayla's plate to hers.

"Hey, what are you doing?" Ayla protested as the maid ruined the perfect display in front of her.

Dolores's eyes were full of hatred as she returned her gaze. "Master ordered me to taste everything you eat, in your presence. I guess he's worried your food could be poisoned. One would wonder why," she replied and stuffed her mouth full of food. She chewed in silence as Ayla digested the new information. Corbin never showed that he cared about her before, not like that. Something had changed, and she wasn't sure if it was for the better or the worse.

Dolores finished her share and turned the empty plate to the corner of the room. Following the movement with her eyes, Ayla spotted a small red dot on the camera she hadn't noticed before. Being under constant surveillance wasn't a pleasant idea. She picked up her fork and paused for a moment, wondering how long it would take for the poison to work if the food was indeed tampered with. Dolores might have seemed fine for now but if it contained a slow-release toxin, it could take much longer.

"Don't worry, the cooks had to taste it too before they put it on the plate and then I took it straight here," the maid voiced her concerns. "If it was slow-release, they would have felt it by the time I got all the way up to this damn penthouse."

Despite the venom in the maid's tone, Ayla allowed herself a small smile, picturing her huffing and puffing to get the elevator button with the huge breakfast tray in her hands. A place this big must have a special person pushing those buttons though. Regardless, the thought of her scurrying along to get the food before it got cold was entertaining. Once Ayla had a few bites of her delightful omelette, she was disappointed to see that the hot brew in her cup wasn't coffee but a fragrant herbal tea of some sort.

"You're not allowed caffeine while you're recovering. Something to do with the blood transfusion," Dolores explained with a chuckle. "I imagine it must be so hard for you."

Pretending it didn't matter, Ayla shrugged. "It's fine. I don't mind."

Dolores pushed the overbed table aside and held her hand to her. Frowning, Ayla took it.

"I have to help you with your bathroom stuff before Master returns." A grimace crossed the maid's face as she helped Ayla out of the bed and lugged her towards the small door with a surprising strength. Her hands had a solid grip but without the pain that was caused to her by Sawyer or Asher. The outfit she was wearing was a stark difference from the one she used back in the mansion—it was still a dark dress, but a warm hue of brown as opposed to midnight black. Her hair was still pulled back into a slick bun, but it now held a bright white frangipani flower pinned to the base of the glimmering net. A brooch with another frangipani decorated her chest on the left, a welcome splash of colour among the solid brown of the uniform. There was no white apron or bracelets, or even earrings. Her makeup was subtle.

Within a few minutes, Ayla's morning routine was over. Ayla had to admit that Dolores was excellent at her job. If only she didn't hate her so much, they could have been friends. Ayla sighed as she was tucked back into bed and made to lie down this time.

She didn't have to wait long before Corbin appeared again. Dolores was all smiles and pleasantries as she dragged a wheeled table behind her, with an array of shiny tools on it. Ayla squeezed her eyes shut as she realised what was coming—needles.

If Ayla's fear of confined spaces stopped her in her tracks, her fear of needles left her paralysed. This made it impossible for her to get any blood tests done, and after a while, Darren just gave up. Even the idea of getting a flu vaccine almost made her faint. And now she knew there was no way around it.

A warm touch brushed the skin on the top of her hand and she looked up, unable to move.

"I know you're scared. Darren told me about your problem with needles. But they're the most efficient way to help you recover, Ayla. I'll be right here with you and it's going to be okay. It will only hurt a bit. Just trust me." Corbin looked at her with his kind eyes. There was nothing to be afraid of. She felt Darren in his touch.

A sharp pinch made her yelp and she thrashed against Dolores's grip. The maid held her arm tight, keeping her still as she pushed the needle further up her vein. Tears welled up in Ayla's eyes but a gentle squeeze from Corbin's hand somehow made it more tolerable. She stared blankly at the identical syringe in his own arm that was now connected to hers by a transparent wire.

"Don't they have bags with donor blood?" she inquired as the dark red liquid slowly started flowing towards her.

Corbin shook his head, a strange expression on his face. "Your blood doesn't match any other type. We ran some tests while you were asleep."

"No match for blood type? Then why would yours work?" she asked, blowing a stray strand of hair off her face.

Corbin gently tucked it behind her ear. "The blood bond I created made us compatible. When you were attacked, it was sheer luck that I found you before the damage was irreparable. You did a good job hanging onto life by keeping the pressure on that wound, but there was no way you would have lasted more than a few more minutes.

I'm not a healer, and even if I was, there was only so much I could do, and you were already crossing the Threshold to afterlife. There was only one option left."

Ayla thought about the circle of candles and those strange figures outside of it. That scene felt off, and she couldn't shake the feeling that the thing he had done was terribly wrong. Unnatural. Abominable. It was hard to think of that ritual as a positive, even though he saved her life with it.

"What was it?"

Before replying, Corbin held a long pause. "The knowledge of our ancestors is greatly underestimated. This blood-bonding ritual was hidden in an ancient book I received from one of my clients in the Middle East. It treads a thin line that can easily backfire, if not performed right. If the circle was broken, if a wrong word was used with the wrong intonation, or if you were beyond the realm of the living, it wouldn't have worked."

"You said life for life," Ayla whispered, terrified in a way she couldn't describe. "You offered your life to save mine."

Corbin nodded shortly, his eyes looking deep into hers as if he could read her thoughts. "That's right. And it worked, didn't it?"

Even though he gave her an encouraging smile, something still bothered her. Something she read about a long time ago. "But magic has a price," Ayla said. "What did you give up to do this? What did you do?"

Corbin pulled Ayla towards him, lashes sweeping across her cheek towards her temple, careful to avoid pulling the needle stuck into her arm. Trapped in his embrace, she could hardly breathe. His grip tightened a little more each time she asked him, "What did you do, Corbin? What did you do?"

PART TWO

CHAPTER 19. BLAZE

The small-town library was built to the standards of centuries past. Thick bricks kept in the warmth and blocked out the winter winds. Reflections of the flames dancing in fireplaces illuminated the faces of children who gathered around to listen to his tales. Blaze held a pause before continuing his story.

"And then the dragon jumped right in front of me, and I barely had time to shift," he whispered. Children leaned in, curiosity shining bright in their eyes. "He was as strong as me, and we fought without a break until the sun rose over the horizon. As the day got brighter, the creature grew weaker. It retreated into its cave, threatening with its claws and baring its teeth to scare me away. I couldn't leave, though; as you know, its very existence was a danger to the town, much like this one."

Blaze looked around the little circle, making sure each of his listeners received a friendly smile. Village youths stood behind the children before him, arms crossed over their chests, pretending they weren't interested yet betrayed by the intrigue on their faces. A couple of girls were playfully twisting strands of their silken hair, throwing meaningful glances his way, but he hardly paid them any attention.

"Did you kill it, Blaze?" a little boy asked when he took a pause.

Blaze cocked his head to one side. "Taking a life is no easy feat, my friend. No, I didn't kill it. It was a young dragon, but with a good potential to lead when it matured. Sometimes things happen in the group that makes some of its members escape to the outer world. The runaways would normally go back after a while. In this particular case, I had to intervene as it was bringing grief to the people of the town. In the end, I took the dragon back to its kin and bound it with a vow to never go back."

"A vow for a dragon?" One of the young women in the back chose not to hide her disbelief. She tucked a strand of blond hair behind her ear and raised her chin in defiance. The bright pattern on her dress gave off her status as a single woman looking for a partner. It wouldn't have been a coincidence that she picked this outfit tonight.

He easily located her in the crowd. Much like other girls he'd met under similar circumstances, she shied away from his gaze. Blaze allowed himself a small smile when he replied. He knew that some people believed he was able to read their thoughts, which was a complete myth. Basic knowledge of human psychology was all he needed.

"Yes, precisely. I have more than enough power, so it wasn't that hard. It took me a few days to restore my strength after the whole ordeal, but it was worth it, knowing the town was safe."

The girl averted her eyes, pretending to focus on something else. Blaze knew this scenario by heart. She was hoping that her blatant doubt in his abilities would grant her a better reaction. He used to fall for this trick. Not anymore.

One of the children raised his little hand and Blaze turned his attention to him.

"How come your hair is white?" the little boy inquired.

His exotic looks always attracted people's attention, and people's curiosities could never be satiated unless they asked him certain questions.

"Let's just say that this was an experiment from my childhood that didn't go too well. Got me in a lot of trouble with my parents." He chuckled, and the faces around him brightened. He knew everyone could think of a thing or two that they got reprimanded for, and giggles spread through the little circle. "That's it for now, guys. It's getting late." Blaze rose from his chair and the children followed suit.

The young people at the back of the hall started pushing the chairs back into place and tidying up. A high-pitched voice broke through the noise, stopping Blaze in his tracks.

"How come you don't have a girlfriend?" A little girl with two ginger braids stepped in his way, her eyes caught onto his skin. Little blue hooks.

Both children and adults alike hushed down. Blaze sighed, even though he knew that one was coming. During these talks, he preferred to stick to his adventures and life lessons, keeping his private matters to himself. It never stopped people from asking, though. "Let's just say I am yet to find a girl with the hair that can compare." He flicked his snowy mane from one side to the other in a playful gesture, making the kids giggle.

The little girl persisted. "Is it because of destiny?"

"Maybe." A sad smile crossed Blaze's lips. "After all, my parents were destined for each other. Maybe my other half is out there and she will be revealed to me at some point. Until then, though..." His gaze drifted to the night sky outside the window. They were treading water he was reluctant to swim. "I think that's enough for tonight. When I was a child, my parents never let me stay out after dark. Thank you for coming, everyone. Stay safe."

He turned on his heel and made his way to the table with refreshments, keeping an eye on the children being picked up by their parents who flocked into the hall from the street. Once they were all gone, he allowed himself to relax and took a glass of water. He was always mindful of the little ones who stayed behind. They were the most fragile ones, easy prey for the dark creatures out there.

The young woman with blond hair stayed back to tidy up after the gathering. Blaze stacked the chairs in the corner while she packed away the leftover food and dishes. Every now and then, she threw a promising glance in his direction, but just like during his speech he ignored it. Finally, she stopped and sulked. Blaze walked to the table and picked up the containers with food.

"Where do you want these?"

"The fridge, please. It's in the back room." She gestured to the brown wooden door. Blaze pushed the door inwards with his shoulder and left the community hall. Fitting the plastic containers in the fridge, he couldn't stop the dark thoughts. Yes, he was already twenty-seven, and none of his previous relationships ever worked out. He would have thought the reason would be fate, but as years went by, his destiny was never revealed. He didn't see the visions that his parents spoke to him about when he was still a child. He didn't meet the girl that would change his whole world. The only thing he had were half-blurred dreams of a young woman with golden highlights against chestnut hair. Time went on and she never appeared in his life. Eventually, he gave up on the idea that she was real. Perhaps, she was a fruit of his imagination. A false hope that kept him away from reality. After all, if she was indeed his destiny, she would have come into his life years ago.

When he came back out, the blond girl was still there. For a moment, Blaze hoped she was only waiting for him so she could lock up the place before heading home. He wasn't in the mood to deal with flirting that night, but the girl's determined face told him she had her mind set. There was no easy way out.

She was a good-looking young woman, dressed to impress, with bright eyes and full lips coated with a thin layer of shimmering lip gloss. The town's eye candy, no doubt. Blaze took in her image, deciphering her stance. The way she was leaning on the table, fanning her face with a folded piece of paper, told him this was going to be one of those nights. A girl this pretty wouldn't walk away from a challenge once she decided to seduce someone. He had to be careful in his approach.

The impromptu fan she was using made her hair move back and forth to deepen the alluring look. He held back a chuckle as he had a closer look at the paper. An advertisement for the town butcher's promotions for the month, and the pictures of raw steaks and crumbed lamb cutlets fluttered in front of her perfectly made-up face. However, it was probably the only thing that could serve as a fan and it had to do.

"It's getting late," he said, giving her a chance to save her dignity. Like many others though, the hint wasn't taken seriously.

The girl put the brochure on the table next to her and slowly got up. Her hand nonchalantly brushed her loose hair away, revealing her neck and collarbones worthy of a royal.

"I can offer you some nice tea at my place. I've got some herbal ones that you'll like. Camomile, mint, orange blossom, you name it. Will you join me?" She moved her shoulder, the strap of her bright-patterned dress sliding down. Her eyes found his, and this time she tried to hold his gaze longer.

Blaze closed the door to the back room and shook his head. There was nothing wrong with this young woman. She was attractive and clearly interested. He could have taken this beauty to her place and spent the night in her arms before it was time to leave. He wasn't going to stay, and he hoped she understood there was no future for her, no chance of a relationship. All he could offer was a broken heart. And he was done with that.

"Look. You are incredibly beautiful. I wouldn't be lying if I said that any man would be honoured to have your attention. You've been blessed with the ability to choose whomever you like. Maybe you could use it to pick someone who can offer you more than a one-night stand. You deserve so much more than this. Much more than I can offer."

He slightly bowed, wishing her goodnight, and quietly left without turning back. Pleasure of one night wasn't worth the trouble. In these situations, it was better to rip the bandaid. Be polite yet firm. Help them understand they can make a better choice and move on. Leave before they start with counter-arguments, which can turn into a mentally draining ordeal.

During the brisk walk to his hotel, Blaze recapped the events of the night and planned his next trip. It was reasonably quiet around the area these days, and he was done with recruitment rounds for the season. Maybe it was worth just going somewhere for beauty. Perhaps, putting up a tent by the gorge. Or going to see the waterfalls.

He closed his eyes and thought about the little girl's question. It was true, his parents were destined for each other, and it was the most beautiful union he'd ever seen. They never had any major fights, and all the rare disagreements were settled respectfully. That was the joy of being destined. An almost perfect match of personalities, with just enough difference to keep things interesting.

When he was growing up, Blaze looked at his parents with adoration. They were the symbol of an ideal family and of course, he hoped that he would find his destiny, too. When that didn't happen, he decided to give up and travel. Moving from place to place taught him that there was much evil in the world, and it was in his power to help those in danger. A short career with the Enforcers taught him the tricks of the trade and provided valuable connections until he tired of the politics and left. Becoming a recruiter for the school of magic at Whitestone was a more suitable choice to help him get over realisation that his destiny wasn't real. His gift to read people's auras made it easier to find prospective students. Finding those among regular human population was a challenge that not many others wanted to accept.

Blaze rolled over on his back and stared at the ceiling. It had been a while since he shifted, but he tried to keep the ability on the ready in case he needed it quickly. Every shift required some wind-down time afterwards, leaving him more vulnerable. Maybe tomorrow.

The moment he closed his eyes again, the image of the girl from his dreams popped up in front of him. She was the most beautiful woman he had ever seen, with her hourglass figure, large hazel eyes and soft chestnut hair that went just below her shoulders in waves. Its golden highlights glimmered in the late afternoon sun, and as always he wondered if they were natural.

The girl was wearing a full swimsuit today, midnight black with silver threading that glistened in the rays of summer sun. With her feet in the water of a swimming pool, she was staring into the distance, lost in thought. Blaze leaned towards her, hoping they could chat again. The encounter in the meadow was one of his fondest memories. It was the only time so far he was able to interact with her instead of being a silent observer.

She turned her head in his direction but her eyes looked straight through him. There was something different about her, something off. He tried to come closer but the air grew thick like marmalade and he halted, frowning. Whatever it was, he didn't like it. She didn't use to be out of his reach, even before they spoke. He looked a little closer and finally saw *it*.

It was almost indistinguishable against her dark swim-suit but he managed to make out the outline of the thing that stuck to her. It looked like some form of parasite attached to her heart. Pulsing and heaving, the disgusting creature seemed to taunt him, and the girl was none the wiser. She squinted in his direction but it was clear that even though she felt his presence, she couldn't work it out. Whatever that thing was, it was blocking his connection with her now. Blaze tried approaching the girl again, but the creature pulsed stronger. The air grew thicker, and the girl's face lost some of its colour.

Blaze woke up with a start, his heart pounding in his chest. *It was just a nightmare*, he told himself. *She is just a fruit of my imagination. Not a real person.*

A small white envelope on the bedside table caught his eye when he rolled over to get up. It was odd how he didn't notice it when he got home, but again, he didn't look very hard. His hands shaking, he opened the humble piece of paper.

Dear Blaze,

I cordially invite you to my humble abode for a reading and sincerely hope you can make it.

You don't need to bring anything with you. Make sure you drink plenty of water on the day and dress comfortably.

Regards,

Sybil

He sat down, eyes fixed on the wall, and caught his breath. Sybil was one of the strongest Prophets, and now she was summoning him! This wouldn't happen under ordinary circumstances. He exhaled, and immediately his mind started jumping to questions. Was she going to tell him his destiny? Did it mean his search would finally end? Would he be able to settle at last?

There was no more sleep for him that night. He hurriedly packed his bag and was out of the door before the first roosters. The drive to Sybil's house at Sunset Waters was going to take a couple of days, and he had no time to waste.

CHAPTER 20. AYLA

Ayla leaned back on the smooth tiles of the hot tub and sighed in contentment. Even though the night had already fallen, the place was far from being dark. Dozens of underwater lights changed their colours at her desire, ranging from seductive red to cold white. She had settled on a soothing, iridescent blue. Another quiet, empty night. Half a dozen hot tubs and a large swimming pool, but not a soul in sight. The streets below were bustling with activity, never stopping day or night. This was a different culture, something she would have loved to experience on her own. To enjoy the smells of street food instead of the pool's ever-present chlorine and perfect flowers of the garden. Something she knew she wouldn't be allowed.

"Penny for your thoughts?"

A sudden appearance of Corbin's lean figure outlined by the city lights startled her. Ayla pulled her feet towards her and rushed out of the hot tub. The fact that he came up there himself meant it was time for her to leave.

She grabbed a large white towel off the lounge chair and wrapped it around herself.

"Nothing much. I was just thinking about this city and that it would be nice to see a bit more of it."

He stepped into her personal space. Ayla averted her eyes from his direct gaze. Things had been odd between them since the night of the attack. He tended to be more familiar with her now and spent some time with her every day. Sometimes, she wondered if the attack made him care about her. Or if the change was for his personal reasons. She struggled to remember certain things and it felt like there were gaps in her memory. Inexplicable changes in time of the day. Strange bruises that she noticed on some mornings. Corbin never brought them up as if they weren't there. Maybe it was just her imagination.

"You know why we're staying here, darling. They think you died that night, and I can't risk you being spotted alive and well. You need to be protected."

Ayla sighed, staring behind his back. Down on the water, a beautiful boat under crimson sails was making its routine tour around the harbour. From the brochures in her room, she knew this was an authentic junk boat. One of the most popular tourist attractions here, among so many others.

Corbin traced her gaze. "Looks pretty, doesn't it? They do evening tours of the harbour to see the light show. All the buildings that participate, with the guide talking about them. The exact same things I told you when we watched the very first show, remember? But here, you get to see the whole harbour from the top, without the crowds of overexcited tourists. So much better."

"Thank you," she mumbled, eyes fixed on the crimson sails.

"How about the fireworks for Lunar New Year? This was the best spot in town to watch them instead of elbowing your way through the crowded streets. This city is not for a fragile girl like you. You're much better off here. Safe and sound."

"I understand." No matter how much she wanted a taste of the local culture, all she could ever get were brochures and Corbin's stories, heavily tinted with his opinion that she should always stay locked up. He had a wealth of knowledge that he was happy to share. Local myths and legends, the way the city developed and all the things that brought it to its current glory. Ayla absorbed every word. She had to work hard to hide the sadness of knowing she'd never see any of the sights in person. If Corbin found out, he would stop telling her these stories altogether.

Ayla glanced at a fresh rose with a red ribbon around its stem on one of the seats around the pool. From her calculations, it should have been mid-February. Hong Kong observed most holidays, and of course, Valentine's Day would be a must for hotel guests.

Corbin spotted the rose, too. "The staff need to pay attention when they prepare this space for you," he uttered. A flash of green from the ring on his index finger and the rose dissipated in the air. "I'm sorry this upset you. I'll make sure the rooftop is checked properly next time."

"I'm not upset," she replied, tears welling up in her eyes. Artificial life in full isolation was driving her crazy. "I'm just... so lonely, Corbin. Can I sometimes have my meals downstairs? Outside the usual hours maybe?"

As she expected, Corbin shook his head. "No, darling. I'm sorry but the fewer people know about you, the better. I don't want the hotel staff talking and exposing you to potential danger." He held a pause, carefully studying her face. "I'll try to spend more time with you and see if I can get some... vitamins to cheer you up. How does it sound?"

"No, that's okay. I'm fine," she hurried.

Great, now he wants to drug me so I don't understand what's going on. I shouldn't have said anything. Stupid, stupid Ayla.

"My precious darling," he cooed, stepping even closer. "I only want what's best for you."

Frozen in her spot, Ayla struggled to breathe. She brought this upon herself by complaining.

"I know something is going on. The blood bond we share will alert me of anything unusual." His smooth voice was calm in the stillness of the night, yet the feeling of danger put her senses on high alert. As if she wasn't high-strung already.

Ayla shivered, chasing away the thought of the white-haired man who started appearing in her dreams more frequently. She didn't get a chance to speak to him anymore, but he was an image of security that made her feel better. For some reason, she wanted to keep his existence to herself.

"How come I don't feel anything about things happening with *you*?" She tried to switch the topic. Corbin knew it too well though. He chuckled at her attempt but chose to answer this time.

"Because it was I who initiated the bond and it was one-sided. You weren't conscious enough to participate," he explained.

Ayla held a whimper when he put his finger under her chin and made her look at him. She hated when he did that. *You mean I didn't consent*, she wanted to say but bit her tongue. It wasn't the time to antagonise him. Not now, not ever.

"There's no need to be afraid. You know I'll never hurt you," he soothed.

Despite his reassuring tone, Ayla was terrified. Out of nowhere, a strange memory popped up. Hot liquid on her skin, dripping down her lips. Her hand, covered in blood. Corbin's face, distorted by a grimace of anger.

With a shudder, she tried to step back but an invisible force held her still. She knew better than to try and run away. There was no victory for her.

Corbin captured her gaze with his dark eyes. Without a warning, his presence flooded her thoughts. Ayla wriggled uncomfortably, wishing he would ask before he did that. She cursed herself once again for being so stupid on the fateful day when he offered her freedom. Now he didn't need her consent to do anything. She'd already agreed to whatever he wanted by putting her signature on that document.

"Oh, darling. This must be one of your nightmares. Let me take care of it for you." His eyes grew soft and kind, establishing deeper contact with her. Much faster than before, Ayla relaxed and allowed him to gently touch her memory and make it grow lighter and lighter until there was nothing but an empty spot in its wake. A little hole to join many others.

She didn't care, though. The only thing she wished for was to have her will back. If he had to go through her mind for that, so be it.

Ayla blinked, coming to her senses. It felt cold to be out of his spell, and as always, the procedure left her exhausted. *A mug of hot chocolate would be amazing right now*, she thought, anticipating an idyllic end of the evening. Corbin took good care of her after every session, making sure she was comfortable and warm. He would take her back to the penthouse and wrap her in a heated blanket. Dolores would bring her a sweet hot drink and light up the candles in the room. Corbin would sit next to her, holding her hand until she drifted off to sleep. The next day, things would be good again.

Ayla made a move to step back, but his hand gripped her shoulder, keeping her in place. Corbin chewed his lip, studying her. "That's not it. Sorry sweetie, I need to take another look."

Like a marionette on a string, Ayla nodded. She had no choice, regardless of what he said. There was no other way but to obey him. If she refused, who knew how much worse things could be?

Her body trembled, struggling with added stress as he perforated her mind again. The touch of his thought was firmer than before, as if he was searching for something. Ayla shied away from him as sensations—visual, emotional, olfactory, pain—lost their definition and bled into one excruciating rush. His hands kept her still, one on her forearm, the other holding her neck just under the chin to maintain eye contact. The grip was so strong she could feel her pulse quickening against it. Maybe this was how she kept getting those bruises.

I have to be strong. He'll let me go once he gets what he wants.

Ayla yelped when he penetrated deeper into her memory, paying no attention to her struggle. There was no doubt now that Corbin wouldn't stop, even if he had to hurt her. The pain of his forced presence was blinding as her mind put up a fight to keep some of her will to herself.

"Please," she begged, her voice hoarse against the grasp of iron fingers digging into her flesh. "You're hurting me, Corbin. Please, let me go!"

"Shh, it's okay. Just relax and it won't hurt," he soothed.

Ayla tried to push him away, but he was much stronger. Primal instinct kicked in when she realised he was about to take over her will. In a desperate attempt to escape, she thrashed around, hoping it would break his focus. It didn't work. His grip only grew stronger, steel fingers digging through to the bone. Tears ran down her cheeks as he suppressed her will almost completely.

The image of the white-haired man popped up in her mind and stayed in front of her as if held by invisible binding. Ayla writhed in the steel grip of Corbin's spell as she realised this was what he was looking for. Somehow, she didn't want him to know, and now that he did, she was terrified.

"Who's this?" His voice was calm, but braided with an underlying strain that she'd heard many times before.

Ayla tried to push the image away but it stayed on the spot, as if lit up by a stage light. The pressure she felt from Corbin intensified, leaving her breathless.

"Stop fighting me, you're only going to hurt yourself. Tell me who this is."

She didn't understand why he was willing to hurt her so badly to get an answer. "He said his name was Blaze," she sobbed as Corbin's will crushed her resistance. "I sometimes see him in my dreams. It's nothing more, I swear! I've never seen him before and I don't know who he is. He's just part of a dream."

Saying it out loud, she realised this was a lie. Blaze was more than a dream, she saw it clearly now. The worst thing was that Corbin did too, and now he knew her secret.

He frowned and nearly let her slip for a moment. Ayla tried once again to hide Blaze's image but Corbin quickly restored their connection and put her under his dominance again.

"It's not that simple, Ayla. I think someone is trying to break into your mind with these sweet visions that look innocent enough for you to trust them. Remember how you were attacked, how someone killed Darren, how they are still looking for you. Their hunt hasn't stopped; I get reports of these people lurking all around the world, searching every nook and cranny. They haven't picked up your trace yet and you're safe for now. But I have to protect you, darling. We need to make sure they can't find you."

Why would they be looking for me if they think I'm dead? Isn't that what you told me before?

Ayla didn't get a chance to say her thoughts out loud. Corbin reached deeper into her mind and the image slowly started to fade. Ayla stubbornly held on, refusing to let it go. There was no way Blaze was dangerous, she knew it in her heart. These dreams were the only thing keeping her sane in this lonely life of being locked up for the unforeseeable future. They were her way of being somewhere else, with someone else. And now Corbin wanted to take that away, too.

She tried to think about the night of the attack when she was nearly killed. The person who stabbed her seemed so familiar—no matter how hard she tried, though, she couldn't remember his face or his name that she was sure he had mentioned. Switching her thoughts to another object didn't help, though. Blaze's green eyes in her memory grew dimmer as if Corbin was sweeping over them with an invisible eraser, rubbing away at her only solace. She tried to push back one more time but that made no difference. She had no more strength to fight.

"This boy is a danger to you, don't you understand? Let it go, Ayla. Don't make me force you," he hissed as she wavered on the verge of collapse.

It now felt as if he was ripping the image out of her mind with iron pliers. She screamed, unable to contain the pain, as he went through her mind, destroying each of her visions one by one.

"It's going to be okay. I'll make sure these dreams never return and you'll be safe again."

Ayla's cheeks were soaked with tears by the time he was done. She was shivering all over. A terrible migraine pulsed through her clouded mind. Arms around Corbin's neck, she clung to him as he carried her downstairs into the penthouse. Once he set her down on the fluffed-up pillows in the cosy bed, a cup of steamy hot drink quickly appeared next to her but Ayla barely glanced at it. Every blink felt like an explosion. Her gaze was fixed on one spot on the wall and she hardly noticed someone's hand holding the drink to her lips.

Absent-mindedly, she took a sip. The hot liquid warmed her up and the headache started to slowly release its grip. Her eyelids grew heavy, and it wasn't too long until her head rolled back and merciful darkness descended upon her.

***

Soft grey fog covered the ground just below her ankles. Her *safe place* held no smells, no distractions. The living greyness rubbed against her ankles like a cat, and Ayla smiled at the analogy. The fog felt like an old friend who came to help her recoup and heal. There was no pain, no suffering. Nobody could hurt her here.

Someone was talking in the distance not too far away. Curious, Ayla tiptoed towards the sound.

Corbin was facing her, but he didn't seem to notice her presence. A large black bird was perched on a thick branch in front of him, its feathers unnaturally shiny. It looked like there was a conversation in progress. Ayla stepped closer, unable to contain the desire to learn about this new development. This was the first time she had seen Corbin in her dream. She wondered what it meant.

"Well? What did you find out, Raven?"

The bird gave him a bow and opened its beak. To Ayla's bewilderment, it started speaking as if it was nothing out of the ordinary. "The one called Blaze is thankfully the only one with this name and white hair, so it wasn't that hard to track him. He's from a Mage community somewhere up north. Twenty-seven years of age. Graduated from the school of magic at Whitestone. The only living son to Gordon and Bella Faingold who used to be a powerful union back in their day until both died in a car crash under strange circumstances. It's curious to know that they were destined for each other, which makes their son a strong candidate for repeating the pattern."

Corbin sighed impatiently, tapping his foot on the floor. "Unbelievable. A *Mage*, really?"

"Yes, Master. And a shifter, too. Mage communities know him as the white tiger for his chosen form. Currently unpartnered." The bird held a pause as if deciding whether or not to continue. "With his career..."

"I don't care about his career!" Corbin raised his voice. "Mages are bad news as it is, especially the brainwashed ones with that idiotic belief in Destiny." He scoffed in disgust, starting to pace. "School at Whitestone, is that where they learn their stupid tricks?"

The bird nodded but Corbin didn't seem to need an answer. His expression grew darker as he continued speaking. "Gordon and Bella Faingold. Never heard of them. Might have been famous in their little world, but clearly not that important, otherwise I'd know. Plus a shifter who chose a tiger's form and is currently single. Tricky." He rubbed his chin, lost in thought. "How the hell do I get rid of him?"

"Have him killed, perhaps?" Raven suggested.

Corbin shook his head and narrowed his eyes at the bird. "Are you crazy? We can't meddle with Mage affairs and they shouldn't be meddling with ours. One thing is an innocent chase of someone you believe is your destiny, and a completely different one is murder. It's as bad as declaring war. I'd lose everything, all that I still have left after the poor girl proved to be a failure and undermined my authority in front of everyone. No, that won't work."

"Maybe it's for the best, Master. We can make it look like it's been your plan all along. Giving her away can be a way for you to save face and restore your reputation."

Corbin took a deep breath. When he spoke again, his voice was calm, with only a slight undertone of rage. "Nobody is taking what's mine. There's no way I'm letting her go. Not after what I've done."

"Master... She's a hopeless *null*. Her only use would be to serve and provide you pleasure, but there are slaves who will do that much better. They will jump at your every command without the need to force them. Just like the old days. Why keep her at all? Let the Mage deal with this problem."

Corbin shook his head. "She is special in a way you won't understand. Ever since she walked into my study and I smelled her sweet fear, I've wanted to give her the gift of pain. Every day, I kept reminding myself that Darren's heritage is not to be touched, that he had warned me she was too fragile for play. When I had to punish her at the Gala, I was sure that Sawyer had set me up. He was hoping I wouldn't be able to contain myself, but that didn't work. When she collapsed after the mere 10 lashes, I knew she was different from others. Her pain gave me a high I'd never experienced before, but she couldn't take it. When she made me angry a few weeks later and I slapped her, it triggered something. I barely stopped myself from doing it again, and I hoped that staying away from her would help. It's excruciating to be around her now when all I want is to protect her and at the same time make her suffer. It's tearing me apart."

"Master... you're not... in love with her, are you?"

"That would be ironic, wouldn't it?" He let out a bitter chuckle. "She's my curse, Raven. I bound her to me with the blood ritual. I took her memories and gave her nothing but suffering. I knew she was fragile, yet I pushed and pushed until she broke down. I kept punishing her for nothing, really. She didn't do anything wrong. Her sheer existence is what's making me weak. But I can't let her die. And I can't let the Mage boy have her, either."

He chewed his lip, digging his hands into his hair, before finally making a decision. "Call the staff at my estate in Lyons first thing tomorrow and have them set it up. Once it's ready, we'll move there. The boy is never going to find her, and even if he does, she won't recognize him. Tonight, I erased all her memories of him. Permanently."

Ayla tried to make sense of it but something was blocking her thoughts. She struggled to process the information as her mind encountered nothing but grey fog, much like the one that was hugging her ankles. Some time ago, Corbin had mentioned something about temporarily taking painful memories, and she was now sure that was what he did to 'help' people and what made them want to pay anything to get more. Erasing memories permanently was a taboo, or so she thought.

"Master... This is uncharted territory. I'm concerned about how far this dark path is leading you," Raven pleaded, stretching and folding its wings in an attempt to make its point more valid.

"I didn't ask for your opinion. I know what I'm doing, and she'll be okay. We'll just need to pay her some extra attention the next few days, as I expect her to be sick for a little while. But it will pass. She'll be fine."

"The Prophet summoned that Mage for a reading," the bird uttered. "Something tells me we're going to have a problem on our tail sometime soon."

"We'll deal with him then," Corbin replied.

Ayla looked closer but his face changed its shape and started twisting and turning, becoming a large blur. The strange stretching entity was all that was left in front of her. Its tentacles of pure black were reaching for her, almost grabbing onto her dress, and Ayla screamed trying to get away.

She woke up covered in a cold sweat, trembling from head to toe. Corbin was sitting on the bed next to her, his hands on her shoulders, and Ayla realised he'd been trying to shake her awake.

"It's okay, Ayla, you're safe." For the briefest moment, a shadow of guilt flitted in his eyes.

Trying to catch her breath, she listened to her inner self. Something was begging for her to move away from him. She couldn't understand why, though. He was there to help, he was worried about her.

"Your body is still adjusting to the blood bond. It's going to get better soon. I promise."

His words made perfect sense, yet felt wrong somehow. She searched for the answer in her mind but the attempt blew up in her face.

A terrible migraine bloomed in her head. Corbin gently put his hand on her forehead and looked her in the eye again. He spoke softly, and his eyes grew large and calm until she was immersed in the feeling of security. Soft haze rose around her, but at least the pain was gone. Fluffy grey clouds lifted her above the ground and carried her away.

CHAPTER 21. BLAZE

The old, weathered building loomed in front of him. Simple brickwork gave away the craftsmen of the previous generations when things were built to last. The two columns adorning the front entrance had sculptures of sitting lions with lush manes and bared teeth. Intricate ironwork on the wooden door could have made somebody believe the place was enchanted. Blaze knew better though. The Prophet had no use for spells.

He took a deep breath before approaching the tall door. That was it. Only a few more steps and he would obtain the knowledge that would change his whole life. That would shape his future every step of the way until his time ran out. What if there was no future for him? The Prophet could just tell him that he was supposed to keep fighting creatures of the night and bringing students to the school of magic at Whitestone, maybe to go back to the Force. Never to settle. Never to love. Always alone, tormented by deceitful visions of the girl who didn't exist.

With a sharp exhale, he pushed the door and it opened with surprising ease. The hallway was clear and spacious, with brass lights on the walls giving off a warm glow. He walked past the paintings that depicted landscapes and battles, flowers and lovers, men wearing crowns, and half-naked women. There was only one door at the end of it. He stepped into the spacious room and looked around.

Large French windows let through plenty of natural light. Heavy curtains were pulled up to make sure not a single ray of sun missed out. A few paintings on the floor leaned against furniture, some still unfinished. There was an easel in the furthest corner, with a colour-splashed apron hanging on it and a half-dry palette on the small cast iron table nearby.

Paintings occupied most of the wall space, too. Watching them more closely, Blaze could tell how the artist's mastery was developing. From softer touches of portraits to strong strokes on the landscapes, colouring the blue and green hues of the ocean in its various states. Painting storms was the most difficult of all, and it was enchanting to watch these pictures progress with realism.

The last painting had the most presence, and not just because it was the largest one in the room. Dark waves were rising to blackened skies, threatening to destroy everything in their path. Their underbellies showed muddy waters with tiny pieces of driftwood and algae trapped in a sinister dance. Blaze noticed something new with every passing minute, perceiving a tiny white sail struggling with the harsh weather somewhere on the horizon, lopsided as the forces of nature nearly devoured it—but for now, it was still there, with a tiny spark of light under the mast.

Blaze suppressed a shiver. He knew that everything he saw in the house carried a special meaning. The Prophet displayed a different set-up for every guest, and that picture must have been telling a story. A story he didn't particularly like.

Someone cleared their throat. Blaze switched his attention to a small fragile-looking lady whose presence he completely missed when he first walked in. She beckoned him to a leather-bound chair at the white wooden table. He took the seat with a respectful bow and an apology for being inattentive.

The Prophet gave him a kind smile and gestured around. "Do you like my paintings?" She spoke with the expected tone of an older lady, slightly high-pitched and perfect for telling bedtime stories to a circle of curious children.

Blaze smiled at the thought, remembering his own experience not so long ago. This was a brilliant setup. He could only wonder what would come out of this visit. "They are most impressive," he responded politely, cursing the small talk for keeping him from his goal. "One would wonder how many years of experience and careful crafting they would take. Especially the one that has captured my attention."

The Prophet chuckled at the unasked question in his sentence. She gestured to the small teapot and a couple of delicate porcelain cups on the table. Following the hint, he took the warm white handle and poured the steamy drink into both cups. The Prophet nodded in approval, picking up hers, and took a tiny sip.

"Have some tea with me, and then we'll talk."

This was part of the challenge. When he was a child, his parents taught him the proper etiquette for many things in life, including manners for a reading. Before going forward with her wisdom, the Prophet would offer a refreshment or a snack setting up a special test.

Blaze drew a breath to calm his nerves. He couldn't betray his impatience now. Her house, her rules. He emptied his thoughts and took a flavourful sip.

Nothing happened. A silence settled in the room as the Prophet sat still, with her eyes closed. Blaze fixed his gaze on the picture behind her, watching the white sail of the tiny ship dancing in the imaginary wind. Or was it?

A gust of salty air threw sharp specks of sand in his face. Blaze looked around, his senses on high alert. Tall waves crashed into the muddled sand of the beach, splashing his boots with ice-cold water. Directly to his left, a lighthouse loomed over the writhing waters, its top barely alight. The white sail on the horizon fluttered in the storm, thrown around like a toy.

Blaze hurried towards the lighthouse, through the rusty door, up the squeaky stairs. As he walked into the small room on the top, he realised that he must have imagined the illumination. The light was off. Wild wind was spinning the sparse furniture across the room. Looking out of the broken window, he saw the white dot almost submerged under the violent waters.

He drew a breath and summoned his power. As always, it easily responded to his call. The ball of iridescent white fire hovered above his hand as he looked around for ideas. First of all, he had to repair the window. A thin thread from his hand flew towards the glass, restoring it in a matter of seconds. Next, he turned towards the large floodlight. This one took a lot more of his power, as if a dark force was keeping it off. Blaze wasn't used to giving up, though. More and more magic went from his hands into the void until a bright light came on, ripping through the night like a supernova.

There was no time for a break to collect his thoughts. It took a few moments for his vision to adjust as he turned the light towards the storm. Once the black dots stopped dancing in his eyes, he took a look outside the lighthouse. The outcome was stunning. The tiny sail had settled on the rough and the waves went down until the surface became a glimmering mirror under the light of the moon.

"Bravo," the Prophet's high-pitched voice said in his ear.

Blaze blinked and found himself back in the large living room, with an empty cup in his hand. The old lady looked at him kindly, her smile reflecting in the wrinkles around her eyes. "Very different approach. Why didn't you try to settle the storm itself?" She cocked her head to one side.

Blaze intertwined his fingers, thinking about an answer, but he could not think of anything beyond instinct or subconscious. "I'm not too sure," he finally answered. "Possibly because I'm not particularly good at weather?"

The Prophet chuckled. These were just pleasantries before the big reveal. Blaze already knew he passed the test; it was time for him to get the reading that would potentially change his whole life.

"Well, I believe congratulations are in order. You have indeed passed and I can see that you're worthy. There's a little problem though." The Prophet held an unnerving pause before continuing. "I can show you what you've been seeking for years. Your destiny. There are many questions and not many answers. The path is in the fog and I can't see it. Today you can decide to go forward or to walk away." She looked him in the eye, waiting.

Blaze nodded, his throat dry. This was the moment he had been anticipating. There was no backing out now.

Sybil's warm hand touched his for a moment, and a heavy wave suddenly covered him in darkness.

It was almost pitch black there. Blaze turned his head to one side, then the other, but couldn't see a thing. The space felt tight yet roomy. Neither hot nor cold. The only sound, his heartbeat that didn't belong in this silence. He made a step forward, then another. There was no movement in the still air—he was walking but not getting anywhere. An icicle of frozen reality, trapped between worlds. Blaze focused his thoughts on his goal. Strange anticipation filled the space, and suddenly he stumbled out of it and into a brightly lit room.

The girl with chestnut hair and golden highlights was lying on the bed, buried in soft pillows and blankets. With a smile, Blaze stepped closer. It was good to see her again; every night he didn't dream about her was a night wasted. Seeing her now made him long for her even more.

Her hand slipped from under the covers and hung lifelessly off the bed. Only then did Blaze understand something was wrong. The whole atmosphere felt sick, and he didn't feel it straight away through his joy of seeing her. He knew it now, though. The girl... Ayla... she wasn't well.

Once again, he couldn't get any closer than a few steps. Annoyed, he kept trying to push through the thick barrier, knowing that it wasn't going to work. Ayla looked much paler than before, and the dark blob sucking the life out of her heart grew bigger. The bed sheets flew away as she thrashed around in agony and finally woke up screaming. Sitting up on the bed, she wrapped her arms around her, shivering all over, sweat beading her forehead. Blaze wanted nothing more than to comfort her, to cut that disgusting thing off her chest and chase away her nightmares.

"You saw her present," a high-pitched voice said in his ear. "In your dreams before, you saw her past."

Images swirled in front of him in a rapid dance. There was one he never understood before, where she was a young girl in a bright yellow dress, someone cuddling her and giving her a small teddy bear. Her picture on a few locket-like portraits given out to cloaked figures. One of them held her hand to lead her away. Two of those figures looked painfully familiar, and it didn't take him long to notice the wild ginger curls that peeked through the hood of one of them. His mother. The figure on her left had the muscular build of his father. What did they have to do with this little girl?

Before he could wonder more, the image changed again. Ayla was sitting on a bench in a dark park, waiting for someone. Another vision replaced it in an instant. She was in a small bakery, tasting hot buns, smiling at the old couple who were saying something to her. Another image. Another. Yet another. All of them were dreams of her he had before but in rapid succession.

Once they all flew before his eyes, a silence took over. The Prophet's voice sounded clear in the stillness of the dark.

"Now you will see what her future may bring."

CHAPTER 22. AYLA

Ayla startled awake, trying to catch her breath. This nightmare was so intense it sent her rolling out of her bed and onto the floor. Grateful for the interruption, she dragged her knees to her chest and wrapped her arms around them. *I'm okay, it's just a dream. I'm okay. I'm okay.*

Her heartbeat took over all the other sounds, pulsing in her ears like the drums of war. The door flew open as Corbin rushed in, turning on the soft light by the bed. He lowered himself to the floor opposite her, deep concern reflecting in his dark eyes.

"Hey, it's alright, Ayla. You're safe," he said, giving her shoulders a gentle rub. This used to help when she just started having nightmares, but it didn't work anymore. Every night things got a little worse and she needed more time to calm down. Corbin was getting more reluctant to use magic, which annoyed her to no end. Why have the ability if you weren't going to use it?

Tonight was the hardest. She couldn't remember the worst part of the dream, but the feeling of free fall somewhere into the pit of darkness was still fresh. She shuddered, tightening the grip on her knees, as if curling into a tighter ball was going to help. It only worked for a second, and then the fear took over again.

Corbin took his hand away as something attracted his attention. Ayla followed his gaze and silently cursed herself. She should have known he'd see it. Even a tiny detail was enough for him to find out anything he wanted to know.

"What's this?" He pointed at the tiny red dot on the side of her sheets that only became visible because of her fall. She didn't have to reply, and he didn't expect her to. Corbin stood up and pulled the blanket off the bed, uncovering the whole scene of her crime. She was going to get into so much trouble!

The sheets were covered with smudged red spots, some small, some bigger, but none big enough yet. She didn't try to hide them very hard as she was going to take the sheets off the bed the next morning and take them to the laundry herself, before the maid discovered them. A silly thought, considering how little she could do lately, with her physical strength seemingly decreasing every day. But the relief was there. Physical pain helped her block out the black hole in her mind that was sucking the life out of her. Those tiny cuts helped more than they harmed, right?

The terror from her nightmare was still holding her in its grip as Corbin threw the blankets on the floor, searching for the weapon. It was easy to find, too. She had put the sheathed knife under the pillow she normally cuddled to sleep, to keep it within reach if she needed it again. This was something she had wanted to do for a while but never had the guts to try. Last night was the night, and it helped. She only wished she'd discovered it sooner.

Corbin carefully examined the blade before flicking it straight into the polished wood of the bedroom door. The knife pierced it with a loud thud, making her startle. Ayla silently counted to ten and back, too afraid to move. What was he going to do?

I made him angry. He's angry with me.

A strange thought crossed her mind. Maybe if he was angry enough, he could help her finish the job that she was unable to do herself. Maybe he would finally set her free from suffering. After all, he saw her every day. He knew what she was going through, and he knew how to stop this. Maybe he would show the mercy she so desperately needed.

Corbin released an exasperated breath and ran his fingers through his hair before turning back to her, his face composed again. Ayla shuddered when he sat back down on the floor, his aura as dark as the despair in her thoughts.

"Show me your arms," he ordered.

She obeyed, numb with fear. Surely, there was nothing he could do to make things worse, yet she was afraid. Corbin had a bright imagination and could always come up with a form of punishment she might not have thought of.

He studied the crimson cuts on her outstretched arms, his expression dark. Ayla gulped, realising that she might have gone too far. She should have thought this through a little better, knowing his ability to spot the tiniest detail. Corbin didn't stop once he looked her arms over. Following his next command, she lifted the hem of her nightdress to show more cuts on her thighs. Corbin shook his head and pulled her up off the floor.

"They are all fresh. How long have you been having these thoughts?"

"Since the nightmares began," she heard herself respond in a voice she no longer recognised as her own. Hoarse, raspy, nothing like the melodic flow she used to have only a few weeks ago. Or was it months? She didn't keep track of time. It could have been years, for all she knew. Nothing mattered anymore as she was stuck in a neverending circle of pain and fear.

"Why didn't you tell me?"

She didn't reply, stubbornly avoiding his gaze. The blanket and pillows lying around the floor made the room look messy, exposing her dark secrets to the world. There was nothing she could say to make a justifiable response.

"I don't know," she finally whispered to fill the silence. It was difficult to explain that the nightmares that jolted her awake seemed to be getting worse. They came every night, making her terrified of going to bed. She hated that she needed Corbin to be there to calm her down. Every evening now he would sit on her bed, talking to her in a soothing voice until things went fuzzy and warm, helping her drift off to sleep. He brought her peace, but being so dependent on him made her feel even worse. What if he wasn't home the next day? How would she handle being on her own?

Corbin's dark eyes were sad, as if he could tell what she was feeling.

"I'm sorry, darling. I understand how much you're going through right now, but it will get better soon, okay?"

"No, it won't. Can't you see? I feel worse every day and all I do is sleep until a nightmare wakes me, and then beg for your help when the pain hits, and this horrible circle keeps going on and on! But you have the power to release me. You can make it stop." She paused, gulping down the knot in her throat. "Please, Corbin. Please, make it stop."

There, she said it. The moment the words left her lips, an immense weight lifted off her shoulders. That was the favour that she'd been meaning to ask but couldn't work up the courage until now. If he killed her, there would be no more suffering. She would finally be free, he *had to* understand it. There was no reason for her to keep going like this.

"Ayla. You are asking me to end your life." He put both hands on her shoulders, looking straight at her. There was no fuzziness this time; he was being serious. The hurt in his eyes reflected her own pain as if he truly knew what she felt. "I know you're struggling, but I didn't realise you were so close to the edge. I can't do what you're asking, I'm sorry. One thing I can tell you is that I will spend all my time now looking for an answer, a clue, anything to find a remedy that will heal you. Please, darling, hang in a little longer. I'll figure it out, but you have to be strong."

Unable to speak, she lowered her head, bitter tears trickling down her cheeks. Corbin wrapped his arms around her, holding her close. He didn't ask any more questions, and she was glad to have this quiet time to collect her thoughts as she listened to his accelerated heartbeat. Once again, like every time he held her in his arms, she wondered if he told her the truth. Or if her whole life was now a never-ending lie.

Once she stopped sobbing, he gave her another minute to catch her breath before pulling away to look into her eyes again. Ayla sighed. She had been too optimistic, thinking she could convince him. She should have finished the job herself when she had the chance. And now he'd keep a close eye on all potential weapons in her room. The maid will probably bring her pre-cut steak now, and butter her toasts for her. Yuck.

Corbin gently tucked the messy strands of her hair behind her ears before he spoke again. Ayla grimaced as he explained that they were not safe anymore and needed to move. She nodded bleakly and plopped back onto the pillows. It didn't matter where to feel miserable. One place or another. The circle of pain was the same.

Corbin gave her an approving look before getting off her bed. Dolores rushed in to pack things up. She didn't say a single word. A blessing. Ayla wasn't in the mood to tolerate her snarky remarks, too exhausted after exposing her darkest secret to Corbin.

With the efficiency of a hurricane, the maid grabbed Ayla's belongings and shoved them into suitcases. Her black hair in a smooth bun and the impeccably ironed uniform were annoying to the eye. Ayla wondered how she always managed to keep it so tidy. She knew Dolores had no magic, but it sometimes felt like her clothes and hair were enchanted to look neat no matter what.

Ayla thought back to her time at Corbin's mansion and asked herself the question about all the other staff members there. The older maid, the driver, the bodyguards... where were they all? Only Dolores came here. And now they were moving again, and it looked like the hateful maid was coming along. Would there be any other servants in the new house?

Ayla struggled to keep her eyes open until the room was mostly packed. Corbin walked in around lunchtime for the daily check, and Ayla squirmed uncomfortably. The checks made her feel odd, and she didn't like them.

He lowered himself onto the bed next to her and took her hand. She stubbornly fixed her eyes on a pot plant by the door, pretending she didn't know what was about to happen. Corbin sighed and turned her head around to look him in the eye.

"Come on now, darling. You know we need to do this." He patted her hand in an attempt to soothe her. "Tell me your earliest memory."

With a grimace, she started talking. As always, he asked a lot of questions, making her remember important events throughout her life. The more recent period of time was full of haze and brought her the most trouble. She didn't remember moving to the penthouse or reading most of the books she had read. There was no recollection of most of her days at the Academy, except Camilla and Julian, and Eric who had left her. It still caused her a lot of heartache to think about it. After all the great things they shared, all the good times together, she found it hard to imagine what kind of fight would have made him disappear without a trace.

She didn't remember the attack or who the shadow figure was. The only thing left in her mind from that fateful night was the circle of candles and Corbin's sinister words about life for life. It was clear now that he was sensitive to her moods and emotions. He always knew what to do when she was upset or scared - which happened a lot these days.

"You can just see it in my mind if you want," she suddenly realised. It dawned on her after all these days that this was exactly what he did to take her nightmares away. He would reach inside her mind and make them disappear. It didn't last long, but it always worked. Somehow, he only touched those areas, leaving the others alone, which was how he never learned of her dark thoughts.

"It's complicated, Ayla. You have to be able to navigate your memory on your own. I can't keep doing this, it's incredibly risky. You are already hooked on an easy relief, and you know how vulnerable that makes you. We do these checks to make sure you're not getting worse, I told you that before."

She jerked her shoulder in annoyance as she thought about Camilla. How she and so many others judged the poor girl for the addiction she couldn't overcome. Ayla recalled her own disbelief at seeing her friend beg Corbin for "one more session". This didn't seem like something that would have ever happened to Ayla herself. And now that it had, it felt awful to realise she was no better.

Corbin cupped her cheek in his hand, warming her skin. She was no longer hungry after sessions or the check-ups, but he always offered some food and drink anyway. This time, a tall glass with pink lemonade and a plate of freshly cut fruit were waiting on a bedside tray. As he broke eye contact with her, he picked up a piece of juicy watermelon on a tiny fork and pressed it against her lips. Despite her reservations, Ayla obediently took a bite. It was good to do as he said so that she would have a better chance at getting a session later.

Ayla scolded herself for these thoughts but there was no running away from them. Only Corbin could make her forget the nightmares that she couldn't cope with herself. She needed all the help she could get.

Without any warning, another migraine struck her. The silver fork clashed against the metal tray as it fell out of her weakened fingers. With a groan, she flopped back onto the pillows, clutching the sheets so hard that her hands went white. Insufferable pain overwhelmed her, a raging sun inside her head. Merciless, evil. That moment could have lasted a few minutes or a few hours. Ayla could never define where it stopped and peace started. Nor did she know if Corbin did anything to help her.

***

Her eyes opened to the familiar greyness and a sigh of relief escaped her lips. This was the place she liked to be in. There was no pain here, no suffering. The air was still, yet fresh, devoid of background noise. No walls, no limits. Perhaps, this was the peace of the dead. Maybe this was where she was meant to go in the end.

She looked around, curious. Sometimes, she felt another presence as if someone was watching her. No matter how hard she tried though, she could never find the source of this strange feeling. There was no telling if this was indeed a presence or just fragments of her imagination.

"That's the last of it. Let's get moving." Corbin's voice sounded as clear as always in her visions. The bird sat still on the perch in front of him.

"Is Ayla asleep?" Raven asked.

"Yes. She's getting worse." Corbin sighed, ruffling his hair. Dark circles weighed down his eyes, something Ayla hadn't noticed before. Maybe she didn't see them, too absorbed in her own pain. Or maybe it was only true here, in her own little world.

"You were warned, Master. Those visions were vital to her integrity. If you'd taken them temporarily, you would have pulled it off. And now it will only go downhill from here."

Corbin pulled the bird by its shiny black tail. "I gave you human life, Raven. Everything you are is thanks to me. Don't forget your loyalties," he hissed. His rage passed in a moment though. He released the grip and Raven slumped forward, nearly falling from its perch.

"She will be your demise, Master. You know as much as I do that the Prophet will tell the truth. This girl destroys everything she touches. She ruined Master Darren's life and your reputation. There's a curse hanging above her head, and no amount of black magic will make it disappear. She's leading you further and further down the path of darkness. It's time you let her go. Let the boy take this burden off your hands so that you can be free again."

"I don't want him anywhere near her. I took her and I'm keeping her. She's mine!"

Ayla's hair stood on end. Even when she had thought she'd seen the worst of him, he showed that there was always more to be afraid of. The bird, however, didn't seem too concerned. Ruffling its feathers, it fearlessly glared at Corbin.

"She belongs to you, yes. But those migraines and nightmares are getting worse. You feel it through the blood bond, Master, it's affecting you too. Don't you see that? You know in your heart that she's ailing because you blocked her connection to him. Taking the painful memories only helps for a short time. You see that she needs sessions more frequently now. You know that she can't handle it anymore, you saw yourself what she tried to do! Let the boy come, and see if the so-called destiny helps her. After all, what have you got to lose?"

Corbin growled, his face a grimace of pain. He turned around and walked away, as the bird flew off the perch to disappear in the darkness in front of him. Ayla tried to follow them but something pulled her back. Echoing voices filled the space. Stretching figures laughed as they danced in an odd circle around her, casting their clawed tentacles in her direction, getting closer with each attempt.

Ayla woke herself up with a scream and nearly fell off the unfamiliar bed. Reaching for the light on the bedside table where it was supposed to be, her fingers found nothing. She sat up and felt the sheets around her for any pointers of what this could be.

Bright light blinded her as someone flicked the switch. Blinking the black and red spots away, she was annoyed to see it was the hateful maid. There was something in her hands, and only once she approached the bed did Ayla make out that it was a vial of some sort.

Dolores picked the frosted glass off the bedside table and put a few drops from the vial into the still water. The room immediately filled up with the smell of medicine.

Ayla wrinkled her nose. "Valerian? Really?"

The maid shoved the glass into her hands. "Really. Drink it or not, up to you."

With a defeated sigh, Ayla accepted the glass and took a few sips. Everything Dolores did for her seemed to be an effort. But at least seeing her unwelcome face made her almost forget about the emotional turmoil she felt when she woke up.

"Where's Corbin?" She tried to fill the awkward silence as Dolores stood by her side, waiting for her to finish the drink. It was unnerving how she sometimes did that. Standing still to wait for her to do something. Or showing up randomly, as she did now.

"Master isn't here tonight as he has more pressing matters to attend to." The maid opened the palm of her hand. "Are you done?"

Ayla stalled. There wasn't much information she could ever get out of the maid. However, there were so many questions she wanted to ask, and nobody gave her answers. "Who is Raven?" she blurted, watching the maid for a reaction.

Dolores's face finally showed that she was capable of emotion. Her features changed drastically as she heard the question. The look of surprise revealed she was shaken, but that only lasted for a moment. She quickly scooped the glass from Ayla's hand and scoffed at her as if brushing off an annoying child.

"It's a bird black of feather. Surely, you know that."

Turning on her heel, the maid nearly flew out of the room, switching off the lights and leaving Ayla alone again. This time, sleep didn't come. This time, there were no nightmares.

CHAPTER 23. BLAZE

"Now you will see what her future may bring," the Prophet cautioned. She opened the palms of her hands in an inviting gesture and Blaze mirrored her movement. Without any other warning, his mind was invaded by other visions.

The girl was standing on the rooftop, the wind ruffling her hair. Her white gown looked like a nightdress, made from semi-transparent material. The desperation on her face was so vivid it seeped through the screen of darkness separating them. She wavered in the moving air and took a step forward, her weightless body easily gliding down to the ground. He didn't need to see the rest to know the end.

The vision switched to another, with her being so sick she couldn't move. Her chest rose once and stopped. There were about half a dozen sombre pictures like these, each piercing his heart with pain he had never felt before.

The tune suddenly changed, and light shone into his eyes. Ayla was laughing, holding a small child in her arms. Blaze smiled, recognising his own features in the little girl's face and her cheeky grin as she hugged her mother back. Another picture swam in his line of sight, where he was holding Ayla's hand and whispering something in her ear. Where she put her head on his shoulder and he wrapped his arm around her.

Many more happy moments went by, lifting his mood and bringing back hope. The last vision left him puzzled. Ayla was standing in a hallway of sorts, a serious expression on her face. Soft grey fog was rising from the floor, covering her legs, but she didn't seem bothered. She looked around as if this was normal, and lifted her arm. The fog followed her movement and quickly buried her under it.

For some reason, this vision was the strongest of all. Puzzled, Blaze looked at the Prophet, wondering if she would explain its meaning.

"This girl is under the protection of a Sorcerer who watches her like a hawk. He will mask her aura everywhere they go, but you still have a chance to find her. I'll give you a guide that will show you the way, but it will only work in her immediate vicinity. It can still be used as a regular photo though." She placed a small picture of Ayla on the table between them. Blaze picked it up, studying the girl's delicate features. She almost looked alive, and he could have sworn he saw her chest rise ever so slightly as if she was breathing. Apart from that, she was perfectly still, like any regular picture.

"She's not one of *them*, is she?" Sorcerers were a sensitive topic in his community. Any discussions about them were avoided by most. Some children even grew up without knowing about their existence until they went to the school of magic at Whitestone and learned about the other kind of magic users. The ones who took slaves and lived a strange lifestyle, unacceptable for most Mages.

A sly smile fleeted across the Prophet's lips as she sat back with her arms crossed on her chest.

"Of course not, you should know that. By the irony of fate, she ended up in the wrong hands. But no, Blaze, she's one of us. And of all people, you are the only one who can go into a Sorcerer's lair and get something he treasures above anything in the world."

Blaze crossed his arms too, frowning. He didn't expect it to be easy to find his destined one, but having to deal with Sorcerers wasn't something he thought of.

Seeing his reservation, the Prophet threw her silver locks back, threading her fingers through them. When she spoke again, there was no hidden smile in her voice.

"You can walk away. She will stay by the Sorcerer's side until she dies, which won't be too long at the stage she's at. Or you can take her to Whitestone and she will heal among other Mages. You can just leave it at that. However, if you do decide to Join with her, it won't be easy either."

Puffing his cheeks, Blaze let out a deep breath. Now there was more to it? Dealing with a Sorcerer wasn't enough?

"Joining with your destined one is easy, isn't it? We'll both know it once we meet," he declared. At least, that was what his parents told him when he was growing up. When you see the one you're meant to be with, you just know it and they do, too. It only took Gordon and Bella a second. That was something that other people called love at first sight, which of course it wasn't. It was much more than that.

"Not in your case. See, the Sorcerer found out about her innocent visions. He felt threatened that she might slip out of his grip so he removed all her memories of you. This careless gesture of jealousy and anger caused serious damage to her mind. She no longer sees you in her dreams. When you two finally meet in person, she won't remember you. She will still feel the pull of destiny but without knowing what it is she might get scared and run away. You'll have to be very careful in your approach. Think about it as if you were courting a regular girl, but with higher stakes."

"Right. Will you at least tell me what her powers are? So I'm aware of what to expect." Blaze already started planning his way around the unexpected obstacles. If the Sorcerer treasured Ayla so much, it would be tricky to get her out of his hands. He had to come up with a solution, a valid argument to persuade him to give her away. For Plan B, he'd need to make sure he was at the peak of his power, in case things went sour and he had to fight. No matter how strong Sorcerers were, once their connection to the magic artefact was severed, they lost a lot of their power. From his vast knowledge of the other kind of magic users, Blaze knew that it would most likely be a graduation ring received from the Sorcerers' Academy, usually worn on the index finger of their dominant hand.

"Oh, that's another problem. Her powers are hidden in a haze that even I can't see through." The Prophet sounded pensive as she took a short pause. "I believe that Joining will unlock her gift, but there is no way of knowing what to expect. She can be so unique that no one will be able to teach her. Or she can be no more than a Breeder. Or powerful beyond belief. We won't know until it happens, and it's your choice what to do with it. I'll give you a warning though." She leaned forward, and Blaze mirrored her move. "The Sorcerer played many tricks with her mind, and some things are broken beyond repair. Unlocking her power may end up driving her insane. And if her powers are strong... the Council won't tolerate a mad Mage in the community."

Blaze straightened his back and looked into the Prophet's pale blue eyes.

"I'm not afraid of a scared little girl, Sybil. I will keep things under control, should she get in trouble."

The Prophet smiled in approval, and Blaze felt the weight lift off his chest. He made his choice now. He did have a destiny to fulfil, after all. It just took time to get to him, but his life had a purpose. That was all he ever wanted.

The glass clinked against the polished steel surface, and the bartender swiftly appeared with a crystal carafe full of sparkling water. Blaze nodded and the clear liquid refilled his drink. The girl behind the bar fluttered her long eyelashes at him as she put the carafe away.

"Are you sure you wouldn't like some wine, sir?" she asked in a gentle high-pitched voice that was undoubtedly reserved for the most treasured customers. Blaze wasn't a regular in this bar; in fact, this was probably the first and last time he was going to come here. Hong Kong was a lovely city to visit, but he couldn't fully enjoy the sights when his target was still so far out of his reach.

Blaze's gaze fell upon the crimson sails of a decorated junk boat swanning on the calm waters of the bay behind the large windows of the bar. He couldn't hear the speaker, but he knew this was one of the tours the boat offered around the harbour. Aqua Luna. A romantic name for a beautiful boat. He wondered if one day he would be able to rent it for just himself and Ayla when he'd finally found her. Take her on a sunset tour around all of Hong Kong's islands. See that happy smile on her face again. And then, show her around the city and explore the plethora of wonders it so generously shared with its guests. Give her the life she was meant to have.

A few shimmering lanterns rose in the air, bringing a smile to his face. The first full moon of the first lunar month. Spring Lantern Festival. Soon, the sky would be full of these shimmering dots. Symbols of hope and reconciliation. And forgiveness. Blaze scoffed, thinking about Corbin. This one's lantern would never fly. He was beyond redemption for everything he had done.

Blaze reminded himself to focus on the task at hand. He turned back to the friendly bartender, accepting the refill. The girl's delicate fingers brushed against his hand, lingering just a fraction of a second longer than was necessary to pass the drink. Despite being used to the tactic, he still allowed her a small smile in acknowledgement of her effort.

"Maybe later, but thank you. I was wondering if you'd be able to help me though."

The girl's face lit up with a hopeful smile as she leaned on the bar towards him. Soft and pleasant like a cat's purr: "Of course. Anything you need." Her hand slid on the bench, stopping mere centimetres away from his as she slowly lowered her gaze to his lips and back up to his eyes, letting him make the next move.

Blaze reached into his front pocket. He used to take these offers when he was much younger, especially right after he lost his parents in a car crash. There was no other way to deal with the giant hole in his heart other than try to forget it in the arms of gorgeous strangers. And drinking. Lots of drinking.

The visions of Ayla made it stop, and he never went back.

"I'm looking for this girl." He tapped his finger on the counter and the bartender begrudgingly turned her attention to the picture he laid in front of her. Ayla's face on the portrait was startled as if she was afraid of something, and Blaze once again admired the craftsmanship of the Prophet. His destined one was so beautiful, with her expression different every time he looked at the little image. He smiled at her dreamily as if she could see him.

"Sorry. Never seen her before." The bartender shook her head, taking her elbows off the bench and clearly losing interest. It was Blaze's turn to lean on the bar.

"Please," he said in his friendliest voice. "She's being held against her will and her life is in danger. She was with a tall man with black hair and dark eyes. I know she stayed in this hotel but she's been taken somewhere else. I need to find her before it's too late."

The bartender shook her head again and excused herself to serve other customers. Blaze sighed in exasperation and covered the picture with his hand. It took him forever to decipher the place where he saw Ayla in his last vision, on the rooftop of a skyscraper. When he arrived there, she was gone. The hotel staff wasn't much help. They frowned at his questions as if there were a gap in their memories, until one of the porters remembered briefly carrying a lost suitcase to the expensive black car where he caught a glimpse of the girl's golden highlights and the face of the man she was with. The hotel's bar was Blaze's last hope.

He played his meeting with the Prophet over and over in his head, never coming to anything new. His hand caressing the edge of Ayla's portrait, he took another sip of his sparkling water.

How do I find you, sweetheart? Give me just one more clue, I don't need much. Show me where you are and I'll do the rest. Let me help you.

Someone's presence interrupted his thoughts. Blaze opened his eyes, a polite excuse on the tip of his tongue. He wasn't in the mood for chitchat, and now was the worst time to deal with flirty ladies. He needed to go back to his room and think of possible ways to continue his search. There was no way he was letting Ayla die at the hand of the cruel Sorcerer.

A slender girl in a black jacket with a hood over her head lowered herself onto the chair next to him. Ignoring the jealous looks from the bartender, she settled with the confident grace of someone who knew their game. Head cocked to the side, she studied him as if she deciding whether he was worth speaking with. A different approach, but none of the ordinary either.

"Can I help you?" he asked absent-mindedly, still immersed in his thoughts. After the girl coughed delicately, he turned his head and took a proper look at her.

It had been a long time since he had seen a Familiar, and the first time he'd encountered one in human form. Blaze quickly scanned the crowd but there was no sign of magic aura apart from hers and his own. It was odd for him not to have noticed it before, and he silently scorned himself. He should be more careful. Now more than ever.

The girl chuckled at his astonishment and took off the hood, revealing shiny black hair tied up into a perfect bun. Her youthful face looked smug, yet he felt that behind that mask she was nervous. A Familiar without a Master anywhere in the vicinity. What an odd encounter.

"No. But I can help *you*," she said, pointing at the picture. Blaze's breath stuck in his throat. He had suffered failure after failure, and now someone was finally offering assistance. Unless it was a cruel joke or a trick to lure him further away from his chase. After all, he didn't know this Familiar and could only guess what her agenda was.

Seeing his reservation, the girl grinned. "My name is Raven, and I know exactly where you can find Ayla."

Blaze froze on the spot. He had never told anyone Ayla's name. How could Raven know it?

Unless she belonged to the dark Sorcerer. It made perfect sense. This was how she knew Ayla's whereabouts, and it wouldn't have been hard to track him if they knew what to look for. Blaze was sure the Sorcerer kept an eye on his progress, otherwise, why would he move Ayla out of a perfectly safe hotel? This didn't answer the question of why the Familiar was there now, talking to her Master's enemy.

"Why would I believe you?"

Raven scoffed, pulling the hood over her head again. "I don't care if you do. That girl needs to disappear from my Master's life, and I can't let her die, for it will destroy him. Take her away and make sure she never comes back. That's all I want. Your choice."

She got up, straightening her jacket. Leaving his empty glass on the table with a generous tip under it, Blaze got up too. Raven gestured towards the back door, taking a swift look around the busy bar as if making sure nobody could recognize her.

"The portal is open. I'll tell you the rest on the way, but we have to hurry. We don't have much time."

CHAPTER 24. AYLA

A doe tore across the orchard, two wolves in close pursuit—or perhaps, they were pursued by another animal sharp of tooth and claw. No, no. A squirrel jumped from tree branch to tree branch, dropping one acorn cupped in its tiny hands with every extension of its haunches. Yes, Ayla liked that story much better. She looked down at her bowl. The porridge tasted delightful. Ayla savoured every spoonful, daydreaming her morning entertainment, before turning her attention to the maid as she welcomed the morning into her room in swift, nervous moves. The open window brought in the crisp spring air infused with the sweet fragrance of cherry blossom. Ayla stared at the empty bowl, considering asking for seconds. She hadn't felt hungry for weeks—or was it months?—and this almost-forgotten sensation made her wonder.

Corbin showed up for the daily check-up right after breakfast. She didn't mind it as much as all other times, though. In a matter of minutes, she finished with all the answers. He looked at her, puzzled, a grimace of worry on his face. She wondered if he was nervous, too. Something strange was in the atmosphere today. Ayla wasn't sure if she liked it.

"Is everything okay?" she asked in her softest voice. The day was so glorious, so uplifting that there was no room for worry in it. Corbin pointed at her pillows and she realised she'd been sitting up the whole time.

"Yes. You're feeling better? Any headaches today?"

She giggled and threw the sheets off the bed. The strange new energy filled her body, and she dared to put her feet down on the dark oak floor. A refreshing change from the suffocating embrace of the blankets. It felt amazing to be fully awake, without the fog clouding her vision. Without the agonising migraines. Without the dread she felt every time before bed now. They were all gone, and she was happy.

"Nope! I think I'm finally getting better, just like you said I would!"

Corbin's hand darted towards her to keep her from falling as she got off the bed, putting her weight onto both feet. There was no need for precaution, though. Ayla felt as strong as before her strange illness. It was gone without a trace.

The whole day went smoothly. Ayla spent it all on her feet, enjoying the new vigour that filled her heart with light. She found joy in the smallest things—a pretty white dress she chose to wear, the delicate pink of the textured tiles in her bathroom, the painted flowers on the teapot that was served with lunch. A smile never left her lips as she danced around the unfamiliar rooms of the new house.

This was another mansion, but much smaller than the one she was first brought in. It had two floors, with the bedrooms upstairs and the entertainment area and Corbin's study downstairs. There was a fireplace in the living room, empty and silent on a sunny day. Spring had set its reign, and it was only a matter of weeks until nights would get warm and pleasant.

The orchard outside bestowed upon her a blessing, a sort of unspoken awareness of cyclical beauty. Ayla enjoyed walking around and breathing in the fresh, clean air. Nobody stopped her from going out this time. Dolores was nowhere to be seen, and Corbin was busy in his study. A stark contrast to hers, his mood seemed foul. As the sun went down, Ayla's heart fluttered with strange anticipation. Something was going to happen that night, she felt it in her bones. When twilight descended upon the orchard, she ran to the house, unable to contain her excitement.

At dinner, she served herself a generous helping of roasted vegetables and a slice of juicy pork with crispy crackling. Dolores seemed nervous as her eyes kept darting towards the door when her Master wasn't looking. He was lost in thought though, and didn't pay any attention to the maid.

Ayla finished her plate and reached for a second helping. She was hungry like a wolf, as if something was telling her to eat in advance. Corbin hardly had a bite, and his concerned expression grew darker by the minute. Unsure about his reasons, she preferred to keep her observations to herself, digging into the indulgent meal. Once finished, she put the fork and knife neatly on the plate and patted her stomach.

"I don't think I can eat any more." Her eyelids were getting heavy after all the food, and she thought favourably about getting under clean, crisp sheets and going to sleep. Only happy things were floating in her mind that night. There was no fear of impending nightmares that were waiting for her the second she closed her eyes. No migraine still. No urge to ask Corbin for another session to take the painful memories of the midnight dread. She felt healed, and it was wonderful.

The short walk upstairs was a delightful ending to the evening. Ayla barely managed to wash her face before getting too tired to stay up. She climbed into the bed and buried herself in the warm blankets.

It felt like only a moment passed when something woke her up. Ayla opened her eyes and listened, strange anticipation filling her again. Someone else was in the house. And she needed to see who.

***

Blaze stepped onto the solid stones of the path in front of the house and looked around. The night was cold but windless, and he was comfortable in his leather jacket. He felt determined with all his actions and didn't allow any doubt to get into his mind. Of course she would come with him. That was her destiny.

Raven had told him everything. She herself was a Familiar to a Sorcerer who nursed her back to life when she was nothing but a wounded bird. Familiars weren't easy to come by, and Blaze wasn't aware it was possible to give them a human form. However, being well connected to his own primal nature, he could always spot someone similar to himself.

Familiars were loyal servants to their Masters. Having one go astray wasn't unheard of but it was highly unlikely.

"Why would I believe it's not a trap?" He asked her during a brisk walk out of the bar. In the dark corner of the street, she stopped and turned around. Her hood was still covering her head, and he now understood that she was simply scared to be recognised by anyone who knew Corbin and his loyal maid.

"Believe what you want, Mage. I tell you what needs to be told. Ayla has been with us for six months now and never showed even a spark of magic, no matter how hard she tried. And boy did she try, I tell you. From other Familiars, I learned about others like her, who were told they had magic but were never able to use it. My Master wouldn't believe it, of course. The only way I can convince him is to show it." She threw a quick look behind his back in the alley, but there was only a lone rat clicking its tiny claws as it ran across the paved surface from one house to another. "She was expelled from the Sorcerers' Academy and Corbin was going to get her back in, but someone else came into play. There is a group of individuals who want her dead—I believe that's from your side. One of them was a Sorcerer's Apprentice whom I didn't recognise, and others, I believe, were Mages. Such cooperation is questionable at best... but anyway, let's stay on topic. What I'm trying to say is that these people attacked and nearly killed Ayla. It was only thanks to my Master's intervention that she is still alive. He created a blood bond between them through an ancient ritual that tied their lives together. So if you do get into a fight, make sure he stays alive because his death will automatically end her life, too."

Blaze let out a heavy sigh, keeping his ears open to any unusual sounds. It was still possible that the Familiar was stalling to keep him from his search, and potentially to have someone attack him in this dark alley. He was wary that a fight would take some of his energy. He needed all that he had for the inevitable confrontation with the Sorcerer. Especially if the conflict escalated.

"That explains a lot," he said cautiously as he noticed Raven tapping her foot on the cobblestones in an impatient rhythm. "Why would you be telling me all this? Betrayal of your Master will cause you serious problems."

Raven held a pause.

"There are bigger things at stake, Mage. I don't know how or why, but my Master became obsessed with this girl. He was only supposed to take her in and keep her safe until she figured out her talents and went her own way. I've always kept my distance, but it is clear that she doesn't belong with us. Master would never let her go on his own accord, no matter how bad her condition is. Take her away, Mage. Convince him. I don't want her to trouble him anymore."

She told him about the house on the outskirts of town, hidden behind a large cherry orchard. There were charms to keep it out of sight as well, and only the person who knew exactly where to go would be able to get through. The best time would be to show up the next night, when the full moon brightened the sky and enhanced his power to increase his chances against the Sorcerer.

Unable to sleep that night, Blaze kept playing their conversation in his mind again and again. There were still questions that were left unanswered. Why was Corbin obsessed with someone without magical powers? If he truly was, that would explain why he didn't want Ayla to die when she was attacked. Creating a blood bond was no easy feat. Blaze had heard of those rituals of dark magic that went back centuries. Sorcerers were always prone to corruption when it came to power. That was one of the major differences between them and Mages.

The sun came up, bringing along a glorious morning and a solution to his problem. Blaze knew exactly what to do. He needed to organise a place for Ayla to stay until she recovered and warmed up to him.

The day flew by in just a moment. Blaze arranged for Ayla's accommodation at the student campus of White-stone School of Magic where he had once lived himself. This took most of his time. Once done with the major organisational problem, it was easy to take care of others. Packing up and transporting his bags to the community. Putting together a small backpack with necessities for the night, including a set of warm clothes for Ayla in case it was cold. She wouldn't need anything in the new house. He made sure it was set up to grant her every wish. She would be safe there.

The night took over the silent city as Blaze walked out on the road that led outwards. He always preferred walk-ing to driving, and tonight was a good night for it. There were only a few fast-moving clouds in the sky, and the full moon appeared in all its glory. Under its soothing light, his skin tingled, radiating a pale glow. His powers were now completely restored and he felt assured.

There was nobody else around as he kept walking towards the hills. Very soon, he caught sight of the cherry orchard by the road. The night was cold but the tiny buds were slowly turning into flowers that speckled the darkness with tiny white dots. Exactly as Raven described.

Blaze stepped under the tree canopy. His steps did not echo, and a sense of eerie magic hung strong in the air. Without hesitation, Blaze kept moving forward, knowing that the exit wasn't far away. In precisely ten steps, just like Raven advised, it was over. Clear night sky appeared over his head again, and the delicate sounds of the night sprung back to life.

Something warm in his pocket diverted his attention from the stone mansion in front of him. Taking the portrait out, he smiled seeing Ayla's face. She looked so real it was surprising she couldn't see him. Blaze suppressed a boyish urge to throw a pebble in one of the windows to see how her expression would change. In such proximity to her, the portrait showed exactly what she was like at this very moment. But he needed to focus. As he knew from his vision, Ayla was easily frightened and he only had one chance.

Blaze's hand lay on the button of the doorbell. That was it. His destiny was waiting. All he needed to do was to come in and claim it.

Before he had a chance to ring, the door opened and
a pair of sparkling dark eyes appeared in front of him.
"Come," the Familiar urged. "It's time."

CHAPTER 25. BLAZE

On the inside, the house looked painfully regular. Plain plastered walls with generic pictures of rustic landscapes, and simple medium-height ceilings. The doors to the rooms downstairs were wooden, painted in ordinary white, and to an outsider's eye everything seemed boring and unremarkable.

Blaze knew it wasn't the case, though. As he crossed the threshold into the house, his skin covered in goosebumps and he tensed up, sensing the magical barrier that had been placed there. A visitor without an invitation wouldn't have been able to get in, and he suspected it wouldn't have been possible to even see the door if he hadn't been given specific instructions. Maybe the Familiar adjusted the house's protection to let him in, or it was fate itself allowing him to reach his target without unnecessary obstacles. Regardless of what it was, he was grateful to have escaped the extra hurdles. Dealing with smaller tasks would take up time and power. On a fateful night like this, he could spare neither.

The Familiar's back in a dark maid's uniform disappeared behind the bend of the hallway. He took a deep breath and cleared his thoughts, calling upon his power. The white bloom of raw energy danced in front of his eyes and slowly disappeared as he allowed it to re-absorb into his open hand. The Familiar was right. On the night of a full moon, he was more powerful than usual. This was partially due to his essence as a shifter. His mother was to thank for the other part of it, having birthed him under a full moon. Linking the beginning of his life to the majestic celestial in its full glory was the best gift she could have given him.

With his head held high, he kept walking along the wall in the Familiar's steps, cautious of any hidden traps. He was stepping on the exact same spots she had stepped on, always keeping his eyes and ears open for anything unusual. Nothing else seemed amiss in the house—it was quiet like a predator ready to attack.

The tall, slender Sorcerer was waiting for him in the large living room. Black fires in his eyes were a raging inferno, clearly indicating his attitude to the midnight visitor.

Blaze stopped a few steps away and quickly scanned the room. There didn't seem to be any other danger than the Sorcerer himself, but that might have been a false sensation. He didn't know what his counterpart was capable of, and was prepared to meet any surprises with a force of his own.

In his mind, he checked the power was still at his command. Magic was tingling on his fingertips exactly how it was supposed to be. It never betrayed him before, and it wasn't going to let him down this time if things were to turn sour.

The Sorcerer gave him a crooked smile as if he noticed the check-up.

"So, you're the Mage." His low voice echoed in the half-empty room.

Blaze returned the gesture with a small bow, visible enough to identify it as one to show respect to the host but small enough to let him know it was nothing more than a tribute to tradition.

"Indeed," he replied, cautiously scanning the room for danger again and again. If there was nothing there, it didn't mean the Sorcerer couldn't make things appear. He learned enough about Corbin to know he had immense power, allowing him not to use spells anymore but bind his will to an enchanted object directly. Blaze ran a quick check of his opponent's aura. There it was, the amulet ring that Corbin wore on his right index finger. A single brass band depicting a bird. A crow, or a raven, close to his own nature. After all, his name, Corbin, meant 'crow'.

The Sorcerer was silent, studying him with a look of distaste on his face. Blaze suppressed a cheeky smile. During his nightly meditation before coming there, he had collected his memories about Ayla. Everything he had ever seen of her in his visions, all the things that could have been useful. He knew that she liked the smell of bergamot and citrus, the colour black and the look of a clean, open face. Mindful of every detail, he incorporated them into his image tonight. His favourite aftershave was exactly that, warm white wood base, heart of lavender and top notes of bergamot with a touch of citrus zest. He always preferred a close shave regardless, and his travel clothes were chosen in black, outlining his figure but still comfortable to move around if it came down to a fight. The Sorcerer's darkened face showed him that he had chosen well. He was confident Ayla would like everything about the way he looked, and hoped it would help him convince her more easily.

"You know who I am and why I'm here," he finally broke the silence as it was starting to look as if the Sorcerer was never going to speak. His opponent's manner of holding a pause was unnerving, but he knew it was part of the trick. Corbin wanted to annoy the newcomer and provoke mistakes. A pleasure Blaze wasn't going to give him.

"I do," Corbin finally replied. "A shifter coming to my house on the night of the full moon. What a coincidence. However, I don't have what you want. You've wasted your time, I'm afraid."

Blaze shook his head, disappointed in the turn this conversation was taking. The Sorcerer wanted to make it difficult when it didn't have to be. The growing warmth in his front pocket alerted him of the painful proximity to his target. He still needed to be careful, though.

"I'm not sure what you mean, Sorcerer. The girl I'm looking for is in this house. She's so close I can almost hear her heartbeat." As Corbin was silent again, Blaze continued. "You know who I am and what I came here to do. Let her go with me to be among people like her, to the place where she belongs, where she will heal. I can give her a full life of happiness and joy. Something she'll never have here."

"It was you Mages who murdered her adoptive father and attempted to kill her, too. She's only alive now thanks to my intervention. Why would I trust a word you say?"

Corbin cracked his knuckles and grinned, watching for Blaze's reaction. *Careful now*, Blaze told himself. *He's just testing me. I need to persuade him to give me a chance, and we might still avoid bloodshed.*

"This is her destiny," he stated firmly, chasing away the thoughts of someone from his own ranks trying to kill Ayla. That simply wasn't possible. The Sorcerer was trying to trick him, no doubt. "Give me one chance, Sorcerer. If she recognises her fate and comes with me, let her go. I swear I'll keep her safe. If she rejects me, I'll leave."

"And never come anywhere near her again." Corbin rolled his shoulders and held his hand to him. "Do we have an agreement?"

"And if she follows me, you will stay away yourself," Blaze retorted, returning a firm handshake. This wasn't something he thought would happen, but for now, it was good enough. He wondered how he could talk to Ayla now. Was the Sorcerer going to call her?

Tracing his gaze to the stairs leading to the second floor, Corbin chuckled as if reading his thoughts.

"If this is destiny as you say, she'll come on her own. I won't be making it easy for you, my friend."

His smug smile faded when the white dress appeared on the top of the stairs. Blaze made a few steps closer and stopped. There she was, finally in the flesh. Standing there hesitant, eyes wide on her pale face, her beautiful hair loose on her shoulders. She locked eyes with him immediately, and he knew that no matter what happened now, he couldn't let her look away. The moment they broke eye contact, she would be lost to him forever.

For a few seconds that felt like an eternity, she wavered on the stairs before finally giving up her reservations. One painful step at a time, she shortened the distance between them. Blaze kept himself from rushing towards her to take her in his arms and inhale her sweet smell, like in some of his visions. To reassure her of her safety and to carry her away, far from this gloomy house and its dark host with his secrets and strange rituals. He reminded himself to stay put.

I made my choice. Now she has to make hers.

It wasn't easy to give up control like this. Blaze always liked to make sure things got done properly. This girl *had* to come with him. The sheer thought of her potentially rejecting him was devastating. No, she wouldn't do that. He'd travelled far and wide to see her now, and there was no room for error.

Admiring her grace, he couldn't stop the feeling that this was it. The moment he'd been preparing for all his life. This beautiful girl who was meant for him by destiny itself. She had been the reason why he never settled in any other relationship. She was the one he had always loved, he saw it clearly now. It hurt so bad to know that Ayla didn't remember him at all. There was no spark of recognition in her hazel eyes. But at least she was walking towards him and not running away. Not yet.

He inhaled the sweet smell of her presence, registering her pheromones for the first time as she came nearer. The hairs on his arms stood on end as an overpowering desire took over.

There was no time for hesitation. Keeping himself still in the iron grip of his will, Blaze tried to shake off the strange spell. The animal inside him had never been this strong. *She is yours. Take her now! Do whatever you want, nothing will stop you.*

He took a small breath, trying to clear his mind. *No. I won't be another perpetrator in her life. What the hell is wrong with me, even considering this? After everything she's been through?*

Seconds flew by, each like an eternity. Blaze was catching on her slightest movement, stifling his raging desire to pounce on her. It seemed that a couple of times she nearly looked away at something behind his back, undoubtedly that unlikeable Sorcerer who would probably do anything to distract her and break their connection. With an enormous effort, Blaze managed to stay in place and not grab her in desperation.

Come on, my sweetheart. I know you want to follow me, to leave this wretched place. I swear I won't hurt you. Come to me and I'll take you away.

He realised he'd been holding his breath until her tiny foot in an elegant sandal left the last step. There it was, the moment of truth. In person, she was even smaller than in his visions, a fragile, delicate flower that could be broken so easily. Her chest was rising and falling in shallow movements. The pupils of her eyes were wide, and Blaze felt a sharp pang in his heart when he realised it was fear. She was afraid of him, of his power over her. She wanted to run away and the only thing keeping her in place was his gaze. What had that monster done to her? *Or is it the monster in me that she fears?*

Please don't be scared. I won't harm you, he wanted to say but knew it would only frighten her. She was so close it almost physically hurt not to yield to the temptation to touch her. To slide his fingers through the smooth locks of her hair, to gently trace her face and feel the warmth of her supple skin under his hand. To wrap her in a loving embrace and never let go. Or to do something much worse.

Blaze breathed out, suppressing these unusual thoughts. It was time to speak. He only had one chance to convince her to leave with him, and he had to tread carefully. She came this far but she could just as easily flee. The animal inside him wasn't giving up. He had to keep that under control, too.

"Hello, Ayla," the greeting slipped off his tongue and he enjoyed the way her name sounded when he said it out loud for the first time. Her large eyes grew wider in response. "My name is Blaze. I've come here to take you to your new home. A place where you'll meet people just like you. Where you'll be accepted for who you are, and where you won't be a misfit anymore. I only need your consent."

She didn't reply. Tiny beads of sweat formed on her forehead and she shivered as if kissed by an icy breeze. Once again, Blaze stopped himself from reaching out to touch her.

Please, don't be afraid. Just say yes and I'll do the rest. You won't have anything to fear once you're out of here, I swear.

Oh no, be afraid, be very afraid, the primal stepped in. *Do you know what a tiger can do to a tiny little thing like you? Of course, I won't kill you. I'll keep you just alive enough so I can do it again and again.*

Stop, Blaze ordered to himself. He was shocked by the things that were going through his head, as if a demon was whispering them straight into his mind. How would he even consider approaching his loved one in his tiger shape, seeing her as prey? That was sick and incredibly dangerous.

It's her pheromones. She's terrified, it's a full moon and I haven't shifted for weeks. That's all there is to it. She's my destined one. A human being, whom I will cherish and nurture back to health. I won't torture her and I won't hurt her. I'll never be like him.

This was all wrong. Blaze had always believed that when the time came, his destined one would recognise him and things would go smoothly straight from the start. He never thought that his animal vein would course in such an odd way. Moments were flying by and Ayla was still silent. Her breathing shallow, hazel eyes pleading for mercy. He had to do something before the connection was lost. He was running out of time.

"It's okay if you don't want to talk. You can just nod if you agree," he added, watching her intently. With a visible strain, she lowered her head ever so slightly and raised it again. "Come, I'll show you the way."

The relief was immense. Ayla seemed more relaxed now that she'd made her decision. Blaze frowned, noticing dark bruises on her neck. *That monster has to pay for what he's done. What the hell is wrong with him?* Stifling the need to attack the Sorcerer, he turned around and walked towards the exit, ignoring his opponent's enraged face. The aura of hatred was strong in the room, and Blaze was glad to be out of there. He opened the door and led Ayla into the glorious night. Her presence felt warm and uplifting. The demon in his mind went quiet. Of course, the Prophet was right. Blaze had never felt like he belonged with someone until this night, under the majestic light of the full moon that sang in his blood, filling him with power. He threw a sideways glance at his tiny companion, admiring her features and the neutral expression on her beautiful face. He felt much better now that she'd calmed down. Maybe it really was her original fear that provoked those strange impulses in him. He hoped she didn't get too overwhelmed by the feelings she experienced. There was no way he could tell what it was like for her, considering she had no recollection of their previous encounters.

One step at a time. I won't rush you, sweetheart. Take all the time that you need. I know you'll come to me when you're ready.

Step after step echoed on the empty road and then along the streets of the sleeping town. Neither of the companions uttered a word. A dozen thoughts raced through Blaze's mind. He was worried about Ayla settling into the new place, if she was going to like the house he had chosen for her and if she would be able to make friends. He knew that even though she agreed to follow him tonight, the hard part wasn't over yet. He still had to win her over, as much as it pained him to realise that he was a perfect stranger to her. That the pull of destiny could frighten and hurt her if she decided to fight it.

Looking at her slender figure in the light white dress, he suppressed the urge to get out the warm cashmere wrap he had prepared for her. Even though there was no wind, the night air was cold. Ayla didn't seem to be bothered by it, though, and after a short pause he decided to let it go. It wasn't the time to try and touch her. Not just yet, and probably not for quite a while.

One thing was clear at least. The Sorcerer was gone and they never had to see him again. There was no place for him in Ayla's life anymore. That chapter was over.

EPILOGUE

A strange numbness suppressed the thoughts in her head. She couldn't explain anything that happened tonight. Her random decision to follow this stranger. Her mixed feelings about the future. Corbin's silence as she left. Falling into step with the white-haired man, Ayla asked herself questions she had no answers to. Maybe he tricked her with some kind of illusion. Or put a spell on her to make her come with him.

She shook her head. No, this stranger didn't look like someone who would do that—but again, who did? She hadn't seen many people cast spells, and couldn't be sure of this one. Blaze said he was a wizard... a Mage? As if it was somehow different from a Sorcerer. It was too much to think about, but her head didn't hurt as she would expect it to. After all the weeks of her illness, she didn't feel sick at all. Her step was light. Her breathing, easy. Despite all the questions in her head, it felt natural to walk along the moonlit streets with this man.

Ayla suddenly realised Blaze was talking. Maybe he had been this whole time, she didn't know.

He said, "Sorry we had to walk all this way. Mages aren't allowed to open portals in the vicinity of Sorcerer's homes, and vice versa. We're out of his area now, so it won't be too long."

He stopped and turned his hand palm up. A bright white light popped into the night and hovered over his skin. "This is what our magic looks like. You'll learn to connect with yours and will be able to do this in no time."

The white ball spun around as if showing off. Ayla smiled, feeling a subtle pull towards it. Something inside her responded to this little display. She wanted to touch it but held herself back. First, she'd need to learn all she could about this and then she could give in to her curiosity. Besides, she only just met this man. No matter how friendly he seemed, he could still be dangerous.

The glowing ball took off from the Mage's hand, twirling and growing in size. A gentle shimmer passed through it like a ripple. A faint smell of ozone filled her nostrils. Eyes wide, she stared at the light slowly expanding into an open door that brightened the night. She turned to the Mage, a silent question in her gaze.

He smiled and stretched his gloved hand towards her. "This is a portal that will take us to your new home. Don't be afraid. I'll walk through it with you."

Ayla glanced back over the roofs of the quiet French town, picturing Corbin's mansion that lay beyond the blossoming cherries. Her past life, familiar and comfortable, yet miserable. She thought about her illness and the dark thoughts. About her dependency on Corbin's powers. That chapter was over. She had to be brave and trust that this would be a better one.

A desperate howl touched her ears almost on the edge of hearing. A scream that sounded somewhat like a crow's cawing, high-pitched in excruciating pain. Ayla shuddered, looking away from the cityscape and the orchard beyond. It was time for her to leave. No more dark magic. No more pain. No more secrets.

With a sharp exhale, she accepted the hand in soft calf-skin leather. Nothing happened. She matched Blaze's step through the glowing door. An unexpected sensation of cool water glided over her but disappeared as quickly as it emerged. Surprised, Ayla checked her bare arms for condensation but there was no sign of water on them. A quiet pop behind made her look back.

The door wasn't there anymore. Her gaze met nothing but a wall of lush trees, their tops silver under the light of the full moon. Turning around, she saw the slated roofs of a small town, sleepy and peaceful at this time of night. This was her new home. Ayla realised she was still holding the man's hand and rushed to let go with a quick step back. His expression was calm, and there was nothing but kindness in those emerald eyes. No sign of an animal that scared her before. Did she imagine that?

Wouldn't be surprised if I did.

Ayla opened her mouth to ask a question, but no sound escaped. Frowning at herself, she tried again. No luck. She looked into his eyes, searching for an explanation. A wave of unexpected shyness came down upon her. She quickly averted her gaze, pretending to focus on the path under her feet. The feeling was contradictory to anything she had experienced. She was never shy in a man's presence, not like that. Even when she just started dating. Being unable to speak was something else entirely.

Luckily, Blaze didn't ask any questions. With a wide gesture, he invited her to follow the path towards the town. "This is Whitestone, one of the safest Mage communities. You'll have your own house that will provide you with anything you need." They walked down the path, with Ayla digesting the idea of now living here. "The magic in the house will match your moods and you'll find all the things to make you comfortable. Tomorrow, someone will come over and tell you more about the community. If you want, you can take a tour or you can stay in. There's no rush to do anything."

A small, white-painted house swam into her line of vision. Blaze went up the steps of the porch and pushed the door open. "This is it, Ayla. Your new home."

Ayla exhaled and walked in. Dim lights came to life, illuminating the open kitchen and dining area with a small fireplace and a modest table in the middle. It was warm, but not too warm. The essence of lavender and mint reigned in the air, making her feel at ease. She looked around with a surprised smile. It felt exactly as Blaze said. Just what she needed after the ordeal of the night.

Her smile faded when she glanced at the kitchen bench. There, right in the middle, sat a fruit basket heaped with oranges. One of them rolled out of its nest and off the bench, all the way towards her to nudge her feet. Ayla reached for it. Her thoughts shot to another time, back in her old life, when a stray orange announced her meeting with Darren and the beginning of a brighter, better time. The earliest of her memories. Oh, was this a sign that things were about to be okay?

Or was this the beginning of a new cycle of pain?

TO BE CONTINUED

ALSO BY ALENA JAMES

The Mage's Destiny – Book Two of the Mistwalker Series

Latest updates are available on www.alenajames.com

ACKNOWLEDGMENTS

I would like to express eternal gratitude to my family. My wonderful parents who raised me and provided for the best childhood and education possible. My fantastic brother who supported my ideas of writing. My grandparents and extended family who were there for me.

Big thanks to the people in my life who inspired me and shaped my views of the world in the way that made the Mistwalker Series a reality. You know who you are!

Shout out to my editor, Krystal Nichol, whose support has been immense, and to the team of cover art designers at MiblArt who worked tirelessly to produce a stunning cover. My gratitude expands to the lovely reviewers who took time to leave their thoughts on my book to help my little enterprise grow, and to alpha and beta readers who helped shape my work to the best it could be. Big thanks to all my loyal followers on social media who help promote my books to new audiences.

Last but not least, a heartfelt thanks to all of you, my amazing readers, who took a leap of faith and supported a debut author! This means the world to me. By buying my work you inspire me to keep writing and follow my dream.